Praise for the Books of J. C. Eaton

"A sparkling addition to the Wine Trail Mystery series. A toast to protagonist Norrie and Two Witches Winery, where the characters shine and the mystery flows. This novel is a perfect blend of suspense and fun!"

—Carlene O'Neil, author of the Cypress Cove Mysteries,
on *Chardonnayed to Rest*

"A thoroughly entertaining series debut, with enjoyable yet realistic characters and enough plot twists—and dead ends—to appeal from beginning to end."

—*Booklist,* starred review,
on *Booked 4 Murder*

"Filled with clues that make you go 'Huh?' and a list of potential subjects that range from the charming to the witty to the intense. Readers root for Phee as she goes up against a killer who may not stop until Phee is taken out well before her time. Enjoy this laugh-out-loud funny mystery that will make you scream for the authors to get busy on the next one."

—*Suspense Magazine*
on *Molded 4 Murder*

Books by J. C. Eaton

The Wine Trail Mysteries

A Riesling to Die
Chardonnayed to Rest
Pinot Red or Dead?
Sauvigone for Good
Divide and Concord
Death, Dismay and Rosé

The Sophie Kimball Mysteries

Booked 4 Murder
Ditched 4 Murder
Staged 4 Murder
Botched 4 Murder
Molded 4 Murder
Dressed Up 4 Murder

The Marcie Rayner Mysteries

Murder in the Crooked Eye Brewery
Murder at the Mystery Castle

Death,
Dismay
and
Rosé

J. C. Eaton

BEYOND THE PAGE
PUBLISHING

Death, Dismay and Rosé
J. C. Eaton
Copyright © 2020 J. C. Eaton
Cover design and illustration by Dar Albert, Wicked Smart Designs

Beyond the Page Books
are published by
Beyond the Page Publishing
www.beyondthepagepub.com

ISBN: 978-1-950461-78-3

To our fearless great nephew, Jeremy Lynes, who defied the odds all those years ago and kissed the haunted gravestone in Penn Yan's Lakeview Cemetery. You continue to amaze us with your zest for life and love of family.

Acknowledgments

Our gratitude goes out to the relentless beta readers who have been by our side all these years. Your tech skills, advice, and keen eyes kept us afloat. Kudos to Larry Finkelstein, Gale Leach, Susan Morrow, and Susan Schwartz all the way in Australia.

Special thanks to Rachel Marlatt Donner, for giving us the title to this mystery. Boy, does it ever fit!

And a very special thanks to all the contributors on the VW Automatic Register forum. We learned so much about removing VW engines that it might just become part of our new skill set. If only in our novels.

We are so fortunate to be part of the "Cozy Mystery Crew" of authors who work together to support one another. We're glad to be part of this crew. You're amazing: Ellen Byron, Becky Clark, Vicki Delany, Mary Feliz, Tina Kashian, Libby Klein, Olivia Matthews, Elizabeth Penney, Shari Randall, Linda Reilly, and Abby L. Vandiver.

Without our incredible team of agent, Dawn Dowdle from Blue Ridge Literary Agency, and editor, Bill Harris, from Beyond the Page Publishing, this mystery would not have come to fruition. We are so fortunate to have you in our corner.

Thank you, Beyond the Page Publishing for getting this mystery out there, and to the booksellers, librarians, and readers whose energy keeps us penning whodunits well into the night.

Chapter 1

Norrie's House,
Penn Yan, New York

I flipped the kitchen wall calendar from May to June and shouted to Charlie, "Only thirty more days till my sentence is over." The big brindle Plott hound barely cast me a glance and continued to guzzle his kibble. My sentence referred to the year I committed to overseeing the family winery while my sister, Francine, and her entomologist husband, Jason, traipsed through the Costa Rican rain forests in search of some elusive insect. All part of a grant Jason got from the New York State Agricultural Experiment Station at Cornell University.

Hooray for Jason. He got a grant and I got stuck dealing with more murders on the Seneca Lake Wine Trail than I could ever imagine in my real occupation as a romance and mystery screenwriter for a Canadian film company. I sublet my cozy apartment near Little Italy and returned to our family farmhouse on Two Witches Hill in Penn Yan, New York, adjacent to our winery that bore the Two Witches name.

For years, Francine and I begged our parents to change the name of the winery but our parents, who are now comfortably enjoying retirement in Myrtle Beach, South Carolina, adamantly refused. Needless to say, Francine and I were teased relentlessly with all sorts of witch references. Of course, the fact that I just had to dye my hair orange and purple for Halloween in my sophomore year didn't help.

Now, with a Sharpie marker in one hand and my cup of morning coffee in the other, I reached over to circle June thirtieth. That's when I spied the small moon images on the calendar page and froze. I put the coffee cup down for fear of spilling it and took a closer look. Sure enough, under June twenty-first, beneath the words *summer begins*, was a full moon.

Wonderful. As if I don't have enough to deal with. Now the curse of the full moon on the summer solstice.

It was a ridiculous Penn Yan legend that probably got started two centuries ago when someone tried to cover up a murder. The curse was right up there with the "kiss of death" gravestone curse that still lingers over the Penn Yan Cemetery on Lake Road. That curse, I think, was meant to keep kids away from the grave markers, but all it did was

1

encourage them to dare each other to place a kiss on Elinor McLandon's grave, circa 1802, and see if she would materialize and take them with her to the netherworld.

The solstice legend wasn't all that different. Apparently, if a full moon occurred the same date as the summer solstice, the two witches, who once lived on our hill, would return from the dead and snuff the life out of someone in their sleep. The legend even specified the location—within a five-mile radius from the top of Two Witches Hill. There was a lot of lakefront in that area, including a popular vacation spot, Kashong Point. It was idiotic nonsense, but still somewhat chilling in a bizarre sort of way.

I snatched my iPhone off the table and googled the last date of a summer solstice that coincided with the full moon. It was on a Monday in 1948. Rosalee Marbelton from Terrace Wineries was old enough to remember that date but she wasn't living here back then. I groaned and tried to think. That's when it dawned on me. Gladys Pipp might be able to help. Gladys was the secretary for the Yates County Sheriff's Office and knew more about the goings-on in the county than the deputies who were paid to deal with them.

Maybe I was being silly, but if no one was smothered in their sleep back in 1948, I could pooh-pooh the whole thing and tell everyone else to do the same. I looked at the clock and saw it was a little after eight. Gladys was bound to be at work, especially on a Monday morning, so I phoned her.

"Norrie! I haven't heard from you in a while. Is everything all right at the winery?" she asked once she finished with the usual spiel of "if this is an emergency, hang up and dial . . . ."

"Great! Everything's great. Thirty days and Francine will be taking over the helm. She needs to make more jellies and jams."

Gladys was a regular fan of my sister's assorted berry jams and, much as I hate to admit it, I used lots of those jars to eke information out of her when I needed it. Besides, she was the only friendly face in that entire office.

"So, what's up?" she asked.

"I know this is a long shot, but you wouldn't happen to know of anyone who was smothered to death in their sleep back in nineteen forty-eight, do you?"

"Oh, no. Not you, too."

"What do you mean?"

"I need to keep my voice low. Listen, Deputy Hickman was in here a few minutes ago asking the same question. Said he wanted to be prepared in case the summer solstice curse reappears. Thinks someone might use it as a cover-up for them to commit murder. Had me pull up the obits from Google, but it was worthless. Now he's sending me to the Yates County Historical Society to go through their records. He even got a deputy to cover my desk while I'm gone. Can you believe it?"

"Yeah, I can. That curse originated with the two witches who lived on our hill centuries ago. Those kinds of tales can really scare the tourists right out of here or bring in throngs of loonies. Hmm, that gives me an idea. I'm meeting a friend of mine in Geneva for lunch today. I'll drop by the Geneva Historical Society on my way home and see what their archives say. We can touch base later, okay?"

"Sounds good to me. Listen, I wouldn't put a whole lot of credence into those things. They're only good for one thing—late-night ghost stories around the campfire."

"I hope you're right."

When I got off the phone with Gladys, I took a quick shower and got down to my real job. I had a screenplay due to my producer in two weeks. Actually, to the screenplay analyst who worked for my producer. Then it would be bounced back to me for revisions and his little "just a thought" notes that were more annoying than anything else. I never knew if he wanted me to change anything or if he merely wanted to point things out.

• • •

At a little before eleven, I closed my laptop and headed to the tasting room before taking off to meet Godfrey Klein for lunch at Tim Horton's. Godfrey was an entomologist who worked alongside my brother-in-law at the Experiment Station. He was also the only person who kept in touch with Jason and Francine via a satellite phone from Cornell. He was also the only person I ever kissed on the lips for no apparent reason other than a spur-of-the-moment impulse. And while nothing like that happened again, mainly because I was, and still am, dating a lawyer who works in Geneva, I still have mixed feelings about Godfrey. Good thing I'll be back in Manhattan in July. I like writing drama, not living it.

It felt wonderful to walk down the hill to our winery building in comfortable sandals instead of the heavy boots that seemed to be glued to my feet all winter long. Living in Penn Yan meant dealing with three seasons—snow, mud, and humidity. With mud season out of way, I could look forward to pesky mosquitos, no-see-ums, and frizzy hair. No wonder I moved to the city.

Surprisingly, the tasting room was busier than usual for a midmorning Monday on the first of June. Lizzie, our bookkeeper and cashier, lifted her wire-rimmed glasses from her nose and called out, "Good morning, Norrie. Did you happen to notice the June calendar?"

"Thirty fun-filled days?"

"Shh! I'm referring to the summer solstice. It falls on a full moon. Not that I believe in all that mumbo-jumbo but—"

Just then, Glenda emerged from the kitchen with a full rack of wineglasses. She immediately put them on the nearest tasting room table and rushed over to me. "The full moon falls on the summer solstice. It's not too late, Norrie," she said as she brushed a long strand of pink and silver hair from her face. "Zenora and I can smudge this place in less than an hour. It's wide open so we can move clockwise while we gently wave the sage stick smoke around the room. The winery can't afford to take any chances. Especially since it sits right on the same property where those two witches lived."

"That was centuries ago and none of us really know if they were witches in the actual sense of the word or maybe two hormonal sisters with bad attitudes." *Like the one I'm about to have if this keeps up.*

Glenda clasped her hands so tight I swore her knuckles were going to turn white. "If you must know, I have an awful premonition about this. And I'm not the only one. Zenora dreamt she saw a dead body floating on the lake."

"Good. At least it wasn't on our property. Tell your friend Zenora we can't risk setting the place on fire with her ritual sage sticks. The séance last summer and the ear-piercing chants around my house were bad enough. We'll be fine. It's only a ghostly legend meant to give little kids goose bumps."

"I'm not so sure," she replied. "Promise me you'll think about it."

"Oh, I'll think about it. I have no choice. By the way, has anyone seen Cammy?" I stretched my neck and looked around the tasting room. Roger was at his table with four customers and Sam was chatting with a full crew at his table.

"In the kitchen," Glenda said. "Loading the dishwasher. It's been a busy morning. Glad she's the tasting room manager and not me. Nonstop customers. Fred and Emma can deal with them at the bistro. Whoa, I'd better get a move on. A few more just came in the door."

With that, Glenda grabbed the glass rack from the vacant table and proceeded to unload the glasses at her spot while motioning for the new arrivals to join her for a tasting.

"You know," Lizzie said, "it might not hurt to appease her. Glenda's a gentle soul and she really believes in all that new age stuff."

"My sister and I believed in Santa Claus but my father didn't go running out there to build a shed for the reindeer."

"No, but your brother-in-law built one for that Nigerian dwarf goat of his."

"Ugh. Alvin. Don't remind me. Hmm, come to think of it, if those ghostly witches do appear on the solstice, one look at Alvin and they'll be hightailing it off this hill like nobody's business. Especially if he starts spitting."

Lizzie laughed. "I tend to agree."

Chapter 2

I walked into the kitchen, and sure enough Cammy was busy loading and unloading the dishwasher. She didn't hear me at first and all but dropped a rack of wineglasses when she turned around.

"Sorry," I said. "Didn't mean to sneak up on you. I should have coughed or something."

"It's fine. Believe it or not, we were slammed this morning with customers out of nowhere. I mean, yeah, the weather's been terrific, but Mondays are usually slow. At least it kept Glenda from rattling us about that full moon curse of the two witches or whatever the heck it is. Remember, I'm from Geneva, not Penn Yan. We have our own imbecilic rumors and curses."

"This one followed me all the way through childhood, past puberty, and now well into adulthood. Anyway, I just stopped in to say hello. I'm meeting Godfrey for lunch in a half hour and better get moving."

Cammy raised her thick, dark eyebrows. "Just lunch?"

"He's a friend. Like Theo and Don from next door."

"Theo and Don are a couple. Godfrey's, well . . . you know. Available."

"I want to find out more about when Francine and Jason are coming home. Godfrey's been on the satellite phone with them. That's all. I'm not about to muddy the waters as far as Bradley is concerned. Hunky lawyers don't appear on your doorstep every day."

"I wouldn't know. The only thing that appears on my doorstep, other than bird droppings, is the occasional delivery from Amazon. Oh, before I forget, Madeline Martinez from the Wineries of the West left you a message. She'll be by today to drop off tickets for the annual WOW Winemakers Dinner in July. I think it's nice that the six wineries in our section of the lake formed that little group. Great way to promote our wines."

"And catch up on the local gossip. Don and Theo draw straws to see which one of them gets stuck attending the meetings. At least the dinner's being hosted at her winery and not here. Did she say who was catering? I must have dozed off at that meeting."

"Chez Claude from Rochester."

"No kidding. Too bad Francine and Jason won't be back in time for it."

"Don't worry, there'll be tons of events for them to attend, like it or not."

I told Cammy I'd be by the next day and took off to meet Godfrey at Tim Horton's. True, it was a small chain restaurant, but they had the best cappuccinos as far as I was concerned, and a decent selection of soups, sandwiches, and pastries.

Godfrey was seated by the front window when I walked in and motioned me over. In spite of his receding hairline and slightly overweight physique, he exuded a certain charm that I couldn't quite explain.

"Tell me the good news," I said as I sat down. "What time's their flight getting in?"

He had a sheepish look on his face and cupped a fist inside his other hand. "Yeah, about that . . . as you know, they've made tremendous progress on the global species database, but it wasn't until recently that they spotted the Haemagogus, epithet unnamed to date, in a small riverbed not far from the—"

I pressed both hands against the table and leaned in. "What are you saying? They found the damn thing and now have to stick around to visit with its relatives?"

Godfrey took a deep breath. "Try to stay calm. Francine said you might overreact."

Oh, if I have to extend my watch one more month I'll overreact all right. I'll be on the next flight down to Costa Rica with a Costco-size bottle of Raid in my luggage.

"And what's with the 'epithet unnamed'?"

"That honor could go to your brother-in-law. The species would be named after him. Like the Haemagogus clarki, named after Dr. Herbert C. Clark, who eradicated yellow fever."

I rolled my eyes and stood. "I need to get a cup of coffee and a sandwich. I'll order whatever you want since I'm going to the counter."

"Turkey, avocado, and bacon club. Oh, and a mocha, too."

"Fine," I grumbled. "Turkey, avocado and bacon it is."

I was practically smoldering when I reached the counter to place our orders. A deal was a deal and it was for one year. *I have a life, too. And it belongs in Manhattan.* I was so engrossed watching the deli guy prepare our sandwiches that I didn't notice Godfrey directly behind me. He put a hand on my shoulder and leaned forward. "We're not talking longer than another week or two at most. They need to establish the range. Then Jason will turn over the findings to another team of entomologists."

"A week or two?"

"Uh-huh. You can handle that, can't you?"

I let out a groan. "I suppose. Besides, with the way my luck's been, there'll be another murder at or near our winery and I'll be stuck dealing with it."

"Another murder? What makes you say that?"

"Ever hear of the full moon on the summer solstice curse?"

Godfrey shook his head. "Is that a short story or something?"

"Don't I wish. It's an old legend with its roots firmly planted on our property."

Just then the deli guy handed me our tray and I moved to the cash register. Godfrey skirted around me and got to the register before me. "I've got it. It's the least I can do. Come on, tell me about this curse when we get back to our table."

Between bites of my ham sandwich and sips of my coffee, I told Godfrey about the remote possibility someone within a five-mile radius of our hill would be smothered to death the night of the full moon/summer solstice.

He all but choked on his turkey and bacon. "This tops the cake. *Really* tops the cake. And Glenda wants to have her wacky friend Zenora cast a spell or something?"

"Not a spell," I said. "A smudging. Like a house purifying thing."

"I suppose I shouldn't offer up a bottle of Clorox, huh?"

I gave him a quick kick under the table and we both laughed. It was comfortable being around Godfrey. I could be myself and not have to worry about impressing him. If I wanted to do that, all I would need to do was find a weird insect.

"Hey, you remember Alex Bollinger, don't you? The entomologist who went with us to that convent in Lodi?"

"Uh-huh. Why?" I asked.

"He and a crew will be camped at Kashong Point starting next week. They're doing a study on the Swede midge. It's a small fly, light brown in color and almost resembles the crane fly. The midge is quite detrimental to all kinds of plant tissue, so we're studying how to prevent the spread into agricultural areas. Not to say, of course, that the crane fly isn't detrimental as well. It most certainly is, but that little bugger's gotten plenty of attention, seeing as how its damage affects golf courses."

I nodded as if any of this meant something to me and continued to chomp on my sandwich.

"If you're interested, we can visit their camp sometime. He's got a few students going as well. Part of their study program."

"The last time Alex wanted me to tag along was in a cockroach-infested apartment building in Ithaca," I said.

"You'll have much more fun at the lake. Heck, our department even has its own boat."

"I'm kind of tied up with a screenplay right now but I'll let you know. Okay?"

"Sounds good."

"Listen, when you talk to Francine, tell her it's a two-week extension at most. If Jason wants his name on something, he can print it on a wine label."

"That's not the same as having a species named after you."

"No, it's better."

● ● ●

It was a little past one when we left Tim Horton's. I drove directly to the Geneva Historical Society on Main Street and parked on the opposite side of the street so I'd be facing the right direction when I drove home. With the exception of an older man walking a small dog, the street was practically deserted. Very different from the fall, when the college students are everywhere.

I walked up the concrete steps to the brick Federal-style building with its arched white doorway and leaded glass side panes. Once a family residence that belonged to the Proutys, the building was later given to the Geneva Historical Society to preserve the area's history. Oddly enough, I actually remembered that spiel from one of the docents during a school field trip years ago.

Off to my right was a former Victorian parlor, and I seemed to recall something about a style merger in this building/museum combination. On a small table in the foyer was a sign that read *Welcome, Visitors. Tours will resume in September. Please feel free to walk about and enjoy our museum. Donations gratefully accepted.* Next to the sign was a small glass jar with a few dollars in it. I reached into my bag and stuffed another one in there before walking down the hallway to the door marked, *Office.* That's when I heard an unmistakable voice.

Madeline Martinez from Billsburrow Winery, just north of Two Witches, was practically shrieking. "You can't be serious. This is the twenty-first century, not the nineteenth. I see no reason why we cannot add three feet to our existing porch cover. We need some relief from that dastardly afternoon sun."

I crept closer to the door, feigning interest in a landscape that hung on the wall adjacent to the office. Next to it was their alarm box, and some idiot had written the disarm code in blue marker next to the company name. I rolled my eyes and went back to the landscape. For a minute I wondered what Madeline was doing at Geneva's historical society, but then I remembered that her winery was in Ontario County, not Yates.

The next voice I heard was a man's. "I'm sorry, Mrs. Martinez, but your house falls under the covenants of the Geneva Historical District. As you recall, Ontario County, as well as Yates County, voted to extend their historical district to include the lake property that stretches from Geneva to Bellona."

"Hurumph. And they extended our real estate taxes to go along with it. Look, I'm not asking for an approval to remodel our farmhouse. All we want is some additional shade."

"Request denied. Of course, you're free to file an appeal with our board. Our next meeting is September sixteenth."

Madeline's voice got louder. "By then it will be snowing."

"One more thing, Mrs. Martinez. Should you decide to make those changes without our approval, you will be fined heavily and you'll have to remove the entire structure. Preserving our county's history is our number-one priority."

"I'd like to tell you what my number-one priority is right now but I'm a lady."

Suddenly, the door swung open and Madeline all but bumped into me.

"Norrie! What are you doing here? I hope you didn't hear all of that."

"Um, it was kind of hard not to."

We stepped away from the office door until we were near the front entrance. "I came here to see if anyone died in nineteen forty-eight under suspicious circumstances," I said. "Of all the ratty things, that lousy full moon summer solstice curse takes place this month. As if we haven't had enough drama on our wine trail this year."

"Goodness. That silly legend was around when I was growing up. People really don't believe it, do they?"

I bit my lip and grimaced. "Oh, yeah. Including one of our own employees. Anyway, I just wanted to check out the archives."

"Then it looks like you'll have to deal with Vance Wexler, the obnoxious little fussbudget I had words with in there. Not only is he the museum's director, but he's the president of the Geneva Historical Society and thinks he's the crown prince of the empire. Good luck with that. Well, approval or not from the *hysterical* society, I plan to have our porch extended, beginning this week. We've got a contractor lined up to do the work. I want it completed in time for the annual Winemakers' Dinner. In fact, I was going to drop off the tickets at your winery this afternoon. I've got to make the rounds."

"Yeah, our tasting room manager, Cammy, mentioned it. Hey, I wouldn't worry too much about the extra three feet. I doubt anyone will notice it from the road."

"Not anyone. That officious Vance Wexler. It wouldn't surprise me one iota if he came by with a yardstick when no one was looking."

"You think he'd do such a thing?"

"I know it. But it may be the last thing he does."

We said goodbye at the door and I headed back down the corridor to meet the infamous Vance Wexler face-to-face.

Chapter 3

Vance Wexler was sitting at a large wooden executive desk that looked as if it was part of the original furniture for the house. He appeared to be in his thirties with a brush cut, light brown mustache and goatee, and slight build.

He looked up from the pile of papers on his desk and rubbed his goatee. "Good afternoon. Do you have an appointment? The museum docents won't be back until the fall and our secretary left to run some errands."

"Oh," I said. "I presumed you were the secretary."

Madeline will get a kick out of this one.

"I happen to be Vance Wexler, the president of the Geneva Historical Society and the museum's director. And you are?"

"Norrie Ellington, co-owner of Two Witches Winery in Penn Yan."

Vance paused for a moment and adjusted the small gold earring in his right ear. "Ah, yes. Two Witches. I seem to remember your winery being in the news a while back. How may I help you?"

"Actually, I'd like us to stay out of the news. I need to look up archival information on obituaries in nineteen forty-eight. To see if there were any unexplained deaths in June. I know the historical society has all of the local newspapers from back then. Much easier than that microfiche at the library." Then I paused and took a gamble. "They haven't finished scanning everything to computer files."

Vance rubbed his hands together and sighed. "Unexplained deaths in June? June of nineteen forty-eight? Mind my asking—What on earth for?"

I shrugged. "To see if a local legend has any credence."

He pushed his chair from the desk and stood. "Follow me. The archive room is downstairs. You'll need to put on white gloves in order to read the newspapers."

I was relieved of one thing. *If* someone was found dead, the death would've taken place during or immediately after the summer solstice. That meant I only had to root through ten or so newspapers, not all thirty.

The archival room consisted of four large tables, a number of uncomfortable chairs, and overhead florescent lighting. Not the most welcoming of work spaces, but I didn't plan on being there long. Vance walked to a cabinet by the back wall and retrieved a pair of white gloves.

"Leave these on the table when you finish."

He then proceeded to open a large armoire, for lack of a better word, and pointed to stacks of newspapers, each positioned according to date.

"This section is for the nineteen forties," he said. "Knock yourself out. When you're finished, leave the newspapers on the table. My secretary will file them appropriately. Oh, and do be careful." He said the word *do* with one of those pseudo-English accents and I nearly gagged. "The paper is old and likely to crumble if you're not careful. The air in this room is kept at a certain humidity level, but still, time takes its toll on fragile papers."

"Thanks, I'll be careful."

He showed me how to retrieve the papers and I was pleasantly surprised that each one was separated by stronger cardboard paper. No notable deaths in the obituary section for the first three days that followed the summer solstice. But then, on the fourth day, off to the right on the front page, was a column titled, "Summer tourist found dead at campground."

The article was brief but contained all the salient details I needed to bring on a migraine. A forty-five-year-old machinist by the name of Eldridge McComb, from Elmira, New York, was found dead in his tent at a campground on Kashong Point. According to the coroner, Eldridge had been smothered in his sleep.

Terrific. There won't be enough sage sticks in the world to pacify Glenda.

I read the other six papers hoping for further news but there was nothing. And no obituary either. I figured that obit was sitting somewhere in an Elmira paper. It didn't matter. I had a name, and a place. Enough for a Google search.

With that, I left the papers and the gloves on the table and returned to the main floor. Vance Wexler's door was closed and I could hear his voice. Something about arrowheads and Kashong Point. A telephone call maybe? Or was the secretary in there? I pulled out one of our Two Witches business cards from my bag and scrawled "Thanks for your help" on the back, followed by a smiley face. Then I put it next to the donation jar on my way out of the building.

By the time I got home, it was two thirty and the sandwich I ate at Tim Horton's seemed like days ago. I pulled out some corn chips and the half-eaten jar of salsa I had in the fridge and made myself a snack. Charlie, who immediately woke up the minute he heard the rustling of the corn chip bag, assumed the begging position at the table.

"Boy, I've spoiled you for Francine and Jason," I told him as I handed him a corn chip. "You'll simply have to wear them down, I suppose, or you'll be stuck with organic non-GMO, non-grain dog food for the next decade."

Just then, the landline rang and I checked the caller ID—YCPSB, the initials for the Yates County Public Safety Building. Gladys Pipp had done her homework, too.

"Norrie, I hope I didn't catch you at a bad time but I was able to track down one person who died suspiciously and another who claimed—are you ready for this?—that a vampire witch, known as a shtriga, tried to smother her with a pillow but she fought her off. All in June of nineteen forty-eight. At Kashong Point. Norrie, are you there?"

"Um, yeah. I'm here all right. I'm just trying to process the last thing you said. About a vampire witch. It wasn't a woman, was it? With a sister who lived on our hill?"

Because that's all I need. Two witches isn't enough. Now one of them has to be a vampire witch.

"The article didn't say. In fact, it made no mention of the woman's name. But the male victim was—"

"Eldridge McComb from Elmira?"

"You found it, too, huh? What paper?"

"Geneva Daily Times," I said. "They went out of print in nineteen fifty-five. Where'd you get your info from?"

Gladys cleared her throat, then chuckled. *"Penn Yan Chronicle Express*, where else? And they're still around. Of course, the paper only comes out once a week. Maybe that's the secret to their longevity."

We compared notes but neither of us had any more information than what I originally found from my own search.

"How did Grizzly Gary, oops, I mean Deputy Hickman, take the news when you told him?" I asked.

"I haven't told him. He's out on call. I don't expect him back until a little before five. Listen, you don't really believe in this nonsense, do you?"

"No, but tales like that tend to ward off some tourists while beckoning the nutcases to visit us. That's the last thing our winery needs. I'm going to see if I can find out more about Eldridge McComb. Maybe his autopsy report showed a medical condition."

"And that shtriga witch?"

I cringed. "Mum's the word as far as I'm concerned. Besides, who else is going to find out about her?"

Bite my tongue. Who else indeed?

• • •

When I got to the tasting room at ten the next day, Cammy informed me that Glenda called in sick, something about needing a ritualistic body purifying that couldn't wait.

"Like a medicinal scrub or something?" I asked. "Or maybe probiotics?"

Cammy shook her head. "More like ward off the evil spirits. Seems one of Zenora's friends from that circle of crazies they hang out with told her about—can you believe this?—a she-witch-vampire who apparently sucks the life out of victims during the full moon summer solstice."

"Hmm, same one who smothers them, or are we dealing with three witches? Two regular and one a bit more of a night creature . . . Oh, what am I saying? This is nuts. Glenda can't possibly believe this."

"Not *can't*. *Does*. Anyway, forget the witches for a minute. Are you all set for the winery meeting at eleven?"

"Oh, my gosh. The winery meeting. I'd completely forgotten, but not to worry. I've got my notes on my desk."

Francine always conducted a winery meeting each month with our three managers: Franz Johannas, the head winemaker, John Grishner, the vineyard manager, and Cammy Rosinetti, the tasting room manager. Mainly, it was a time for us to review the calendar, provide updates in our areas, discuss any concerns we might have, and share new ideas or proposals. Usually the meetings lasted an hour unless Franz got off on some tangent.

I rushed into my office, reviewed my notes, and took a breath. Nothing out of the ordinary. Since that winemaker dinner was taking place at Madeline's Billsburrow Winery, I didn't have to worry about hosting an event. My mind immediately circled back to each of our three areas.

As far as the vineyards were concerned, June was a month for tying down vines. The only holdup would be rain and muddy soil. That would postpone the process, but as far as I knew, no major rainstorms were predicted. Good thing, too, because the vines have to be tied down before the buds swell. Those buds are so fragile, all it takes is one touch and a bud can be knocked off the vine, resulting in the loss of a cane that could produce up to four clusters of grapes or more.

The tasting room was under control. Our summer college students were hired and a few of them had already started to work part-time, allowing our regulars like Roger, Sam, Glenda, and Lizzie to use vacation time. Gift shop inventory for the summer had arrived, and that included an additional design for our T-shirts and sweatshirts. Apparently Alvin was a big hit with kids and visitors wanted souvenirs with his likeness on them. Go figure.

As for the winemaking, I didn't expect any surprises. The summer is when we finish up with last year's wines, so that means lots of bottling in order to prepare the tanks for the fall harvest. Franz, along with Alan and Herbert, the assistant winemakers, knew what they were doing, and as long as I could steer them away from any long dissertations about fermentation, maceration, and any of the other "ations," I'd be okay.

Or so I thought.

Chapter 4

Our meeting began a few minutes past eleven in the small banquet room, adjacent to our tasting room. Cammy set out a pitcher of iced tea and a plate of oatmeal raisin cookies that Emma in our bistro had baked.

It was only the four of us and I didn't expect the meeting to run more than an hour. However, in light of the fact that some people—Glenda mainly, and Deputy Hickman—were getting edgy about the summer solstice falling on the same day as the full moon, I thought I'd cut to the chase and get it over with.

"Um, before we start with calendar events and reports from everyone, I thought I should bring up the subject of the summer solstice."

John took a sip of his iced tea and scratched the back of his head. "It's not that big a deal. In fact, it's like having our own Alexa or Google Echo, only in this case it's Mother Nature reminding us of the time."

Mother Nature? What the heck is he talking about? "Huh?"

"The summer solstice marks the end of the grape growing, or canopy growth, as we refer to it. Simple, really. The berries stop growing and they ripen. The ripening gives them their flavor. The date's usually June twentieth or twenty-first, depending on the calendar. Not a concern. But if you want to know the concern I have, it's heat spikes. Heat spikes result in less acid in the soil and that translates to concerns with balance and longevity for the grapes. Anyway, since we can't do a darn thing about it, we'll have to make adjustments should that situation arise."

"Uh, yeah. Grape ripening and all that," I said. "But this year's summer solstice falls on a full moon and we all know what that means."

Franz looked at John, who in turn shrugged.

"The witch legend," I said. "The stupid Two Witches legend about someone getting smothered in their sleep on the night of the solstice."

At that point, John's eyes widened and he leaned forward. "If this means more crazed tourists tromping through our vineyards on the night of the solstice, we'll have to rope off the rows like last time."

"I'm not worried about that," I said. "I'm worried it will keep them away."

John laughed. "Not on your life. If anything, it will bring them out."

"If you say so. Anyway, we might as well get started with Cammy's overview of the summer calendar."

Since we didn't have any special events planned, Cammy was finished in less than thirty seconds and added a quick update about the tasting room. Then John went on to explain that they were working nonstop to tie down the vines and checking to be sure we had proper drainage in the likely event of summer storms.

When he finished, Franz leaned back in his chair and said, "I'd like to introduce rosé."

He said it as if he was about to introduce some debutante at a cotillion and I blurted out, "Rosé? Rosé the wine?"

Franz looked stunned. "Of course the wine. What else? Don't any of you recall our meeting this past fall when I introduced the topic and gave a brief explanation about the four different methods for producing rosé wines? I distinctly remember explaining about limited skin maceration, direct pressing, blending, and the less popular, albeit effective, saignée method."

Oh, my gosh. Now that he mentions it . . . That was the same time I was working on those screenplay edits for Renee. I must have tuned him out.

"So, as I was saying," Franz went on, "Alan, Herbert, and I decided to use the limited skin maceration process where we allowed the juice to remain with the skins for eight hours. We felt six would be too short and certainly didn't want to exceed the cutoff of forty-eight hours."

Nope. Wouldn't want to exceed that . . .

"We're anxious for aromas of cherry and perhaps watermelon but it's too early to tell, of course. And naturally we would want those aromas to carry over to the taste."

"Um, naturally," I said.

"Since this is a new wine for us, it's being produced in a limited quantity. Dependent upon its success, we'll decide what alterations, if any, we'll need to make next year. Oh, and lest I forget, we're awaiting label approval from the Alcohol and Tobacco Tax and Trade Bureau. Aargh! Bureaucracy! Nothing like the U.S. Treasury to take its time. You know, before 2011, label approval took a week. Now, it's months."

"Rosé's a good addition," Cammy said. "So many of our visitors request Zinfandel and are disappointed when we tell them the grape can't be grown in this region. A nice pink blush wine such as our new rosé is bound to be a hit."

The meeting ended with a reminder about the winemakers' dinner and all three managers, plus the winemaker assistants, Herbert and Alan, planned to attend. Madeline told me they rented one of those enormous wedding tents for the occasion and planned to situate it on the top of their vineyard for a spectacular lake view.

No one mentioned another word about the summer solstice but it still plagued me. When the meeting ended, I grabbed a panini at our bistro and walked home to accomplish two things: the screenplay I was working on and my research on Eldridge McCombs's cause of death.

I spent the rest of the day on my couch toggling back and forth on my laptop between Microsoft Office 2016, where I kept my screenplay, and Google, where I tried desperately to pull up information on Eldridge.

At a little before five, Bradley called. He'd been in Syracuse for the past two days meeting with a prominent family regarding a complicated trust.

"My brain feels like mush," he said. "I can't wait till Friday when we can relax at Port of Call. Maybe take in a late movie if something decent is playing. Then again, I'd probably fall asleep and snore through it, that's how tired I am. By the way, I got a phone message from Madeline Martinez from that winery group of yours. She wanted to know if individuals could sue historical societies. Do you know anything about this? Figured I'd ask before I got back to her. I wasn't sure if it was personal or pertained to your group."

"Personal," I said, "but it could affect anyone in our group should we decide to make exterior alterations on our houses that don't meet the historical standards."

I told him about Madeline's dealings with Vance Wexler and how he brushed her off.

"Okay, I'll give her a buzz. Usually it's the other way around. You know, historical societies suing individuals or entities. Anyway, I'm counting the days until Friday. Miss you."

"Same here. Oh, wait. Don't hang up yet. Any chance you can help me dig up information on Eldridge McComb? He died under suspicious circumstances in nineteen forty-eight. Right here in Kashong Point."

"Is that a relative of yours?"

"Um, no, but he may have been murdered by the former occupants of our hill."

"Hold on. I need to grab a cup of coffee for this one."

By the time I was done, not only did Bradley agree to help me learn more about Eldridge, but told me he had relatives in Elmira, New York, who may have heard something over the years.

"I'd sleep better," I said, "if I knew the guy died of a heart attack or stroke as opposed to having the breath sucked out of him."

"Who wouldn't? I'll make some calls. Pick you up at seven on Friday, okay?"

"Sounds good."

Apparently Bradley wasn't the only one enamored with Port of Call, because not more than a minute or two later, I got another invite. This time from Theo at the Grey Egret, the winery just down from us on the same hill.

"So what do you say, Norrie? Friday at Port of Call? Don's been hankering for their parmesan-encrusted chicken wings in garlic butter. He won't stop talking about it."

"I'll be there but Bradley beat you to it. We've got a date. He's picking me up at seven. But hey, it's casual. I'm sure he won't mind if we grab appetizers together at the bar."

"Sounds like a plan. See you there."

I returned to my screenplay and put Eldridge on hold. He was already dead, unlike my script, which faced a less-than-two-week deadline. In the back of my mind, I hoped Bradley would be able to dig up some dirt on the guy. For a young family lawyer in Geneva, Bradley seemed to have a zillion connections everywhere. Maybe that's because he partnered with Marvin Souza, one of the most prominent attorneys in the Finger Lakes. And one of the orneriest.

By seven fifteen I was starving, but it was slim pickings in the fridge. I scrambled up eggs with feta cheese and tried to convince myself it was a gourmet dinner. Then I made a run to Wegmans and stocked up on real food like fruits, fresh vegetables, sliced beef and chicken tenders—because I was too lazy to cut the meat myself for stir-frying—as well as assorted pastas, sauces, and cheeses. For good measure, I made sure to pick up the usual snack food and three small containers of ice cream. Charlie had more than enough kibble since I had gotten to the farm store the week before, but to be on the safe side, I bought him a giant box of organic, made-in-the-U.S.A. dog biscuits.

The jaunt to Hamilton Street in Geneva would have taken me less than an hour if it wasn't for one thing—the checkout fiasco. I was two customers down on the line when I spied Vance Wexler unloading his groceries onto the conveyer belt. He didn't have that many items, but as soon as each item was scanned, he stopped the cashier to verify the price against some app he had on his phone.

The man directly behind me could be heard uttering expletives I'd rather not mention, but when Vance accused the cashier of "price-gouging him to death" and a manager had to be called over, I figured Madeline may have had the right idea in the first place—legal action. I swear, the entire line probably felt like applauding when he finally left.

"If I didn't need this job," the cashier told the woman ahead of me, "I'd poke a large hole in each of his grocery bags."

"Oh, honey," she said, "I'd do more than that."

When I left Wegmans, I wondered how many people Vance Wexler managed to tick off in a given day. Heck, counting myself and Madeline, plus the people in the checkout line, he had already reached at least five. With those odds, I would have hated to see the full day's tally.

Chapter 5

The next few days were pretty uneventful except for a Friday morning phone call from Godfrey Klein asking me if I wanted to visit the field study site on Kashong Point where Alex Bollinger set up shop with an assistant entomologist and some students.

"It's a fascinating study, really," he said. "Are you aware that there are three population peaks from May to June? Of course, farther north in Ontario, the peaks are spread out and can last until September."

"Um, yeah. Fascinating. But why Kashong Point?"

"It's centrally located to all of those farms that produce broccoli, cauliflower, and cabbage."

"I see."

Godfrey's voice was more animated than usual. "Alex is working in conjunction with the Center for Invasive Species at the University of Georgia. It's a joint grant and the setup is amazing. They have the latest computer technology in their field station."

"You mean in tents? The setup is in a tent like in *M.A.S.H.*?"

"Come to think of it, that's a good way to describe it, only we're in the twenty-first century now, not mid-twentieth. So what do you say? Are you interested?"

I did a mental eye roll and was glad we were on a landline and not Facetime. "Uh, how can anyone not be interested? But I'm really stuck cranking out this screenplay. It's due in less than two weeks so I'm kind of tethered to my laptop and the couch."

"No problem. Alex's study will still be going on once you get that screenplay in. You can join us later this month."

Unless a tsunami wipes out Seneca Lake, I'm stuck. "Sounds good."

At noon I stopped by the winery to see how things were going. Other than Glenda mouthing "It's not too late" when I passed by her tasting room table, everything was business as usual. I grabbed a chicken salad sandwich on rye and returned home to eat it while I reviewed my screenplay notes.

By five thirty I was wiped out and called it quits for the day. I jumped in the shower and got ready for my dinner out with Bradley. I snagged an emerald green gauzy sheath dress from Francine's closet, and grabbed a lightweight cardigan in case it got cooler on the deck.

When Bradley and I arrived at Port of Call, Theo and Don were already at the bar and motioned for us to join them. A huge platter of mixed appetizers took up most of the bar space.

"Looks like we may be here a while," Theo said. "Even with reservations they're backed up. Eat up. We can always order more."

Don looked around the room and moaned. "As long as they don't run out of my parmesan-encrusted wings, I'll be fine."

We spent the next few minutes talking about the looming summer solstice and some telescoping ladder that Theo just *had* to buy, when Bradley suddenly stopped nibbling on the Jamaican beef tender he was holding. "Eldridge McComb. I was so mired under at work today I completely forgot about it."

Don gave him a funny look. "Is that someone we're supposed to know? Don't tell me it's some jerk from the Department of Agriculture about new winery regulations. What did they do? Send information out to all the local attorneys?"

Bradley and I tripped over each other's words. "No, he died in nineteen—suspicious death—found at Kashong Poi—happened on a full moon solstice—"

"Will one of you stop talking and the other one explain? I feel like I'm watching a Ping-Pong match," Don said.

I took a deep breath and reiterated everything I knew about Eldridge McComb. Then Bradley added the proverbial icing on the cake.

"My great aunt lives in Elmira and remembered hearing about Eldridge when she was a little girl. About five or six years old. Said her parents and all the neighbors talked about it for days on end. What she overheard scared the daylights out of her for years and she insisted on sleeping with the lights on."

I felt as if someone had punched me in the gut. "What story?"

"The guy had gone camping with a few buddies of his, and when he didn't get up for breakfast the next morning, they went to check on him. Dead as a doorknob. No sign of a struggle. And he was in perfectly good health. My aunt recalls hearing her mother say 'the hand of death reached out and got him.' Hell, that would have kept me up nights, too."

"Any chance you could track down a death certificate?"

Bradley flashed an enormous smile and took out his cell phone. "I can do better. I can show it to you. You can thank Marvin the next time you see him."

I took the phone from his hand and enlarged the photo. Under "Cause of Death" was one word—*Undetermined*. I handed the phone back to Bradley. "That means they didn't find any reason for him to suddenly stop breathing. Right?"

"It doesn't mean there wasn't one, Norrie. It just means they couldn't determine a cause. It was nineteen forty-eight. They didn't have the resources they do today. Look, I wouldn't worry about it if I were you. It's just a coincidence, that's all. Try to put it out of your mind."

"Bradley's right," Theo said. "All of this is poppycock. The full moon. The solstice. The witches' curse. Hey, maybe you can put it in one of your screenplays."

"Nice try. I write romance, not horror."

"No," Don said. "Horror is waiting for a table to open up. Will you look at that crowd?"

I turned my head to face the double sliding doors that led out to the giant wraparound deck. "Yep, it's packed all right. But something's opening up. I see people moving away from a table. I see—Oh, hell no. Three times in one week? That's Vance Wexler leaving the table and walking toward us. Oops. My mistake. He's headed for the exit. It's only a few feet away. Whew. I told all of you about him, didn't I?"

"And then some," Theo said. "At least we're in the Yates County Historical District, not Ontario."

Suddenly, a heavyset man with a ruddy complexion made a beeline for Vance. The man appeared to be in his late forties or perhaps early fifties, and his voice was so loud that he could be heard above the restaurant and bar chatter.

"Mr. Wexler! Don't try giving me the slip. My wife said she thought it was you at that table but I wasn't about to interrupt anyone's dinner. Now that you're leaving, perhaps we can have a conversation about your denial for our backyard pool application."

Vance turned away from the man and started for the door. "Make an appointment with my secretary."

"And wait another week? This has gone on long enough." The man sidestepped Vance and blocked the door. "It's for a backyard swimming pool, for crying out loud. Backyard! No one can see it from the road. It won't interfere with your historical preservation or whatever the hell it is you've got going on."

"I'm afraid there's nothing I can do. Late-nineteenth-century houses cannot have swimming pools on their property."

"I'm not living in the nineteenth century, I'm living now. According to the letter we received about our appeal, you were the deciding voice."

"Indeed. And now please get out of my way."

"This isn't over, Mr. Wexler. Not by a long shot. And I'd watch my back if I were you."

"Is that a threat?"

"It's a piece of advice. Take it."

The four of us held our collective breaths as Vance hurried out of the restaurant. We didn't make a sound until the ruddy-faced man had brushed by our seats and was out of earshot. Don stretched his neck and didn't turn back to the bar for a few seconds. "Hmm, I think I've seen that man before, I just can't place him. Rats. This is going to plague me all night."

"Maybe not," Theo said. "Looks like your order for those garlic butter parmesan wings is on its way."

Chapter 6

If anyone did the plaguing, it was Vance Wexler. For a man I hadn't met in the eleven months I'd been babysitting Two Witches, he certainly made up for it this past week. Madeline was fit to be tied, the cashier at Wegmans had reached her apex, and the man who wanted to install a pool was one step away from combustion. But none of that compared to the issue that Alex Bollinger from the Experiment Station faced.

Godfrey called me midweek to see if I wanted to "pop over and check out the field station on Kashong Point."

"It's still drizzling," I said, looking past the couch at the window that faced the winery. I had moved from my usual couch position with the laptop to a small tray table and high-back chair. "And the ground's pretty muddy after the past four days of rain. Maybe we can do it another time."

"Yeah, you're probably right. Besides, Alex is in quite the mood about that historical society expedition. They're tromping all over the place with no regard for his research."

"Historical expedition? Tromping all over? What are you talking about?"

"I thought I told you. No, wait, come to think of it, I mentioned it to my landlady. Sorry. I'm getting so absentminded lately. Anyway, seems the Geneva Historical Society got approval from the county board to scour and search for Native American arrowheads and similar artifacts that get washed up from the lake. Had the approval for months but were waiting on a solid rainstorm so the creeks would swell and the arrowheads would be more visible on the lakefront."

"At least the rain is good for something. I know the grapevines don't like it when the soil gets wet. If they had their way, those vines would be happy in a dry-weather climate all year-round. And our vineyard manager isn't all too thrilled either. Something about decreased sugar level and having to spray for more pesky insects . . ."

Godfrey cleared his throat and continued to talk. "A crew of six or seven would-be anthropologists pitched their tents on the higher ground just below the Kashong conservation area. A stone's throw from Alex's setup. According to Alex, it's been a nightmare."

"You mean they're interfering with the insect study?"

"If you ask Alex, he'd tell you they're sabotaging it. Yesterday he got into a huge row with the president of the historical society and wound up telling him that the New York State Conservation Department trumps the city board of directors any day of the week."

"The president? Vance Wexler? *That* president?"

"Could be. Alex was too busy spouting off. Said he had a good mind to wallop that haughty son-of-a-gun in the face."

"Yeah, it had to be Vance. I only met the guy last week and from what I could tell, Alex will need to take a number."

Godfrey laughed. "I'll give you a call in a few days. Maybe the ground will dry out by then."

"Sounds good. Hey, if you wind up hearing from my sister, remind her that I only agreed to another week or two."

"Think Bastille Day. That's July fourteenth. The French got their independence, maybe you'll get yours."

"Fine. Not one minute past Bastille Day. Tell her that."

Other than my sister and brother-in-law, I think the only one happy with me staying longer in Penn Yan was my subletter. It meant she didn't have to return to her mother's house and launch a mega search for a new place right away.

It was midmorning and I was getting fidgety considering I'd been writing since seven thirty. I was about to get myself a snack when my phone rang. For a second I'd forgotten where I put the darned thing, but the ringtone was so loud I followed it all the way to the kitchen table.

"Norrie! It's Cammy. Did you see the front page of the *Penn Yan Chronicle Express*? Lizzie brought it in."

"I only read it when it's lying around the winery. Why?"

"Two Witches is on the front page. Not the major headline, but the column off to the right. Where everyone sees it."

"Did Franz send them something about our new rosé? He's supposed to clear that stuff with me."

"Not the rosé. The full moon falling on the summer solstice. The headline reads, 'Will Two Witches Curse Return on the Solstice?'"

"Oh, crap. What else does it say?"

Cammy made a half-hum, half-moan sound. "Er, nothing we don't already know. Explains about the curse and mentions one suspicious death back in nineteen forty-eight. That's about it."

Guess the paper did its homework, too.

27

"Think it will keep tourists away or bring out the crazies?"

"Oh, the crazies for sure. Glenda's taken to dabbing herself with biblical oils but that's not surprising. Anyway, just thought you should know. Are you going to stop by here today?"

"Um, maybe later in the afternoon. I'm still trudging through that screenplay."

"No worries. Catch you later."

When I got off the phone, I sent a text message to John. Short and sweet. "Rope off those rows ASAP." He'd understand. They read the *Chronicle Express* like everyone else in Penn Yan.

The summer solstice was nine days away, counting the day itself, and it couldn't come fast enough as far as I was concerned. I just wanted to get the whole stupid thing over with so I could go on with my life without worrying about curses from the beyond. Or more specifically, from our hill.

• • •

In retrospect, maybe I shouldn't have been in such a hurry after all. In the nine days preceding the lunar and calendar event, I'd had two dinners out with Bradley and one at Don and Theo's. I had successfully managed to avoid an outing with Godfrey to check on the Swede midge study at Kashong Point, and was thrilled that our WOW, or Wineries of the West, meeting had been postponed until after the solstice because Madeline, who usually hosts the meeting, was too busy conferring with her lawyer, and complaining to anyone else who would listen, about her letter of architectural denial from the Geneva Historical Society.

Both Two Witches and the Grey Egret saw an uptick in customers during the few days leading up to the solstice. We also had a record number of sales for our witch-themed T-shirts. Still, I was uneasy. In fact, I found myself checking out all sorts of astronomical websites, including NASA and Space.com, not to mention *The Old Farmer's Almanac*. I needed to be prepared.

According to NASA, the summer solstice would begin at precisely eleven fifty-two a.m. in our neck of the woods. The sun would reach its farthest point from earth at that time and wahoo! That night, the full moon would show up and, if superstition and legend held, some poor unsuspecting soul would take his or her last breath. Needless to say, I was so jumpy the morning of the solstice that I couldn't sit still. Thank goodness I had finished my screenplay and shot it off to my script analyst a few days before.

"All we have to do is hold our breath until tomorrow morning," I announced to Cammy, Glenda, Sam, Lizzie, and Roger when I walked into the tasting room at ten.

Glenda looked ashen. "That's not all we have to do. We have to purify the room. Cleanse it of malevolent spirits."

Sam, who stood next to her by a wine rack, gave her a nudge. "There's a bottle of Lysol under the sink. Knock yourself out."

"It's not funny," Glenda said. "I'll do the best I can by quietly chanting in between customers."

I rubbed my temples and walked toward them. "Fine. As long as you don't scare them off."

Given the article in the paper and the nonstop local gossip, our tasting room tables were packed all day long. It was a good thing, because I needed to keep busy. I rotated among the tables, allowing the regulars to take breaks and grab lunch.

When it finally got to closing time, Glenda grabbed me by the wrist and asked, "Do you want one of us to stay with you tonight? We all live past that five-mile radius but you don't."

"I'll be fine. Charlie passes gas all night. It wakes me up every hour on the hour."

"We could do a phone tree thing. You know, call you every hour on the hour to make sure you're still—"

"I know. Breathing. Like I said, I'll be fine."

The five-mile radius. Whoever thought of that! With the exception of Madeline's place, all the wineries in WOW were in a five-mile radius. And Alex's crew was at the epicenter. Maybe I should've given Glenda *his* cell number.

All of us left the winery at the same time and Cammy locked the doors behind me. I took my time walking back up the hill to the house. Although the rains had stopped days ago, it was still humid and miserable outside. So much for those delightful breezes the tourist brochures rave about.

I stir-fried beef in a combination of soy and oyster's sauces and added broccoli to convince myself it was a healthy dinner. Healthy or not, Charlie enjoyed the small portion I added to his kibble and sacked out on the floor as soon as he was done.

When I finished with the dishes, I checked out Facebook, answered some emails, and surfed the internet. Bradley called at a little past eight and was stuck in the office with Marvin. Something about a family trust with tentacles. I briefly considered inviting him over to spend the night but thought otherwise. One thing would lead to another, and I'd be returning to Manhattan by Bastille Day. At least according to Godfrey.

For the next hour, I moved from surfing the internet to surfing the TV and finally landed on an old sci-fi movie that had scared the daylights out of Francine and me—*Invasion of the Body Snatchers*. If you didn't want the Martians, or whoever they were, to get you and destroy your emotions, you had to force yourself to stay awake. If you fell asleep, it would be too late. You'd wake up a virtual zombie.

I thought about it for a moment and shuddered. Was it that different from the Two Witches curse? Fall asleep and risk being smothered to death. I checked the time on my iPhone and half expected Glenda to call, begging me to pull an all-nighter or douse myself in some foul-smelling herbs. Instead, I switched the channel and wound up watching one of my mother's favorites, *Auntie Mame*, starring Rosalind Russell.

When I woke up, it was past one and I stumbled up the stairs to my bed. I shoved Charlie off to the side and pulled down the lightweight cover. "If anyone or anything comes into this room, growl or something, will you?"

Chapter 7

The hazy sunshine cast a direct beam across my bed and into my eyes. Comatose, I reached across the nightstand and checked my iPhone. It read 5:29 a.m. *Good. I've lived to see another day*. I leaned back on my pillow and pulled the worn cotton sheet over my head, too lazy to pull the curtains.

Another hour slipped by and I had no choice but to get up. Charlie nudged my head with his and made deep guttural sounds. I knew he wanted me to open the doggie door and get him some kibble. Too bad they don't make an Alexa or Google Echo for that.

By seven fifteen, I was at the kitchen table with a cup of Dunkin' Medium Roast in my hand, compliments of the Keurig. Charlie had already returned from his jaunt outside and had gobbled most of his kibble. That's when the landline rang and the caller ID indicated it was Stephanie Ipswich from Gable Hill Winery.

My morning voice was soft and creaky. "Hullo?"

"Oh, good, you're up. Derek and I didn't get a wink of sleep. The twins were in our bed all night. Petrified that a horrible witch from your hill was going to murder them. For your information, that story's been going around the elementary school all month."

Stephanie and her husband owned the winery on the next road over from ours. They had twin first-grade boys and a mother-in-law who was a saint to take care of them.

"Is that why you called?"

"No, but I thought I'd start with that. I called because a few of Hanson's cows got out of their enclosure this morning. That's only a hop, skip, and a jump to our place and yours if those bovines stick to the top of the hill. I wanted to let you know in case that Plott hound of yours sees them and goes nuts."

"Yeesh. Charlie won't go nuts but our vineyard manager will. I'll send him a text right now. Thanks for letting me know."

"Any time. Uh, you don't put any credence into that stuff, do you? About the full moon and the solstice?"

"Hey, we're still breathing and I imagine everyone else is, too, so no, I don't. Tell your kids those stories are a bunch of bologna."

"Already tried. At their age they tend to believe the schoolyard talk

31

before anything Derek and I say."

I laughed. "Catch you later."

The next call came just as I finished smearing jam on my toast. This time it was from Theo.

"Hey, Norrie. Don and I wanted to let you know Rosalee Marbleton is alive and well at Terrace Wineries. Don had a funny feeling and insisted we call her this morning. She all but went ballistic. Spouted off that just because she's, and I quote, 'a woman of a certain age,' didn't mean she was 'circling the drain.' Don tried to explain that he was checking on our neighbors over that full moon deal but she didn't buy it. Anyway, thought you should know."

"Stephanie and Derek are still breathing, too. She called because Hanson's cows got out again."

Suddenly, the sound of sirens came from everywhere. I heard them loud and clear from my phone connection with Theo and equally loud from my own living room. The noise seemed to reverberate off of our hill.

"Can you hear that?" Theo asked. "Looks like an entire brigade's headed south on Route 14. I see at least one fire truck and two sheriff cars."

"Must be one heck of an accident, huh?"

"Yeah, and so early in the morning. I don't think it's a fire or there'd be more fire trucks. Then again, if they're responding out of Bellona or Penn Yan, they'd be coming from the other direction."

"Hope it's not one of the wineries."

"Guess we'll know soon enough."

I went back to my breakfast and followed up with a brisk shower. Since I'd met my screen analyst's deadline, the only thing I had on my agenda, other than helping out in the tasting room, was to submit a proposal for a future screenplay. I figured I'd work on that for the next day or so and then send it in.

By nine thirty I had made myself comfortable on the couch and sifted through some old notes from Renee regarding favored locations. Seaside towns. Beachy towns. Coastal towns . . . Atlantic or Pacific, it didn't matter. I wondered if perhaps she'd changed one litter box too many and got nostalgic. But what the heck. If she wanted a beach-themed romance, that's what she'd get.

No sooner had I reached for my laptop than another phone call came in. Usually, I don't get as many calls in a week, let alone in a single morning. It was Godfrey and he spoke faster than usual. "I'm on my way to Kashong Point. Alex called. There's a situation going on."

"What do you mean? Some of the specimens got loose or something? Oh, no, don't tell me those arrowhead scavengers messed with the field lab."

"Worse. Much worse. One of those scavengers was found dead in his tent this morning."

The words *dead* and *tent* had an edge that cut right through me. I immediately thought of Eldridge McComb and gasped. "How? Who? When?"

"All Alex would say was that someone discovered the body shortly after dawn when their expedition director from the historical society didn't show up at their campfire for breakfast. It was Vance Wexler, the guy who he had it out with a few days ago."

Yeesh. Talk about karma coming back to bite you.

"Vance Wexler? Dead? Did Alex say what happened?"

"He said that his crew was scattered between the shore and the field tent. They had already eaten and were fast at work when they heard someone scream, 'Vance is dead. Vance is dead.'"

"Then what?"

"What else? They dropped everything and rushed to the scene. Alex said it was utter chaos. Someone, he doesn't know who, dialed nine-one-one, and the next thing he knew the place was flooded with sheriff deputies and even a fire truck."

The sirens. The barrage on Route 14. That explains it. Not an accident. Not a fire.

"Everyone's being held for questioning. The historical society members and Alex's crew. It doesn't look good, Norrie. Alex said there wasn't a single person in the area who didn't hear him arguing with Vance."

"That doesn't mean anything. Lots of people argued with Vance. In fact, Theo, Don, Bradley, and I watched a full-blown shouting fest at Port of Call not that long ago."

"But this happened on-site."

"Alex didn't happen to see Vance's body, did he?"

"No, one of the historical society volunteers did. Told everyone there was no outward sign of blood or a struggle, but the person didn't pull back the covers to see if maybe Vance had been stabbed or shot."

"Is the body still there?"

"No. It, I mean Vance, was placed on a gurney and loaded into the coroner's van. Alex said he felt numb watching the whole thing. Look, I don't know if they'll let anyone near the scene but I'm hoping I can wield some clout and talk with Alex. Feel like taking a ride?"

I slammed my laptop shut and shoved Renee's notes to the corner of the couch. "I'm ready to go. See you when you get here. Um, drive to the winery building. I'll meet you out front."

"On my way. Give me fifteen to twenty minutes."

Charlie, who was asleep near the couch, looked up as I gathered Renee's notes and stuck them under a large bowl on the kitchen table. "You've got plenty of fresh water and some more kibble. Be a good boy."

With that, I grabbed my bag, locked the door behind me and literally power-walked my way down the hill to the winery. It wouldn't open for another few minutes but cars were already in the parking lot. I took a deep breath, stepped inside, and took in the scene.

Cammy, Glenda, Sam, and Roger were all making minor adjustments to their tasting room tables and Lizzie was hunched over by the computer/cash register. Across the room, at the bistro, I could make out Fred and Emma behind the counter.

"Hey, Norrie," Cammy shouted. "Looks like everyone survived the night."

I walked toward her and in my softest voice possible replied, "Not everyone."

Apparently my voice wasn't soft enough because next thing I knew, Sam called out, "Don't tell me the Two Witches curse returned for another season."

In that instant, Glenda grabbed the table as if she was about to swoon but managed to steady herself instead. "What are you saying?"

"Vance Wexler from the Geneva Historical Society was found dead in his tent at Kashong Point. I'm going there now with Godfrey. He was the one who called me. Their department is conducting an insect study there."

Sam scratched his head and chuckled. "And Godfrey thinks those bugs might have killed the guy?"

"Don't be absurd. It was the solstice curse. The full moon solstice curse," Glenda said. "Mark my words. There'll be no sign of foul play. Zenora predicted this would happen. She's very attuned to the occult."

Wonderful. Let's have the Yates County Sheriff's Office add her to their payroll. "I'll let you know what I find out. Meanwhile, don't mention this to our guests."

Who was I kidding? It'll be all over social media before Godfrey and I even get down the driveway.

Chapter 8

I'd seen Kashong Point on busy days—picnics, parties, camp events, and even weddings. But I'd never seen it as harried and frenetic as it looked when Godfrey and I turned off of Route 14 and approached the circular drive that opened up to the area. Cars were parked everywhere and people were milling all about. I imagine the owners of the homes that faced the driveway weren't all that thrilled with the traffic.

Godfrey continued past the driveway and down the road to the left where Alex's field station was set up. It was adjacent to the shoreline and a few yards away from private residences according to Godfrey.

"Holy hell," he said. "Look straight ahead. They've got everything cordoned off except for the lake itself."

Sure enough, there was enough crime scene tape to stretch from here to Idaho. Just past the tape, at least two dozen people were moving about, forming small clusters that grew and then disappeared in seconds as the crowd shifted.

About twenty feet away I spied two Yates County Sheriff's Office vehicles. Parked without the lights flashing. Godfrey pulled the car off to the side, carefully wedging it between two other cars that lined the road.

"I'm taking my chances," he said, "and ducking under the tape. I need to find Alex. What's the worst they can do to me? Tell me to go home?"

"Or arrest you for interfering with a crime scene. Been there before. Come on, let's do it. There are so many people here, those deputies won't know the difference."

We moved quickly, skirting the crowd that had now shifted closer to the smaller tents that comprised the historical society's campsite. At least I was fairly certain it was their campsite because Godfrey told me Alex's crew was staying in a large, modern structure.

Just then, Godfrey caught sight of Alex and waved. "Over here!"

Within seconds, Alex charged toward us, pausing once to look behind. "I'm supposed to remain with my students and—" He pointed to a small group of people who were seated on some picnic benches and then reached his hand out to shake mine. "Godfrey drag you into this?"

I nodded. "I wouldn't exactly call it dragging. I kind of have a vested interest."

"Forget the vested interest for a minute," Godfrey said. Then he faced Alex. "What's with Cassie? I thought Arvin Pincus was the admin assistant for this project."

Alex looked behind again and then turned back. "He was. Until he wound up with a bad case of poison oak from that spider mite study in Watkins Glen. He talked Cassie into taking his place."

"Yeesh. I've never seen her outside the lab. Guess there's a first time for everything."

"Yeah, including an unexplained death right under our noses. So help me, if they find he was stabbed, shot, or choked to death, I may be spending the night in the county lockup. Vance and I got into one doozy of an argument yesterday afternoon, and worse yet, we had a major verbal altercation last night. Everyone must have heard us."

I brushed a strand of hair from my brow and stepped closer to Alex. "That doesn't mean anything."

"Tell that to Deputy Hickman. I gave him my preliminary statement, along with the rest of my crew. After that, we were directed to sit and wait while they question the members of Vance's team and the other campers in the area who happened to pick the wrong weekend for a vacation."

"Look, until they know anything substantial, it's all speculation. Did you notify the department head?"

"I sent a text. It's Saturday. He probably won't read it until Monday morning. Maybe that's just as well."

"You've got an alibi. You were in your field tent all night with your crew."

Alex shook his head. "Not much of an alibi. Everyone was sleeping. No one can say for certain if any of us snuck out and did away with Vance Wexler."

I was about to say something when Deputy Hickman thundered across the open field and moved like a bulldozer in our direction. None of us were facing the area where the sheriff vehicles were parked so we didn't see him coming. Not that it mattered. *He* saw *us* and that was enough.

The deep-set lines on his face, coupled with a steely look, were not a welcoming sight. "Miss Ellington! What are you doing at this crime scene?"

"I'm with the Cornell Entomology Department from the Experiment Station. They're conducting a study on the Swedish Midget Fly."

As soon as I said that, I thought Godfrey and Alex were going to choke, but that didn't stop me. "Very detrimental to broccoli."

The deputy rolled his eyes and turned to Godfrey. "And you are?"

"Dr. Godfrey Klein, entomologist. Dr. Bollinger is my colleague and I came to check on the field study. It's a very sensitive study." Then Godfrey looked around as if he was taking in the crime tape for the first time. "Dr. Bollinger isn't in any sort of trouble, is he? I only just arrived."

"If you must know, we're investigating an unexplained death that occurred sometime last night, according to the coroner. But I suppose you've already been informed." He stared directly at Alex. "We'll know more once an autopsy's been performed and toxicology results are in. Meantime, we're questioning Dr. Bollinger and his crew, along with the victim's associates." Then he looked directly at me. "If I didn't know better, Miss Ellington, I would swear you have a sheriff's scanner in your kitchen and one at your bedside. You seem to be drawn to crime scenes like moths to a candle."

I swallowed and shrugged. "Dr. Klein works with my brother-in-law, Jason Keane, who's still in Costa Rica, as you know."

"Harrumph. Only too well."

"If you don't mind," I asked, "you said 'crime scene.' Why is this a crime scene?"

Deputy Hickman stretched his arms back and for a minute I thought the buttons on his shirt would pop. "Unexplained deaths are always treated as such until lab results and medical history prove otherwise." Then he rubbed his chin and sighed. "I know why you're really here, Miss Ellington. Don't think for one minute I've been living under a rock. Correct me if I'm wrong. Insect study or not, and heaven knows what *that* has to do with your winery, but nonetheless, as soon as you found out about this death, you couldn't wait to pry."

Then he shot looks at Alex and Godfrey and mumbled, "Everyone's got a damn cell phone these days," before turning back to me. "You came here to find out for yourself if the death we're investigating has anything to do with that full moon solstice curse that emanated from your winery's folklore. Does that about sum it up?"

"Well, to be honest—"

Just then, he looked past me toward the road. "Oh, hell's bells!" he shouted. "This is all I need."

I turned to face the circular drive and widened my eyes as Channel 13 WHAM's van pulled directly up to the cordoned-off area. It was immediately followed by Channel 8's van and Channel 10's.

"Um, I guess we'd better get going," I said, but Deputy Hickman didn't hear me. He was already three or four yards in front of me charging toward those vans like a bull moose after a female in heat.

Godfrey gave Alex a tap on the shoulder and told him to "hang in there." "They don't know anything right now, so until they do, I wouldn't worry about it," he said. "By tonight, that historical society team will have taken down its tents and returned to Geneva. At least you'll be able to conduct your study in peace."

"Let's hope so," Alex said. "At least I got my chuckle for the day. Swedish Midget Flies. Good going, Norrie."

I grimaced. "I was close, wasn't I?"

Alex walked back to the bench, where his students and Cassie were waiting. I elbowed Godfrey and pointed to the road. "Looks like Deputy Hickman's having a face-off with those reporters. Guess we'd better get out of here before one of them recognizes me from the winery and shoves a microphone in my face."

"Good idea."

● ● ●

"Keep me posted about Alex," I said when Godfrey dropped me off in front of the winery. "I don't think he has anything to worry about but you never know. Maybe Vance had some sort of a medical condition and that's why he died in his sleep. *If* he died in his sleep. Guess we really don't know that either. But one thing I do know, those TV stations want viewers and nothing brings them in like an old death curse."

The minute I stepped foot in the door, I was besieged with questions. Unfortunately, they were all flung at me in the form of hushed whispers as I passed by the tasting room tables on my way to the bistro to grab something to eat.

"How did he die?"

"Was anyone arrested?"

"Did you see the body?"

"Don't know, no, and no," I managed to whisper back. I didn't want the customers, who were engrossed in wine tasting, to lose interest.

When I had taken my last bite of the brisket on brioche bun, I pulled Cammy aside and gave her the rundown. I would have shared the info with Fred and Emma but the bistro was packed.

"I ran into Deputy Hickman when we got there," I told her. "They don't have a clue what happened, but according to the scuttlebutt, there was no visible blood or signs of a struggle. Of course, Vance had a blanket on him so if he was shot or stabbed, only the coroner would know."

Cammy pulled on the dark green ribbon that secured her bun. "It won't matter. A man was found dead on the night of the full moon summer solstice. If that's not enough to get the rumors flying, nothing will."

"Oh, it'll be more than rumors. Three news vans were on the scene."

"Look on the bright side. Maybe we'll sell more Two Witches T-shirts."

Chapter 9

By six ten, every TV station in the Greater Rochester and Syracuse areas had homed in on "the spooky death of Geneva Historical Society's president." It didn't matter that the forensic report hadn't been issued, the postmortem kept under lock and key, and the toxicology report in limbo for the next two weeks. What mattered was attracting viewers, and nothing lured them in like the premise of a suspicious death with paranormal overtones.

Truth is, I expected as much from those reporters. Bradley all but said the same thing when I spoke with him earlier in the afternoon. "It's all about ratings. Once an official determination about the cause of death has been made, it will die down."

"Maybe the cause of death, but not the suspects if it was foul play. Face it, those deputies take the easy way out, and what's easier than pointing a finger at Alex Bollinger. He certainly had the opportunity. Not to mention motive. Vance's team of lakeshore-tromping amateur archeologists were wreaking havoc on his insect study. And as for means, if Vance was a sound sleeper it wouldn't have been all that difficult to suffocate him with a pillow."

"Hmm, now that you mention it, Alex really should seek legal counsel. I'm sure the Experiment Station has someone on retainer."

"There's also Madeline Martinez. She sort of made a veiled threat to Vance regarding his denial of their porch expansion. Who the heck knows if that bugger didn't write it down somewhere. Along with every other threat he's gotten as a result of his obtuse attitude regarding improvements to homes in the historical district."

"I'm sure the Yates County Sheriff's Office will look into it along with Ontario's since Vance was employed in Geneva."

"Oh, they'll look into it all right, but the little ball on the roulette wheel is headed straight for Alex and I can't sit back and twiddle my thumbs."

"Uh, what exactly did you have in mind?"

"Only the usual snooping around. Relax. Nothing that would violate state or federal laws. I got all my edits done on that screenplay, so until it comes bouncing back from the script analyst, I've got some time to look into Vance's unfortunate demise."

"Be careful. I don't want to be looking into *your* unfortunate demise. Okay?"

"Uh-huh."

"So we're still on for dinner next weekend?" he asked.

"Wouldn't miss it. And this time it will just be a table for two."

When the news anchors finally finished their bantering about Vance Wexler, I called Theo and Don, hoping they had finished up at their winery and had gone home for the night.

Sure enough, Theo picked up. "Hey, Norrie, talk about good timing. Don and I just got in the door. Got your earlier text about Vance but we were too busy in the tasting room to get back to you. I imagine it was quite the scene at Kashong Point given all those emergency response vehicles."

"Listen, I wouldn't ask you this if I didn't think it was really, really important. I need you to reprise your role as one of the Hardy Boys. Take your pick."

"Uh-oh. I'm afraid to ask."

"One of Jason and Godfrey's coworkers, Alex Bollinger, might be taken in as a suspect. A bunch of historical society amateurs were collecting arrowheads at Kashong Point and interfering with Alex's field study on some sort of crane fly. He and Vance got into a big brouhaha that everyone overheard. Next morning Vance is dead in his tent."

"Yeesh. I see where this is going. What is it exactly that you want me to do?"

"Alex wasn't the only one who got into it with Vance. Madeline did, too. I even overheard her in his office when I went to check out those archives for nineteen forty-eight deaths. He gave her a hard time about her porch extension request and she kind of went ballistic on him."

"Okay, okay, but what does this have to do with me? Or should I say *my help*?"

"Yeah, about that. Look, from what I've seen of Vance Wexler, the guy was a meticulous, prissy fussbudget who most likely kept track of every single dealing he had with the residents in the historical district. We've got to get our hands on his notes before the sheriff's deputies do. It's the only way we can find out if there were other, more viable, suspects than Alex or Madeline."

"First off, wouldn't the deputies be doing that? Second, and more importantly, how do you propose we accomplish that little feat?"

Just then I heard Don's voice in the background. "What do you want me to nuke? The gnocchi and asparagus or the mushroom ravioli?"

"Whatever you want. Be right there!"

Then Theo was back on the phone. "Sorry, Don's getting dinner on."

"I know, I heard. Listen, I'll wager Deputy Hickman and whatever crew of deputies he called in are still at Kashong Point interviewing campers and residents. By now they've finished up with the entomology crew and those amateur archeologists. In order for him to review Vance's notes and check his computer, he would need to work with Ontario County's Sheriff Office and they would need a warrant."

"Oh, dear God, no. Do not tell me you want me to break into Vance's office and steal his notes."

"Not steal. Make copies with my iPhone."

"But break in, right? It may be a misdemeanor but you can still go to jail."

"A misdemeanor, huh? Not a felony? Hmm, that's better than what I thought."

"It's only a felony if the breaking and entering resulted in burglary. Oh, for heaven's sake. What am I saying? It's all bad. Bad! Bad! Bad!"

"Theo, I'll never live with myself if Alex gets arrested. Or Madeline gets pulled in on some trumped-up charges. Look, it'll be light out for at least another hour and a half. The sun won't set till almost nine. Once we're inside, we can use a flashlight."

"And how do you propose we get inside? I'm sure the place is armed even if you jimmy the lock."

"Trust me, I know how to disarm it. Look, I'm going there no matter what. If we do get caught, I'll say you went over there to stop me."

"I wish I'd never promised your sister and brother-in-law I'd keep an eye on you."

"So that's a yes?"

"It's a yes. A reluctant yes."

"What are you going to tell Don?"

"I'm going to make sure he has our lawyer's number on speed dial."

"I'll be in front of your house in forty-five minutes. Is that enough time?"

"Yeah, I'll choke down the gnocchi or ravioli and hope I don't wind up with indigestion."

• • •

Theo stood on their front porch and waved as soon as I pulled up. He opened the passenger door, slid in, and reached for the seat belt.

"I used the hand vac," I said, "and got rid of most of Charlie's hair. For a hound dog, he sure sheds a lot."

"Got news for you. Isolde is worse. That long cat hair is everywhere. So, want to review the plan with me? I'm not really keen on standing in front of the place while you fiddle with the lock."

"Relax. I have no intention of messing with the lock. When I was in Vance's office I noticed the double-hung windows weren't latched. That room faces the lake so no one will see us climb in. Once we get inside, we should have thirty to sixty seconds to punch in the alarm code."

"Unless he latched the windows before he left for the day."

"Don't be such a pessimist. Everything will go as planned."

Or not.

Sure enough, the narrow window on the back of the building wasn't latched, and with some effort on Theo's part and mine, we were able to lift it so that the next sound we heard was a robotic voice. "Disarm system now. Disarm system now."

"Wait here. Don't crawl in. I'm on my way to the panel."

It was a good thing we had gotten there before the sun went down. There was enough light coming through the side windows in the building for me to get to the alarm box and tap in the four numbers that someone thoughtfully left in full view.

"Hoist yourself up," I said as soon as I walked back into Vance's office. "Then close the window."

Theo didn't waste a second. "Let's make this quick. We'll look around his desk and that four-drawer file cabinet behind it. Geez, I think the heavy curtains weigh more than the window itself. They're horrible. Floor-length and dismal green. I think Scarlett O'Hara once wore them if I'm not mistaken."

"I brought my flashlight but so far, so good. Look, I have a better idea. You start with the cabinets and I'll scan the desk."

"Forget the cabinets. They're locked."

"Not anymore." I held up a small key that I removed from a minuscule drawer to the left of Vance's executive desk. "Francine has a similar desk, and believe me, I used to get into it all the time when we were kids."

Sure enough the key unlocked the file cabinets, and for the next fifteen or twenty minutes, Theo busied himself pulling out file folders and perusing them while I was on the lookout for anything that resembled a notebook.

"I'm not having any luck," I said. "How good are you at getting into a computer without a password?"

"Seriously? That's your next step?"

"Uh-huh. At least it's a PC and not a Mac. I have no idea how to operate a Mac."

"Probably the same way. Listen, there's all sorts of files here: maps, photographs, blueprints . . . I'm looking for one that says 'Permit Applications.'"

"Good. Keep looking."

I took a breath and typed "Password" onto the computer. When that failed, I typed variations of Vance's name, and when that didn't work, I typed variations and initials for Geneva Historical Society. I even typed the numbers for the historical society's address. Then I noticed a framed photo of a yellow car on his desk. It didn't look like any model I'd seen.

"Psst! Theo! Stop what you're doing for a second. Do you have any idea what kind of car this is?"

Theo walked toward the desk and picked up the frame. "It's an old Karmann Ghia. Looks like the late nineteen sixties. I had an uncle who used to have one of those. It's probably worth some bucks by now. And why are you stopping to look at photos?"

"Spell Karmann Ghia."

Theo eyeballed the computer and leaned over my shoulder. "You think?" He immediately tapped in the letters that spelled the make of the car, and within seconds a screensaver with that very car appeared on the monitor.

I grabbed Theo's wrist and shook it. "Bingo! We hit pay dirt! Now all I need to do is open Microsoft Word and pray to the gods he kept his notes in a neatly marked file."

"Pray fast. It's getting darker outside."

Chapter 10

"Found it," Theo called out. He held up a manila folder that he had just pulled from the file cabinet and waved it in the air. "Actually, there's more than one. The files date back ten years and the folders all read 'Applications.' I'm going to start with this year and see what I find. Any chance there's some blank paper on his desk and a pen or pencil? I'll write down the names and addresses of the applications that were denied while you fiddle with Microsoft Office."

"Here, use these Post-it notes that were on the desk."

I handed him a few pens from the top of Vance's desk in case one of them was out of ink, and then I went back to the monitor. If Theo thought he had plenty of files to check out, it was nothing compared to the Word documents on Vance's computer. Folders such as Taxes, Associations, Letters, Grants, Museum Loan Pieces, and even one marked Local Restaurant Menus. Sheesh.

"I've got to use your flashlight, Norrie. It's getting pitch-black in here."

I stood, stretched, and handed him my flashlight. "I can't believe it's almost nine. Drat. I haven't found a single thing that would help Alex."

"Keep looking. A guy like that was bound to have a 'tell-all' file."

"Yeah, or one for covering his bu— Oh my gosh, I can't believe I didn't pull that file up. The one marked CYA. Give me a second."

I clicked the file, and in a heartbeat a list of names appeared along with a notation that read "Date or dates of incidents." Under each name was an explanation, some longer than three paragraphs, about the issues related to that person.

I cringed. "This is way too much stuff to write down." *Hell. Why on earth didn't I think of bringing a flash drive?*

It wasn't the first time I went full speed ahead without thinking things through. That was the difference between my sister and me. Francine always took cautious, measured steps while I plunged headfirst into whatever situation I was caught up in.

"It'll take too long if I use my iPhone to snap photos. I'll have to print it out unless you've got a flash drive on you."

"A flash drive? Seriously? This was last-minute. I'm lucky I have my driver's license on me."

"Never mind. It can't be that long, can it?"

"Let's hope not. Maybe the guy went for the CliffsNotes version." Theo put the Post-it pad back on the desk. "Well, I'm finished at my end. All we have to do is wait while those pages print and then we can get the heck out of here."

The grinding sound of Vance's Canon copier overshadowed the creaking, whistling sounds that emanated from the building itself and its HVAC system. At least it was a laser printer.

"This shouldn't take much longer," I said. "I mean, how many people could he have ticked off?"

"If you ask me—"

And then Theo stopped talking. The copier still cranked out sheets of paper but there was another noise—the unmistakable sound of a key turning the dead-bolt lock in a door. I froze and held my breath. In that instant, two things happened. The copier stopped making copies and the light in the hallway flooded under the closed door to Vance's office.

I moved quickly to where Theo was standing and didn't say a word. Just then we heard voices and they seemed to be coming from the corridor.

The first was a woman's voice followed by a man's. "That idiotic Doris. Vance wrote the alarm code on the box, and even with it she didn't set the darn thing."

"Well, that was an imbecilic idea to begin with. The code to arm the place is the same code to disarm it. It wouldn't have done any good. You could have written it on Doris Belcher's forehead and she wouldn't know where to find it."

Then the woman again, "Never mind. I can't believe we agreed to meet here."

"Where else did you want to go? Starbucks, where everyone could hear us?" It was a third voice and it belonged to a woman as well.

"We need to get out of sight," I whispered to Theo, "but we'll make too much noise going out the window. Besides, I want to hear what they say."

"Get behind those curtains. We'll each take a side."

I plastered myself behind the curtain and then realized the computer was still on. Tiptoeing, I powered it off along with the printer. Then I gathered the printouts, rolled them into a coil and stuffed them under my jeans before resuming my spot behind curtain number two.

"Might as well go into the conference room," the man said. "I want to get this over with and get home. Damn it. I still can't get over the fact that our names and phone numbers were in Vance's wallet as emergency contacts. Of all things. That call from Ontario County surprised the hell out of me. If that death looks the least bit suspicious, the police will be knocking on our doors and we can kiss those donations goodbye."

Conference room. Donations. These must be the historical society's board members.

In the dark, I turned on my iPhone and used Safari to see exactly who those board members were. In less than fifteen seconds, I had my answer—*unless new members had been appointed.*

"It's the board members," I whispered to Theo.

"Shh. I figured as much."

Then the man's voice again. "We should have done this earlier in the day, when the museum closed, and not have waited till so late."

"I'm sorry. I had a dinner engagement." The first woman's voice.

"Never mind. I say we scour his office before the police and the county sheriff beats us to it. God knows what incriminating stuff Vance collected on all of us. You know how he wrote down every little thing and exaggerated it to the point of no return."

"Curtis is right." The second woman. "I'd bet money Vance kept notes on us. I caught him once with my personal mail in his hand. I had just picked the mail up from my post office box on my way over here and set the pile on the large credenza in the hallway. Then I went to the kitchen to get a cup of coffee. When I got back, I saw him shuffling through my mail. I asked him what he was doing and he made a feeble excuse about thinking the mail was for the historical society. Poppycock! He could see those letters were addressed to me."

I looked down at the floor to make sure my sneakers weren't visible. If Theo and I could remain motionless, or close to it, they might not notice us. At least the curtains were those heavy-duty drapes that weighed a ton and not the light and frilly kind or we would have been doomed.

The sudden blinding light as someone flicked the switch forced my eyes shut. Saliva gathered in my mouth and I swore that my heartbeat had increased tenfold.

"Turn on the computer, Mildred," the second woman said. "You're familiar with the system."

"Give me a second. There, it's on. Oh, dear. I can't get in. Vance must have changed the password. He was not supposed to do that. He probably did it when he came back from that weekend trip he took down south somewhere. The password for all of our computers is GHS followed by the person's initials and the year."

Then Curtis's voice: "Did he have any pets? Try one of those names."

Mildred again. "Vance didn't have any pets, remember? Said they made too much of a mess."

"Aargh. Try his birthdate. People always use birthdates."

Then the second woman again. "How is Mildred supposed to know his birthdate?"

Mildred's voice sounded strained. "What about his birth state? It was Tennessee, wasn't it? I remember the interview. No. Wait. Maybe it was Kentucky. Darn it. Well, it was somewhere down south."

"Forget the damn computer," Curtis said. "Let's get a look at his desk drawers. He must have kept a notebook or something in them."

"At least we can get into his file cabinet." It was the second woman speaking. Loud and assertive. "It's the same key for all the file cabinets in our building. The former director thought of that. I'll be right back. I'll get one of the keys from Doris's office. I know where she keeps them."

I wasn't sure how much longer I could remain behind that curtain. My back began to hurt and I found myself shifting my weight from one foot to the other. I wondered how Theo was doing but there was no way to tell.

"I'm baaack . . ."

"That was quick, Agnes," Curtis said.

Agnes. Yep, the same three names I found: Agnes Merryweather, Curtis Bloor, and Mildred Beattle.

"I told you I knew where she kept it."

"You and Mildred check out the cabinet. I'll take a peek at his desk."

The next few minutes were agonizing. A sharp spasm in my back all but resulted in a loud breath but I kept my mouth closed tight and instead clenched my fists so I'd have something to think about other than the proximity of Vance's file cabinet to the window.

Other than the sound of papers being shuffled and the occasional groan, it was pretty quiet. Then Curtis spoke. "Not a damn thing in his desk except for a bunch of binders from our committees. I glanced at them. Nothing to write home about. Any better luck with the file cabinet, Mildred?"

"No, not a gosh-darned thing. Unless Agnes found something."

I watched as Agnes shoved some papers into her bra when Mildred wasn't looking. Maybe she did find something after all. Lucky her. If so, she was pretty secretive about it. "Any incriminating notes about us must be on that computer of his." Agnes sounded irritated.

"Look," Curtis said. "As long as the three of us stick together should we be questioned about our relationship with him, we'll be fine. Board members squabble with each other all the time."

"But he blew those squabbles out of proportion. Lord knows what's sitting on that computer."

"I know you two ladies wanted to meet as soon as possible, but honestly, we're probably overreacting. Granted, the guy was a snit and gave all of us indigestion, but we weren't at Kashong Point last night. So there goes opportunity right out the window."

"Actually," Agnes said, "I did drive over there, but it was earlier in the afternoon. I wanted to see how their expedition was coming along. Vance made such a big deal about uncovering arrowheads from the Seneca Tribe at Kashanquash, now known as Kashong. That was the name of their village."

"Thank you for the history lesson. Did anyone see you leave?" Curtis asked.

"I don't know. I honestly don't know."

"Best thing we can do under the circumstances is cooperate with law enforcement, but don't give them any ammunition. Answer their questions but keep it short and sweet. You know they'll be hauling us in for questioning. Probably Monday."

"We may have something in our favor," Agnes said.

"What's that?"

"When I went over there, a few of our volunteers said Vance had a knock-down, drag-out fight with one of those entomologists who was busying himself with insects. It wasn't their only verbal altercation from what they said. And if that doesn't shift the focus away from us, I can do one better. Last Monday I was in the back workroom when I heard a woman threaten him. It was a Madeline Martinez from Billsburrow Winery. I asked Vance about it shortly after the woman left. He said she was a disgruntled and disturbed resident."

Curtis chuckled. "Got enough of those. If the deputies question us we can always mention Mrs. Martinez and those entomologists, but I've got one better for you. I say we bring up that old curse from Two Witches Hill. You know, the full moon summer solstice. Nothing like getting the locals all worked up over a death curse. That should take the heat off of us."

I gasped and quickly covered my mouth. *Those buggers!! I can't believe what schemers they are.*

"Was that you, Mildred?"

Rats!

Then Curtis spoke again. "Since we're here we might as well go back to the conference room and come up with some sort of statement for the newspapers about how shocked and saddened we are about Vance's death. Then we'll explain that the vice president, namely me, will be taking over until a new election is held and a new museum director can be hired. Make sure his computer's turned off. I'll get the lights on my way out of here."

The next thing I knew, Theo and I were back in total darkness and Vance's office door slammed an instant later.

I hope they don't take their sweet time composing that statement.

I crept over to where Theo was still huddled behind the curtain and whispered, "Want to make our exit now or wait it out?"

"That window creaks and they'll hear something when we close it behind us. We can't leave it open. The alarm system won't turn on. I'm stiff as a board. What's ten more minutes?"

The ten minutes turned into twenty but we finally heard the robotic voice call out, "Armed Away," followed by a series of annoying beeps.

"That's our cue. Out of here," Theo said. "Hurry up. Those systems only give you twenty or thirty seconds."

It was easier climbing out than getting in, but closing the window took some effort on his part. Luckily, he managed it before the final "System Armed."

"Stay here and don't move," Theo whispered. "We should give them a few minutes before we walk back to your car."

"Do you think they'll be suspicious about a car parked right across the street?"

"Nah. It wasn't the only one. Lots of student housing on Main Street."

I stretched my arms and shook my legs while we waited. "Did you hear those horrible things Vance said about Madeline? And that wretched Agnes will use it to make it look like Madeline had a motive for murder. Yeesh. I had no idea she was in the workroom."

"And what about Curtis? Dredging up that full moon curse to shift the attention off of them."

"Yep. Self-serving bureaucrats for sure."

"Want to know what the worst part is?" Theo asked. "We won't be able to say a word since we'd be hard-pressed to explain how we happened upon that piece of information."

"If it means saving Madeline and Alex I'm willing to take my chances and tell all."

"Come on, Norrie, looks like the coast is clear."

Chapter 11

"What took you so long?" Don asked the second Theo opened the door to their house. "I was half tempted to drive over there myself."

"Three unexpected guests, that's what. But you can relax. Norrie and I didn't get caught. Just don't suggest we buy heavy floor-length curtains for our living room."

"Huh?"

"Long story. Turns out we weren't the only ones interested in what Vance might have had in his notes. The remaining three board members were concerned he had enough dirt on them for a motive to commit murder."

Then he turned to me. "I was sweating bullets. Agnes was inches from my feet. Inches. When I looked down, I could see the heels of her shoes. Brown orthopedic shoes."

"What about me? If Curtis waved his hands any more, he would've socked me in the face."

"How'd you know he was waving his hands? You were behind the curtain."

"I kind of took my chances and sort of peeked."

Then we both laughed.

Don looked at us and put his hands on his hips. "I think the two of you got a big charge out of that clandestine escapade. In fact, I'd go so far as to say it gave you a full-blown rush. Flirting with danger like that."

"I wouldn't exactly call it *danger*," I said. "It wasn't as if we were dangling off a cliff or anything."

"Don't get any ideas. Look, it was a damn good thing no one saw you lurking behind curtain number one and curtain number two. Breaking and entering carries a heavy fine and maybe jail time."

Theo put his hand on Don's shoulder and gave it a pat. "Calm down, big guy. No one got caught."

"Not this time. Anyway, I want to hear all about it." He ushered us to the kitchen table and plunked down some coffee cups and filled them. "Unless you'd rather have wine."

"Coffee's fine," I said. "Theo and I got to hear most of their conversation and I really don't think any of them was responsible for killing Vance. All they want to do is protect their own butts, even if it means lying."

I went on to tell Don what Agnes said regarding Alex and how Curtis insinuated he'd fan the flames about the full moon curse to shift the attention to our winery.

Don didn't look all that surprised. "Let's hope their acting skills stink." Then he looked directly at Theo and back to me. "Please tell me you got what you were looking for."

"The papers are a little creased from being rolled up in my jeans," I said, "but we pulled up Vance's 'incident notes' from his computer. The guy kept a log on anyone who crossed paths with him, and that's not all. Theo's got a list of all the owners of historical homes who were denied applications for improvements. I guarantee, if Vance was murdered, the killer's name is sitting on one of those lists."

Don stood, walked to the pantry and came back with a tin of apricot and raisin rugelach. The minute he opened it, Isolde appeared and jumped on the kitchen counter. Don immediately scooped her up and opened a drawer, where he retrieved a handful of kitty snacks. "Here. Eat these. Tuna morsel treats. You'll like them more than the rugelach."

"He spoils her something awful," Theo said, to which Don replied, "And who soaks bread in warm milk for her?"

I laughed. "I've spoiled Charlie, too. He'll be insufferable by the time Francine and Jason get back. And speaking of insufferable, that may be what got Vance killed. I mean, *if* that's what happened."

Don stroked Isolde's long white and gray fur and shook his head. "You know, we could be spinning our wheels for no reason. Maybe Vance had an underlying medical condition or an allergic reaction to something. It's still an unexplained death as far as Deputy Hickman is concerned."

I nodded. "Yeah, but that's likely to change, and when it does, I want to be ready. At least we've got some time. If the autopsy doesn't point to anything, it will be weeks before the toxicology report does. Meanwhile, I was kind of hoping we could divvy up these names and see if anything pops out at us."

Don grabbed a rugelach and motioned for me to show him the papers that I had placed to the left of my coffee cup. "Mind if I take a peek?"

"Oh, my gosh. Don't tell me you're chomping at the bit to do some sleuthing, too."

"Chomping, no, but curious, yes."

I handed the coiled papers to Don and took a sip of coffee while I waited for his reaction. He thumbed through the first three pages and slapped the side of his cheek. "Vance missed his real opportunity. The guy should've been writing a daytime soap opera. Did either of you read this?"

Theo and I looked at each other and shook our heads. "Who had time to read it?" he asked. "We were too busy finding it, copying it, and getting it the hell out of there. Why? What does it say?"

"First of all, that copier was low on toner. Never mind. I can still make this out. The first one is a blow-by-blow description of a conversation he had with Madeline Martinez regarding her request to extend that porch of hers. His version paints her as a dangerous woman with a short fuse who would 'stop at nothing' to get what she wanted."

Then Don ran his thumb through the remainder of the pile. "The second one is worse. Look, this could take us all night and it's late. Although I must admit, it makes for some compelling bedtime reading. Better than that novel I started."

Theo chucked. "I'm sure Norrie wouldn't mind if you ran into the office and made yourself a copy. Our machine is pretty quick. Then we could all read what it says and compare notes tomorrow after work."

I stood and helped myself to another cup of coffee. "That's a great idea. And while you're at it, can you make me a copy of Theo's list of denials? We can tackle that next."

Don was out of the kitchen and on his way to his office before I had filled my coffee cup. "Does this mean you're joining our makeshift investigation?"

"Arrgh. I suppose so, besides, there were two Hardy Boys, weren't there?"

I winked at Theo. "Yep. Take your pick."

• • •

Don was right about bedtime reading. Even though it was late and Charlie was snoring from his new place in the middle of my bed, I shoved him over to the side, propped another pillow behind my head and one by one went through the pile of papers that documented Vance's unfortunate dealings with the public. It read like *Where'd You Go, Bernadette?* sans the Microsoft references.

Vance saw himself as the last crusader, fighting off throngs of Huns, Visigoths, and Vandals who sought to destroy the final vestige of humanity with their architectural plans for longer and wider porches, patio enclosures, brightly hued paints, and in that one instance, a backyard pool.

With few exceptions, the notes focused on the denials given to the home owners who had the misfortune of living in the Geneva Historical District. Tidbits of conversations were drawn out and embellished to the point where all of these people, including Madeline, appeared to be unhinged and potentially dangerous.

Then again, maybe one of them *was*. I set the pile of papers on my nightstand, having read all but a handful of them, and pulled the cord on the lamp. Seconds later, I was out cold. Had it not been for the phone ringing at eight fifteen, I might have remained that way until noon. I was that exhausted.

"Good morning, Norrie. It's me, Gladys Pipp. I hope I didn't wake you, especially on a Sunday, but I'm heading out shortly for church services. Much better refreshments at the earlier service. Anyway, I wanted to get back to you regarding some more information I dug up at the Yates County Historical Society last Monday but I haven't had a chance. Every time I picked up the phone, Deputy Hickman was looming over my desk. And then that dreadful discovery at Kashong Point yesterday. If that doesn't catapult that Two Witches curse to new heights, nothing will."

"I, um, er . . ."

"I know. I know. You don't have to say a word. I was originally supposed to work the morning shift but wound up staying all day on account of the . . . well, I'm sure you know by now. It was on the news last night. A very brief statement and a photo of Kashong Point, followed by—"

"Don't tell me. Someone mentioned the Two Witches full moon summer solstice curse."

"Well, yes. The news anchors mentioned how coincidental the death was."

"Did they mention the deceased by name?" I asked.

"No, pending notification to next of kin."

"I don't suppose they speculated about the cause of death, did they? Those news anchors speculate about everything. The price of eggs, which celebs had work done, and which foreign countries are messing with our elections."

"No, no mention about cause of death."

"Yeah, it's not as if it was obvious, like a gunshot wound or a stab to the heart. Um, I kind of ran into Deputy Hickman at the scene. One of my friends, who's an entomologist, is doing a study at Kashong Point."

"Dr. Bollinger?"

"Uh-oh. How did you know?"

"He's on a list of . . . well, people that Deputy Hickman needs to speak with further."

"I really hope it turns out to be some underlying medical cause, because the last thing Dr. Bollinger needs is to have his attention taken away from that very important study on water flies, and the last thing Two Witches needs is to have that curse rumor spreading around. One good thing, though. The full moon summer solstice is over."

"That's precisely the reason I called. Oh dear. You may not want to hear this."

"Hear what?"

"When I did my research, I uncovered the rest of the curse."

"The rest of the curse? You mean there's more?"

"I'm afraid so."

Chapter 12

My throat usually has that cracking, croaking feeling when I first get up in the morning, but as soon as Gladys said there was more to the curse, it felt as if every last bit of moisture was sucked dry.

"What do you mean? What are you saying?"

"Oh, dear. I hope this doesn't upset you."

It's never good when someone says they hope something doesn't upset you, because inevitably, it will upset you. I held my breath and waited for her to continue.

"The Yates County Historical Society is privy to archival information that other historical societies can only envy. I was able to read the original land holdings documents dating back to seventeen ninety-six, when a man by the name of David Wagener bought a tract of land that would eventually become Penn Yan. A year later, Adeliza and Derella Marsten from Massachusetts bought a small tract of land on a hill in what is now the Town of Benton."

"The two witches? Those were the two witches?"

"The land holding documents only listed names and dates, but there was a side note next to Adeliza and Derella's names. It seemed to be added later and was a referral to another document—a small leather-bound diary of sorts found in the basement of the original Penn Yan Library. The docent was good enough to let me peruse it. It was mostly recipes for poultices, lists of herbs and their uses, as well as a few recipes for wild mushrooms. Then I noticed pages folded up within other pages and was terrified the paper would crumble. But I couldn't resist. I unfolded the paper and there it was in front of me—the full moon summer solstice curse."

"Do you remember what it said? And what was the other part?"

"I'll do better for you, Norrie. I'll email you the two photos I took of it with my cell phone. I still have your email somewhere. Anyway, I must be going or I'll be late for that service."

"Can you just tell me more or less what the second part of the curse said?"

"Hmm, let me think. I was sure it said, 'When a fortnight cycles past, your breath will be the last. One sip of the partridge's eye and ye are surely to die.'"

"The partridge's eye? What on earth is that?"

"I asked myself the same question so I googled it. It refers to rosé wine. Norrie, are you still on the line?"

"Um, yeah."

"I wouldn't worry about it if I were you, dear. Your winery doesn't produce a rosé."

Oh, crap! Crap! Crap! Crap! We do now! Thank you, Franz.

I was so stunned, all I could muster was a croaky-sounding thank-you before Gladys hung up.

Happy Sunday to me! Now, as if I didn't have enough to worry about, phase two of what seems to be "the never ending curse from Two Witches Hill" just appeared on the horizon. I threw the covers back from the bed, got up, and headed straight for the shower. If nothing else, I'd be clean for what I imagined would be one hell of a long day.

● ● ●

Curse or no curse, Cammy hit me with more glorious news the second I set foot in the winery. She had two pitchers of water for the tasting room tables and set them down before walking toward me.

"Talk about a busy Sunday morning," she said. "Someone from Channel 8 ROC called here about an hour ago requesting an interview with you. Let me see . . . it was—"

"Not Wade Gallagher? He all but ruined Stephanie's reputation last February at that Chocolate and Wine Extravaganza. It better not be him."

"No, it was a woman. Lorraine Stuyvesant. Their programming director. I wrote the number down in the kitchen. They want to do a special on the Two Witches full moon summer solstice curse. When they got wind of that death yesterday at Kashong Point, they sent a team right over there. Couldn't miss an opportunity to attract more viewers."

I groaned. "For all we know, Vance Wexler could have died from sleep apnea or something."

"Exactly. The breath taken right out of him. Not that I believe in all that mumbo-jumbo, but if the networks can keep the viewers tuned in, they'll make the advertisers happy, and that's all that counts. When they finally learn the truth, it won't matter."

"They won't learn it for a while. I doubt they'll get the autopsy results before Tuesday, and as for the toxicology results . . . well, that takes weeks. Face it, we're doomed either way. If the cause of death was foul play, then Deputy Hickman won't just point a finger at Alex Bollinger, he'll point an entire fist. And if it was some kind of natural cause, our winery will be flooded with every new age lunatic and nutcase from here to California. One thing for sure, I'm not about to give any interviews."

Cammy tightened the fuchsia ribbon on her bun. "You may want to give that a second thought. If you do the interview, you can control what's being said. If not, they'll find someone else, and who knows what that will lead to."

"Yeesh. You're right. Guess I'll have to call her after all. But I only intend to talk about what everyone already knows. The nighttime kiss-of-death thing and not a word more."

"What do you mean by 'more'? What else is there?"

"We'd better not talk about it right here. Come on, let's go to the kitchen."

I got right to the point telling Cammy about my wake-up-call conversation with Gladys this morning, including the partridge eye reference.

Cammy's eyes got wider and wider and her jaw actually dropped. "'Fortnight cycles past,' huh? That's two weeks from yesterday. The date of the WOW Winemakers Dinner."

"Uh-huh. So?"

"So you better hope Franz doesn't decide to show off that new rosé of his. It's ironic, isn't it? In a weird sort of way."

"What is?"

"If I remember what those nuns taught us in Ancient History, some Greek king claimed that drinking undiluted wine would drive you insane, and that's when they started making diluted blends from white and red grapes. Now, this twist has the opposite curse. It's the blend that will kill you."

"Well, it won't come near us at the winemakers dinner. Franz was waiting on label approval from the Alcohol and Tobacco Tax and Trade Bureau. Believe me, it won't come by the time of the dinner. And labeling takes forever, even with our modern equipment."

I thought back to when I was in my early teens and Francine and I got stuck hand-labeling bottles of wine. I remember having to soak the labels and use a special glue gun to get them to stick just right. It was a wretched experience and involved most of the winery workers plus anyone else my father could commandeer. Then, as Two Witches began to expand in vineyard acquisition and wine production, my father purchased a semi-automatic pressure-sensitive bottle labeler.

It could label over eight hundred bottles an hour and took all the guesswork out of centering that darn label. Not to mention the wasted labels and sticky glue that was the mainstay of my handiwork.

The tension on Cammy's face dissipated. "That's a relief. About the second part of the curse. Not that I put any credence into it, but why take a chance? I mean, *should* something happen, and I'm not saying it *will*, but should it happen, we don't need people to worry about drinking our wines."

"No, they're too busy worrying about our curses."

Since no one needed my help in the tasting room, I grabbed a bacon and avocado panini at the bistro and returned home to finalize that screenplay proposal I meant to do a few days ago. Unfortunately, the pile of Vance's tell-all notes that I had moved to the kitchen table caught my eye the minute I got in the door, and in an instant I forgot all about that proposal and plunked myself down at the table to read them thoroughly.

With the exception of Charlie going in and out of the doggie door a few times, the house was quiet and still. Too quiet. Too still. I rummaged around the drawer of CDs that Francine and Jason had, and using their old Panasonic, filled all five slots with the Grateful Dead before returning to Vance's musings.

I don't know what I was expecting, but nothing jumped out at me. He was a miserable, picky man who had issues with everyone, it seemed. The only question was which issue got him a ticket to the afterlife.

Then something hit me. Something I should have thought about earlier, but in all the commotion at Kashong Point followed by that little jaunt Theo and I took last night to the historical society, it totally escaped my mind. Until now.

Where was Vance Wexler's car? A bright yellow Karmann Ghia would have stood out among all the SUVs and Jeeps at Kashong Point, yet I didn't remember seeing one. Cars were parked along the road and in the gravel lot by the campground, but for the life of me, the Karmann

Ghia wasn't one of them. I grabbed the landline since it was near the table and called Godfrey.

"Hey, Godfrey, it's me. Norrie. Have you been in touch with Alex?"

"Uh, not since yesterday when we saw him. Why? Did something happen?"

"No, but I may be on to something. Do you remember seeing a bright yellow Karmann Ghia parked along the road or in that campground parking lot when we were at Kashong Point yesterday? It's a mid-century Volkswagen sports car that kind of looks like a Porsche knockoff with big front lights."

"I know what a Karmann Ghia looks like. For a while they were pretty popular when I was in school. Why?"

"Because that's the car Vance Wexler drove and I don't remember seeing it. It would've stood out like a sore thumb."

"I don't recall seeing it, but then again, I wasn't looking. Uh, how do you know what kind of car he drove?"

A little breaking and entering . . . a little snooping around his desk . . .

"Don't blow this out of proportion."

"Oh, no. What?"

"Last night Theo and I snuck into Vance's office at the historical society and there was a photo of it on his desk. It was also the password for his computer."

"Breaking and entering? Computer hacking?"

"More like snooping and sleuthing. Besides, we didn't get caught."

"That's not the point."

"Godfrey, we walked out of there with information that could lead us to Vance's killer. That is, if the coroner says the death was a homicide. It would get Alex off the hook."

"And you and Theo on it."

"Aren't you the least bit curious about what we found out?"

"Petrified as hell is more like it. Whatever you found out could put you in danger if someone were to find out what you did."

"There's no way that will happen. It's not as if the place was bug— Oh, hell."

Chapter 13

That tingling feeling of little hairs sticking up on my arms and legs engulfed me as I tried to remember if I'd seen anything that remotely resembled a surveillance camera at the historical society. Thoughts of Agnes, Mildred, and Curtis reviewing footage was enough to make me shudder. "It's an old building. A historical society. Not a bank or a school."

Godfrey's voice got a tad louder. "No. Worse. A museum. A museum with valuable artifacts."

"You're scaring me. Look, let's say they had surveillance. There wouldn't be a reason for them to review it unless something was stolen or missing, or broken. Listen, getting back to that Karmann Ghia. Can you call Alex and ask if he or any of his students saw it? Or if it's still there?"

"I'll call his cell right now and let you know. If he doesn't answer, it means he's doing something that can't be interrupted."

Wonderful. What do you do with insects that can't be interrupted?

Godfrey went on. "If that's the case I'll leave you a message. You don't plan on any more escapades this weekend, do you?"

"Nope."

Not that I know of.

"Tell me, if that car isn't at Kashong Point, then what?" he asked.

"Then I've got to find out where it is, because it may be the very clue to Vance's demise. Either he drove it there and someone made off with it, or he got a ride with someone and the car's still at his house. Or apartment. Or wherever he lives . . ."

"Norrie, whatever you do, don't go breaking into his house."

"I can't. I have no idea where he lives."

"Good. Keep it that way. Let the sheriff's office deal with it."

"Aargh."

When I got off the phone with Godfrey, I called Theo and Don to remind them that we were going to meet after work in order to discuss our findings from Vance's notes. I offered to pick up a giant pizza with all the works from Cam's in Geneva and Don said they'd bring a blueberry cobbler he had made earlier in the day.

By seven thirty, as we were stuffing ourselves with pizza, I suddenly remembered that I never returned Lorraine Stuyvesant's call from 8 ROC. And in fact, Godfrey hadn't returned mine with the info from Alex.

"Think it's too late to call that programming director?" I asked Theo and Don.

They both shrugged and Don replied, "You have nothing to lose. If it's the station number, she'll get back to you. If it's her cell, you might catch her."

As it turned out, it was her cell. Either that or the woman worked awfully long hours. She was more than pleased I was willing to grant them an interview about the Two Witches curse, although I wasn't quite sure what I could tell them other than what they already knew. Still, it might be good publicity for the winery if I handled it right.

We arranged for her to chat with me at the winery on Wednesday morning and have one of her production assistants film it. I thought back to the last time something was filmed at our winery and recoiled. At least this wasn't a major movie production, or any production for that matter. Only a simple interview.

"We might as well get started on Vance's notes," Theo said, "then we can dive into the dessert."

Just then the landline rang, and it was Godfrey. "Sorry it took so long, Norrie, but Alex and his crew spotted the Tipula paludosa, an exotic species of the European crane fly, and, well, you can't imagine the paperwork it entailed."

Thank goodness.

"Anyway, he said to tell you that one of his students saw that car when he came back from a snack run late Friday afternoon. It was gone the next morning when Vance's body was discovered. Guess this is another part of the puzzle going unsolved, huh?"

"Unsolved but not untouched. It's on my list. But I don't think it's on Deputy Hickman's radar. Maybe I can get one step ahead."

I thought I heard Godfrey groan before I thanked him and told him that I was reviewing the "ill-obtained notes"—his words, not mine—with Don and Theo.

When I got off the phone, I explained about the car and how it could hold a piece of valuable evidence considering it was, after all, Vance's password on his computer and showcased in a frame on his desk.

"Good grief, Norrie," Theo said. "You're piling more stuff into this investigation of yours than Don does at a salad bar."

Don immediately jumped in. "I heard that! I'm right here."

"Fine, fine. Let's get back to what we were originally doing. I made a good dent in the pile of notes Theo and I printed out but didn't have a chance to finish reading them. If you ask me, Vance saw the residents and taxpayers more like enemy combatants than citizens. Just give me a second."

I put the two leftover pizza slices in the fridge and carried the box to the garage, where we kept the garbage cans. When I got back, Don had already organized their pile of papers into three stacks, and I noticed he had marked them with red, yellow, and green dots on top.

"The green dots are notes that are fairly benign," he said. "The others are sorted into higher levels of intensity."

"Start with the one that's nuclear," I said, "and we can go from there. Although I don't remember anything that sent up a red flare. Then again, I still had a small stack to go."

"It's a short note that Vance wrote," Don said, "and refers to someone with the initials R.S. Here, let me read it to you. It says: 'thought of taking out a restraining order but he'd get even. Got too much invested already.' What do you suppose that means?"

My reaction was immediate. "Sounds like he was being threatened and maybe even blackmailed. Question is . . . by who? And why? You know, this note could be Alex's salvation, but we can't very well offer it up."

Theo took the note from Don, studied it for a second and put it down. "Agreed, but rest assured the Ontario and Yates County sheriff's offices will have their teams of techie experts cracking into Vance's computer without needing his password. They'll find that note along with number two on the nuclear list."

"Who's the second-place winner?"

"Madeline," Theo and Don answered in unison.

"Okay, fine. Who's on third?"

Don removed two pieces of paper from the pile and shifted his gaze from one to the other. "It's a tie. A letter from a woman on Snell Road threatening to have him neutered if he didn't acquiesce and grant her request for window planters in the front of her house."

"Yeesh. And the other one?"

"A very similar note from someone on Armstrong Road. It says, "Carport my ass. We need to build a garage. I suggest you reconsider this or you'll be speaking in falsetto permanently.""

I clasped my hands together and tightened them. "The trouble with those two notes is that they're so over-the-top as to lose their credibility. What about the others? The yellow and green dots? All I saw were normal requests that were blown out of proportion."

Don put the papers back on the table. "That about sums it up. Too bad there's no one on that historical society board with the initials R.S."

"Probably listed in his cell phone, which those deputies must have by now if it was anywhere near the body," I said. "Maybe Godfrey and Bradley are right. Maybe those deputies will put two and two together and find out who really was responsible, but I'm not counting on it. The only Hail Mary we have is if the autopsy report shows the real and hopefully natural cause of death."

. . .

It didn't. The preliminary autopsy report on Vance Wexler was released to the media on Tuesday following notification to next of kin, whoever and wherever they lived. All I knew was Vance was single. It hit the noon news on all of the TV stations in Rochester and Syracuse. I know, because it was also on a Facebook feed that I was monkeying around with, having taken a break from my screenplay proposal.

The minute I saw the feed, I plopped the laptop on the coffee table and turned on the TV. Then I moved from channel to channel. Thirteen, ten, eight, and some channels I didn't even know we had. The news was all the same—Vance Wexler succumbed to asphyxiation.

Asphyxiation. What the heck was that supposed to mean? The news anchors danced around the differences between suffocation and asphyxiation, but it all wound up in the same nebulous place. Vance died because his oxygen supply was cut off, and that could have been from natural causes or an outside source. However, there were no indications that his death was caused by the deliberate action on the part of anyone. At least until "further evaluative studies" are conducted. Nice way of saying no one had the slightest idea what did the jerk in.

The news anchors went on to say that toxicology reports were bound to shed more light on this suspicious, for lack of a better word, death. Those results weren't expected for another two weeks, and even then they would be preliminary results because that kind of thing can take months.

Following that announcement about Vance's cause of death, I had a sinking feeling those news anchors would latch on to the full moon summer solstice curse like those crane flies did with broccoli. Good thing I had that interview tomorrow with Lorraine from 8 ROC. Maybe I could water it down so as to diffuse it altogether. Boy, was I wrong.

Chapter 14

Madeline left a message for me at the winery on Wednesday morning to remind me we had a WOW meeting at her place the next day. Something about the winemakers dinner. I made a mental note to show up on time and left it at that. I was way too preoccupied with the interview I was about to have in twenty minutes with Lorraine Stuyvesant, the programming director at 8 ROC. I was petrified about what I was going to tell her, and the hundreds of viewers who were mesmerized about a local curse on Seneca Lake.

Thankfully, I'd snuck away from my screenplay proposal on Monday morning and had gone to the Yates County Historical Society in order to find out more about Adeliza and Derella Marsten, aka our personal answer to Samantha and Endora. Too bad our witches weren't quite as charming as the ones on that old TV sitcom. From what Gladys had told me, the sisters were known to dabble in spells and were somewhat shunned by the churchgoing community. All rumors, of course. However, Gladys had found out one verifiable piece of information. The sisters bought property on our hill in 1797, and that meant there had to be town records dating back to that time.

It took a bit of doing, but I was able to convince one of the docents at the Yates County Historical Society to take a gander at what's behind door number three and track down those records, which were bound to be lurking around in their basement.

While the woman didn't seem to find my sense of humor pleasing, she stopped sorting mailers and agreed to have a look downstairs. Had I known that "have a look" meant donning white gloves while rummaging around dusty shelves and sweeping away pill bugs every few seconds, I might have changed my mind. At least there weren't any visible cobwebs.

Finally she uncovered a worn yellowed book whose binding was falling apart. If that wasn't bad enough, it looked as if it had been recovered from a fire, burnt pages and all.

"Be very careful with this," she said as she handed it to me. "It's irreplaceable. It documents the Town of Benton records from eighteen ten to eighteen fifteen."

"Nothing sooner? Like the late seventeen hundreds?"

She shook her head. "Although the town came into existence in eighteen oh three, the records don't begin until eighteen ten."

Wonderful. Go figure what those two witches were up to between 1797 and 1810. If they even lived that long.

I took the book from her and walked back upstairs, where I spent the next hour trying to make sense of it. Mostly references to creating a mail station and a grist mill, although I did spy what I believed to be one note pertaining to the Marsten sisters in reference to their cultivation of grapes and subsequent wine making, or "spirits of the devil," as the notation said. Then, the clincher—it was dated June eighteenth. A few days before a summer solstice.

Did those two put a curse on someone because they tried to stop them from producing a little homemade wine? If that was the case, it wasn't documented in the town records. I pulled out my iPhone and snapped a photo of the page for future reference and called it a day. At least I'd have some tidbit of truth to embellish during my interview for 8 ROC.

Suddenly I felt a familiar vibration in the pocket of my pants and it shook me out of my reverie about my visit to the Yates County Historical Society on Monday. It was a text message from Godfrey and it said, "Alex at YCPSB. More questioning. Talk to you later." *More questioning. That couldn't be good.* Cold beads of sweat trickled down the back of my neck while the palms of my hands felt sticky and clammy.

"Are you all right, Norrie?" Cammy asked. She rapped on my office door and stuck her head inside. "You haven't said a word since you walked in here an hour ago. I wouldn't have bothered you in your office but Lizzie said you looked as if you were in a daze when you came in this morning."

"Come on in and close the door. Lorraine Stuyvesant from 8 ROC is going to be here any second with a production assistant. I must have temporarily lost my mind because I agreed to be interviewed by her in reference to the Two Witches curse."

"So you agreed after all. I thought you'd adamantly refuse. Whatever possessed you?"

"*Possessed* is a good word. And didn't you say it would be better if I put a spin on the situation so it would end all the speculation about Vance's death being caused by a curse that emanated from our hill? But now I've got to do exactly what I promised myself I wouldn't."

"What do you mean?" she asked.

"Without the curse, Vance's death may point to the murder unless some underlying cause is found. So far, no go. The news just said asphyxiation. That means poor Alex Bollinger is about to be offered up as the number-one suspect. The poor guy is sweating it out right now in the county public safety building. Godfrey sent me a text a few minutes ago. Face it, Alex had motive, means, and opportunity. But he couldn't possibly have murdered Vance. Trouble is, they need a suspect."

"Uh-oh. Are you about to do what I think you are?"

"If you mean am I going to point the finger at those two witches, then the answer is—hell yes! Don't look at me like that. I need to find a way to shift the attention. True, up until now I was concerned that all this witch nonsense would lead to a bunch of lookie-loos traipsing all over the vineyards, but John's got that pretty well under control with ropes and signs."

"If you say so." Cammy opened the office door and quickly shut it. "You may not have to work that hard. Your opening act is in the corridor. I can hear Glenda's voice. Shh . . ."

I stood from my desk and along with Cammy opened the door by a sliver and listened to the conversation.

Glenda's voice sounded wispy and out of breath. "I begged them to smudge the winery with sage and lavender. Witches aren't like ordinary souls. They linger after death."

I closed the door and gave Cammy a poke. "Betcha in two seconds she mentions Zenora and the need for a séance so we can communicate with Vance. Heck, I didn't like communicating with him when he was alive."

"Better not mention that at the interview."

Just then there was a loud rap at the door and we jumped back. Cammy moved quickly to the side of my desk and I literally threw myself into my chair. "Come on in," I announced.

A tall fortyish-looking woman with chin-length dark hair stepped inside. She had a beige top with cuffed three-quarter sleeves, navy slacks and navy pumps. Behind her was a young guy who couldn't have been older than twenty. At least from his appearance. Curly blond hair and an earring. He juggled a TV camera and a tripod.

"Good morning, I'm Lorraine Stuyvesant and this is Chad Montgomery, our cameraman. Thanks so much for agreeing to this interview. It's nice to meet you in person."

"Likewise. I'm Norrie Ellington and this is our tasting room manager, Cammy Rosinetti."

Cammy gave a quick wave and an even quicker hello before racing out of the office. The thud of the door almost made the camera guy drop the tripod.

"Um, however you want to set up in here is fine. Can I offer you anything? Water? Iced tea? Coffee?"

My God. I'm sounding like a flight attendant.

"We're fine," Lorraine said. "We stopped at Tim Horton's on our way over. How about if we pull those two chairs over and we can talk face-to-face as Chad films us."

I immediately dragged my chair out from behind my desk and set it across from the one Cammy had vacated a few seconds ago. When I'd left the house, my hair was perfectly draped on my shoulders and I had added a bit of tinted sunblock to my face. Not enough to cover the light freckles but sufficient enough so my complexion wouldn't appear shiny. Now, given the clammy feeling that had taken over my body, I wasn't too sure.

"This is a recording," Lorraine said, "so you don't have to worry. We can edit out any bloopers. Are you ready to begin?"

I nodded and then remembered something Theo told me: *The camera adds ten pounds to you.* Then I sucked in my stomach and took a quick breath.

"Welcome Channel Eight viewers," Lorraine began. "I'm Lorraine Stuyvesant, and with me today is Norrie Ellington, co-owner of Two Witches Winery in Penn Yan. We're here today to chat about the infamous Two Witches Summer Solstice Curse that may or may not have been responsible for the untimely and unexplained death of Vance Wexler, president of the Geneva Historical Society."

Then, like a burp, I cut in. "Oh, it was responsible, all right. No doubt in my mind. I mean, what else could have happened? It's not as if one of those Cornell entomologists who happened to be at Kashong Point at the same time was responsible."

Lorraine's eyes looked as if they couldn't get any wider. "What entomologists?"

"The ones studying crane flies. Very detrimental to plant tissue."

"I see." Lorraine thumbed through her notes like a banker counting cash. "Yes, our news team noted something to that effect. I wasn't aware the entomologists crossed paths with the crew from Mr. Wexler's historical society."

"Oh, they crossed paths, all right. More like trampled over the delicate field study area, resulting in a very time-consuming recalculation of the population, not to mention the insect behavioral study."

Lorraine looked up from her notes. "Hmm, so maybe Mr. Wexler's untimely demise had more to do with, say, one of those entomologists than the full moon summer solstice curse that's been making the headlines."

Oh, my God! What the heck have I done?

"Oh, no. If anyone's responsible, it's those two witches, Adeliza and Derella Marsten, certainly not Dr. Alex Bollinger."

"Dr. Bollinger?"

"Yes, he's in charge of the insect study. His department works with our vineyard managers to ensure winery pests like the spotted lanternfly are kept under control."

I think it's the lanternfly. Or was it a worm?

"I'm beginning to understand," Lorraine said. "If those amateur archeologists interrupted a valuable field study, there could be scientific as well as financial implications. That does spell out *motive*, doesn't it? That is, if Mr. Wexler's cause of death is deemed a homicide."

The only homicide will be mine if I don't get this turned around fast.

"Vance Wexler's death is still classified as unexplained." *But not for long.*

Chapter 15

I took a deep breath and figuratively threw Adeliza and Derella under the bus like nobody's business. From illicit winemaking to herbal concoctions and heaven knows how many spells, I left little doubt that their full moon summer solstice curse would continue to linger around Seneca Lake until 2062, when the next event of its kind would take place.

And while Lorraine seemed satisfied with my interview, Godfrey wasn't. The three-minute segment aired that night during prime time as part of 8 ROC's human interest programming. And five seconds later Godfrey called, all but jolting me off the couch since I had upped the sound level on the landline.

"Good grief, Norrie! What the hell were you thinking? You let out enough rope to hang the entire entomology department. At least you got the lanternfly part right."

"I'm sorry, Godfrey. Honestly. I tried to do the exact opposite but once I mentioned the field study, everything kind of got out of control."

"Well, maybe it will turn out to be a slow viewing night. Anyway, Alex is a basket case. He wasn't officially charged with murder since the autopsy is still ongoing."

"Ongoing? They released the results to the media."

"Preliminary results. Not the official results. I hate to say it, but I think they're hoping they'll find something that links Alex to Vance's death."

"Like what? There were no signs of a struggle. No bruises. Just plain old suffocation."

"They'll run the DNA around Vance's mouth and nose. Dead skin, dried saliva . . . that sort of thing."

"Then Alex has nothing to worry about."

"Norrie, they were face-to-face arguing. Trace DNA could have wound up on Vance's face."

"Or the real murderer's DNA. *If* it turns out Vance was killed and didn't die of some allergic reaction. Listen, Vance had a boatload of people who were ticked off with him. Theo, Don, and I went through the notes we found in his office. He wrote one of them himself and mentioned taking out a restraining order on someone with the initials R.S. It looked like Vance was concerned that R.S. would get even."

"You think this R.S. might have killed him?"

"It's the best clue we have, only there are no R.S.'s in the Geneva Historical Society. Don got the list and checked. And there were no letters of complaint with anyone who had those initials."

"Think it was personal? Like a girlfriend or boyfriend?"

"Vance seemed too self-absorbed to be dating anyone. And the news said he was single. Oh, my gosh. I can't believe we didn't check his Facebook status. Godfrey, let me call you back. I'm off to pay social media a visit."

I grabbed my laptop and immediately logged in to Facebook. Sure enough, Vance had a profile. Single and not much info. If I wanted to learn more, I'd have to submit a friend request, and well, that was a few days late.

The photos on the left-hand side of the page were vintage cars. Nothing was listed under his bio and his recent posts were about the Seneca Tribe Village on Seneca Lake. I scrolled down and found one post that didn't deal with Ontario or Yates County history. It was about a vintage car race at Watkins Glen and was dated a month ago. Bummer. Nothing I could use and nothing at all about an R.S. To be on the safe side, I checked Instagram, Pinterest, and LinkedIn, but nothing.

No sooner had I shut my laptop than the landline rang again. This time it was Theo and Don, who had also seen my less-than-stellar performance on 8 ROC.

"You may not want to grant any more interviews again, Norrie," Don said. "Unless they're carefully scripted."

"Aargh. I know. I just got off the phone with Godfrey. I'll probably have to buy the entire entomology department lunch one of these days. Listen, we've got two possible leads and a dead end on one of them. You checked the historical society and R.S. wasn't there. I moseyed through social media and those initials didn't appear on anything Vance had on his Facebook page. Which, by the way, wasn't much."

"Theo thought the R.S. could be a local business, so we scoured the online directories for Ontario and Yates counties and came up with a big fat zero. Might as well put that one on hold for a while. What was the other?"

"Vance's car. One of Alex's students saw it at Kashong Point on Friday afternoon but it wasn't there Saturday morning when Vance's body was found."

"Sure it was the right car?" Don asked.

"Not many bright yellow Karmann Ghias floating around. Yeah, I'm sure. I'm going to run down to Kashong Point tomorrow right after our WOW meeting. I figure I can ask around the campground and see if anyone knows anything. Right now, I don't think the sheriff's office is looking for that car."

"When you talk to people, please don't try to pass yourself off as an investigator. We don't have that much money for a bail bondsman."

"I'll tell the truth. That I'm a winery owner and that Vance's unexplained death has some serious implications for our winery due to the Two Witches curse and that I need to track down the flesh-and-blood killer before things get out of hand."

"Norrie, no one really knows if the guy was killed. The autopsy was preliminary and the toxicology report hasn't been finalized."

"Then why is Deputy Hickman badgering Alex? I'll tell you why. His office wants to be poised and ready to make an arrest as soon as that other data is received. Anyway, which one of you plans to be at the WOW meeting tomorrow?"

"Theo does. He drew the short straw. I don't think it will be a long meeting. The only thing on the agenda is the winemakers dinner."

I gulped. "The *written* agenda. You know as well as I do that we'll all get drawn in to discuss some picky little thing that could've been handled by an email."

"Yeah, guess you're right about that. Wonder what it will be this time. Oh, well. Theo will be sure to tell me."

• • •

As it happened, the "picky little thing" turned out to be the Two Witches summer solstice curse and my "unfortunate blunder" during the 8 ROC interview with Lorraine Stuyvesant. At least they waited until our discussion about the winemakers dinner was over.

"Summer blends," Madeline said. "That's what we plan to serve at the winemakers dinner. You all got my memo with the menu. Pan-seared Chilean sea bass with garlic and lemon sauce and Malaysian tamarind prawn. Naturally we need to pair it with white or light wines. We're featuring our Sunbeam Delight, a Niagara grape blend with hints of pineapple, lychee, and papaya. What about the rest of you?"

"Lakeview Breeze for us," Catherine said. "It's a Chardonnay blend."

"Vignoles," Stephanie chimed in.

As they shouted out their selections, I suddenly remembered part two of the summer solstice curse—that bit about drinking rosé and dropping dead. I wasn't exactly sure if those witches meant rosé produced on our hill or rosé from that idiotic five-mile radius. And while the rational part of my brain knew it was a ridiculous notion, the other ninety percent of my brain wasn't all that sure.

Not wanting to sound like Glenda, I sat still and held my breath until they were all done. Four white wine blends and one red. I was so busy tallying them up in my head, I didn't hear Madeline's question.

"Norrie, were you listening?"

"Huh?"

"Do you know what wine you're going to serve? At the winemakers dinner. What wine will Two Witches be bringing?"

Thankfully I remembered Cammy talking about the melon and pear notes in our Cayuga and Riesling blend and how she thought it would be perfect for the winemakers dinner.

"Summer Magic," I said. "It's light and fruity."

Madeline nodded. "Good. Looks like we're all on board for next Saturday. Does anyone want me to review the menu again?"

A collective groan was all Madeline needed to skip over the dinner and launch right into my interview fiasco last night. "Dear me, I wouldn't want to be in that entomologist's shoes. All I can say is thank goodness I kept my diatribes to the verbal kind as far as Mr. Wexler was concerned. Imagine not letting someone extend their porch by three feet."

The next seven or eight minutes were spent with stories about how Vance Wexler made life miserable for anyone in the new historic district who wished to modernize their home. Then Madeline went over the program for the winemakers dinner and how we sold a record number of seats. Forty-nine at the pricey amount of one hundred sixty-five dollars a pop. Glad I didn't have to spring the money for mine. Of course, given the exotic menu and the wines, it was a pretty good deal.

The event would take place rain or shine in the clearing above her vineyard. Finger Lakes Awnings and Pavilions was to arrive the Thursday before to set up the giant white tent complete with tables and chairs. I tried to listen but honestly, Madeline just kept droning on and on about centerpieces and stemware, so I discreetly slipped my iPhone from my pocket and looked down to check my emails. That's when I noticed one with a red flag alert on it.

It was from Cammy and it read, "Better get over here quick. Deputy Hickman has a search warrant for your office."

Chapter 16

"Well, this was certainly a fun meeting," I said, "but I've got to get back to the winery. Yes, indeed. Back to the winery."

Theo gave me a funny look. "Are you okay?"

"Yep. I need to search through that grizzly pile of screenplay notes on my desk. I just remembered a deadline I have."

I stood and started for the door when Theo pushed his chair back. "I'll join you," he said. Then he glanced at the ladies who were seated around Madeline's enclosed porch. "That is, unless there's unfinished business. I don't have to review screenplay notes like Norrie."

Madeline clasped her hands together and gave him a nod. "No, we're all set here. Until next Saturday. Of course, I was hoping everyone would stay and give their opinions on the centerpieces but that's not necessary."

A chorus of "we trust your judgment" and "whatever you decide" immediately followed her comment. I didn't wait for further conversation. I bolted out of the place as if it was about to explode. Theo was at my heels and all but tackled me in Madeline's driveway.

"What's Deputy Hickman doing in your office? Very cryptic. Stephanie probably just figured it out, and it won't take Rosalee long."

"I don't know but you may be next. The only thing I can think of is that someone looked at the surveillance footage from that night in Vance's office and shared it with the Geneva police and the Ontario County Sheriff's Office. And we both know Hickman's working with them on this case."

"Oh, crap! I'd better call Don."

While Theo reached for his cell phone, I texted Cammy, *On my way.* Then I sent another text to Bradley, just in case.

"Don busted a gut when I told him," Theo said. "Grizzly Gary hasn't made it to the Grey Egret but give it time. Call me and let me know what's going on."

"You mean let you know how much bail money I need?"

"You? We'll both need it."

I shot out of Madeline's driveway and down Route 14 in a nanosecond. As tempting as it was to speed my way to Two Witches Hill, I decided to stay within five miles of the speed limit because, heaven knows, I didn't need any more trouble.

Sure enough, Deputy Hickman's official vehicle was parked right in front of the winery. If that wasn't cause to scare wine tasters away, I don't know what would be. I look a breath, ran my hands through my hair like I always do when I'm nervous, and walked inside the building.

Lizzie reached out her hand to my wrist the second I got within range of her. "What's going on? Deputy Hickman showed Cammy and me that search warrant and he's in your office. Thankfully Cammy had the good sense to close the door."

"I'm not sure but it may have something to do with a bit of sleuthing that Theo and I did at the Geneva Historical Society on Saturday night."

"Oh, dear. Nancy Drew was always careful to cover her tracks. Discretion was her middle name."

Terrific. Now she has a middle name.

"Um, yeah, well, she had a good author. Or authors . . ."

Just then Cammy approached the cash register where we were standing and motioned for me to join her in the kitchen. "Hurry up," she whispered. "He doesn't know you're here."

"Do you have any idea what's going on? What he's looking for?"

"Whatever it is, the search warrant's only for your office in the winery. Not your house."

I let that sink in for a minute. If the warrant included my house, Deputy Hickman would be looking for the papers Theo and I copied from Vance's computer files. After all, I could have stashed them in either location. That meant he was snooping through my office for something else. The question was . . . what?

"Did he come alone?"

Cammy nodded. "Uh-huh."

"Well, I can't put this off much longer. I'd better go inside before he ransacks the place."

"Yell if you need me!"

I left the kitchen, walked across the corridor and opened the door to my office. Before I could utter a word, Deputy Hickman stepped away from my desk and spoke. "It was about time you got here. I figured someone on your staff would send out a high alert as soon as I showed up."

"Well, with a search warrant and all, what did you expect? They're petrified I might be arrested. Although for your information, Theo and I—" And then I stopped. Maybe he didn't know about the unorthodox entry into the Geneva Historical Society.

"What were you saying about you and Mr. Buchman?"

"Um, only that we were concerned about anything that would keep visitors away from our wineries. You know, like the witches' curse."

"Nice try, Miss Ellington. I happen to know for a fact that you and Mr. Buchman are in possession of some delicate information that the joint forensic analysis team was unable to retrieve. And if you must know, I have a second search warrant in my possession."

Yippee. A second search warrant.

"Delicate information? What delicate information?"

"Whatever it was you were able to secure from Mr. Wexler's computer during your little spy mission on Saturday. You're lucky the grainy footage from Geneva Historical Society's surveillance system is too blurry for a positive ID."

"Uh, well . . ."

"Before you start denying it was you, let me point out that I'm quite familiar with your mannerisms by now, including that hair tossing habit of yours. Not to mention Mr. Buchman's unique way of lumbering around a room. The Geneva police might not have a clue who the culprits were, but as soon as they forwarded the footage to my office, I knew immediately it was the two of you."

Security footage. Geneva police. How could I have been so stupid? Of course they would be accessing Vance's office. Duh!

"It's not what you think. Oh, what the hell. It's exactly what you think. Theo and I couldn't very well sit back and do nothing when a friend of ours is turning out to be the number-one suspect."

"So you broke into Mr. Wexler's office to see if there was anything on his computer that would point to another suspect?"

I nodded. "His computer, his office files, and even his Facebook page, although I did that at home and there's no crime in that."

"You *do* realize that trained professionals, and I emphasize the word *trained*, know exactly how to extract and analyze that type of information."

"Well, they're not exactly extracting and analyzing that information too well or you wouldn't be in my office with a search warrant."

Deputy Hickman rubbed the back of his neck and groaned.

"Hair tossing and lumbering around don't make for a positive identification," I said. "Although I think Theo would find that description of him somewhat objectionable. And if you must know, we can always deny it was us."

"Miss Ellington, I don't know how else to put this. We're on the same page. Although it's a professional matter for my office, and apparently a personal one for you and your friends. I have no intention of turning you over to the Geneva police for breaking and entering, but if this investigation is going to get off the ground, it would certainly behoove you to share what you've found with us."

"I, um . . ."

"Look, the combined forensic analysis teams from both counties will undoubtedly get into that computer, but why waste valuable time?"

"Does this mean we're working together?"

"Good heavens, no! It means you won't get arrested."

I did a mental eye roll while considering my options. Not that there was anything to consider. "Okay. The password is Karmann Ghia. And all we found were notes Vance, I mean Mr. Wexler, had about people who ticked him off. Which was pretty much everyone. Mostly the folks who had requests for architectural changes to their historical properties. If you want, I can get you the list. And his notes."

"Miss Ellington, please don't tell me you were planning to contact those people because, in addition to breaking and entering, that would be considered interfering with a crime investigation."

I shrugged while he continued to expound on why I needed to mind my own business. When he paused to catch a breath, I looked directly at him. "You think Vance Wexler was murdered, don't you? Even though the first round at the coroner's office didn't confirm that."

"That's why those reports are called *preliminary*. Once we get the toxicology report, we can further substantiate the initial findings."

"Then why continue to press Alex Bollinger?"

"Because his field research team has access to all sorts of toxins in their labs. It may have appeared as if Mr. Wexler succumbed to that idiotic smothering curse, but I guarantee, if he didn't die from a preexisting medical condition, he died at someone's hand and Dr. Bollinger had a darned good motive."

81

Chapter 17

When Deputy Hickman left my office I felt as if someone had punched me in the gut. I immediately sent Bradley another text, *Forget first text. False alarm.* Then I phoned Theo to let him know he was off the hook and told him I was on my way over to Kashong Point to see if I could find out anything about Vance's car.

"After Grizzly Gary told you to back off?"

"He told me not to contact any of the people who were on those notes of Vance's. He didn't make any mention of campers at Kashong Point."

"Just watch your back while you're down there. For all any of us know, one of those campers could have been responsible for Vance's death."

"I'm only going to inquire about the car. How dangerous can that be?"

From now on, I will never, under any circumstance, use a retort like, "How dangerous can that be?" because, as Glenda would put it, "The life forces have a way of answering your question," and in this case, it wasn't the answer I was looking for.

Cammy immediately tackled me once Lizzie gave the all-clear that Deputy Hickman left the winery. "What was he looking for? What did he find? What did you tell him?"

"The good news is no one has to post bail money, but I did have to offer up the password Theo and I figured out for Vance's computer. It was a trade-off—the password in exchange for not getting arrested. You know, breaking and entering into the Geneva Historical Society on Saturday. Go figure the Geneva police would actually be reviewing surveillance footage from Vance's office. Well, I hope they were satisfied because—Oh, my gosh! The other board members were in there as well. I wonder if someone's paying Agnes, Mildred, and Curtis a visit. Oh, well, it doesn't matter. I'm going to grab a sandwich from the bistro and take off for Kashong Point."

"Be careful, okay?"

"If it will make you feel any better, my phone has GPS tracking. If I'm not back here before we close, use it."

"Norrie, I have no idea how to do that. Don't you need special software or something?"

"Hmm, come to think of it, you're probably right. If I'm not back here, call the sheriff's office. Oh, and Theo, too. And Bradley."

"Just get back here."

I devoured a turkey and bacon on rye, washed it down with a Coke and took off for Kashong Point. Not that I had given it much thought earlier in the day, but I was glad I had put on a pair of faded and partially ripped jeans as well as my sneakers instead of sandals. Walking along the beach at Kashong Point with opened-toed shoes was an invitation for cuts and bruises thanks to all of the sharp rocks and glass debris that seem to wind up onshore. Unlike ocean beaches, where soft sand is the norm, lakeside beaches tend to be rocky, marshy, or a combination of both.

It surprised me that Deputy Hickman made no mention about Vance's car, but then again, it wasn't as if he was going to share any part of the official investigation with me. I figured I'd find out one way or another while I did my own bit of detective work.

Kashong Point had its usual share of cars lined up along the circular drive and the parking lot adjacent to the conservation area. A lineup of people with their fishing rods extended into the lake was the first thing that caught my eye as I grabbed the nearest parking spot. In the distance, I could see the area that the entomology department had commandeered for their Swedish fly crane or whatever-it-was study. The only thing missing were those amateur artifact hunters who most likely jumped ship once their captain was found dead.

A few people were sunbathing along the lakeshore while others were either walking their dogs, throwing sticks or balls for their dogs, or yelling at their dogs. In retrospect, I should have brought Charlie along, but with my luck he'd probably find some disgusting dead fish to roll around in.

With so many people all over the place, it was tough to figure out where to begin. I had no idea who might have been here the night before Vance was found dead, but I couldn't afford to stand around and waste time. I made a beeline for an older man who was putting bait on the end of his fishing pole. His scraggly beard and five o'clock shadow made me wonder if he'd been camping for a few days.

"Pardon me," I said, "do you remember seeing a bright yellow Karmann Ghia parked around here last weekend?"

"Sorry. Got here at five this morning. You may want to ask the folks who've got that yurt a few yards down. That's where I got my bait. Nice healthy earthworms. Here, see for yourself."

He held up a plump worm that moved slightly.

"Yep. Well fed. Um, thanks. I'll check it out."

I walked to where some of the tents and lean-tos were pitched and spied the yurt immediately. It was the only one of its kind. A middle-aged woman was grilling some sort of fish on a small Weber and waved when I approached.

"If you're looking to buy bait, we already sold out. Got to get here first thing in the morning. The bait and tackle shops on the lake will have plenty but they'll charge you an arm and a leg."

"Uh, no. Thanks. I'm hoping you can help me. Someone said you've been here for a few days."

She grabbed a pair of tongs and flipped the filets. "Since the Tuesday before last. My husband and I work in Elmira and we always spend our summer vacation camping here. What is it you need?"

"Did you happen to see anyone drive off in a bright yellow Karmann Ghia the morning when a man's body was discovered?"

"Last Saturday?"

"Uh-huh."

She shook her head. "Saw that car *before* Saturday, but come to think of it, not after. Why? Was it stolen?" Then she stopped and furrowed her brow. "Don't tell me it belonged to the dead man. I had a hunch about that. Even told my husband, Darryl, but he said to mind my own beeswax before we get tangled up in this. Bad enough we lost good fishing time while those deputies questioned the daylights out of everyone."

"You wouldn't happen to know if anyone else saw anything, would you?"

"That happened last weekend. Most of the folks who were here are long gone. They only camp for the weekend. Not many of us diehards are left. Hmm, let me think for a minute."

She flipped the fish again and removed two of them from the grill. "You might want to talk to those two hee-haws way over by the old dock. Can't miss 'em. They're the only ones there."

"Hee-haws?"

"The two thirty-somethings who make so much noise it would scare away a herd of buffalo, let alone the fish. They've been showing up every day before dawn and leave when it gets too dark to fish. Seen them a few times on my way to the john before daybreak."

I thanked her and started for the dock. That's when she called me back. "I wouldn't tell them too much if I were you. Something about those two is off but I can't pinpoint it."

Wonderful. Just what I need. Unstable people.

The thirty-somethings also had that lakeside five o'clock shadow. Really noticeable since they both had dark hair. Yep. Nothing spells vacation like putting away your razor for a while and covering most of your hair with generic baseball caps.

"Excuse me, do either of you recall seeing anyone drive off in a bright yellow Karmann Ghia last Friday night? Or early Saturday morning?"

"What's it to you?" the taller one asked. He had just stashed a cell phone in his pocket and gave me a nasty look.

"The car belongs to a friend of mine. It's missing."

"Tell your friend to call the sheriff," the shorter one said.

I read somewhere that the best part of getting away with a lie was to look the person directly in the eye. I took a step closer and glared at him. "She already did that."

He stared back. "Then why isn't she here checking?"

"She's at work. Look, I understand the two of you have been regular fixtures around here so you must know something. You wouldn't want me to—"

"Hey, we don't know anything. Nice talking to you. I'd watch it if I were you. These docks can get awfully slippery."

"Thanks for the warning."

I turned and barely walked two or three steps when I felt something cut me on the back of my ankle. The second I lifted my foot I realized it was a hook from a fishing line. I bent down to remove it, and that was the second someone slammed my back with such force that I lost my balance and fell chest-first from the dock into the waist-deep murky water. Not quite a belly flop but close enough to sting me. At least it was summer and the water temperature couldn't have been lower than a nice seventy degrees. Of course, at the deeper levels it would have been closer to the high thirties. And while I remembered many pleasant swims in this lake while growing up, today wasn't one of them.

Above me, I could hear the thud of footsteps as my assailants thundered off the dock and most likely into their cars for a fast getaway. My first reaction was to reach for my cell phone and pray it hadn't been in the water long enough to ruin it. That's when I remembered I had left it locked in my glove compartment.

I was soaking wet, and if that wasn't bad enough, bits of dirt and dead leaves adhered to every part of my skin and clothing. I was about to head back to where that yurt was when I thought of something. What if that fish-grilling woman tipped these guys off? Or maybe even the earthworm fisherman. I did, after all, see the tall thirty-something put his cell phone in a pocket when I approached him.

There was only one person at Kashong Point I could trust and he was busy categorizing crane flies. Then again, Alex Bollinger owed me one. I put my neck out for him. The least he could do was find me some dry clothes.

Chapter 18

"Yikes! Norrie! What happened? Did you fall out of a boat or what?"

Alex was leaning over what looked like a makeshift drafting table that had small jars of insects—what else?—on it. I had hoofed it all the way from the touristy area at Kashong Point to the conservation area where his team was still working. A few students stopped what they were doing and rushed over to me.

Everyone spoke at once. Questions. Answers. Directives. You name it.

"Do you want a towel?" "Go get her a towel from the tent."

"We've got blankets. Hold on."

"Did your boat capsize?"

"Were you kayaking?" "Will someone get her a damn towel?"

Finally, a girl with tight blond curls and wire-rimmed glasses handed me a dish towel. "Um, you may want to wipe your face. It's got slimy dirt on it."

Gee, you think?

"Forget the face dirt," I said. "Are there any bugs in my hair?"

She shook her head just as another student handed me a larger towel.

"Are you sure you're all right?" Alex asked. "What happened?"

"I'm fine. Just wet. At least it's summer. Um, is there someplace we can speak privately?"

Alex turned to his students and motioned for them to get back to their work. Then he turned to me. "Follow me. I've got some dry clothes in the tent if you don't mind wearing New York State Agricultural Experiment Station–issue sweatshirts and sweatpants."

"Thanks."

On the way to the tent I told him my reason for dropping by Kashong Point and how I must have hit a nerve with those two guys on the dock.

"You think they might have something to do with Vance's death?" he asked.

"Uh-huh. That Karmann Ghia of his didn't disappear on its own. I'm thinking whoever took it might be the person who made sure Vance wasn't about to wake up. I'm surprised the deputies aren't all over it, but then again, it's not as if Deputy Hickman is about to share any information with me."

Alex gave me a pat on my shoulder as we approached the tent. "Norrie, I appreciate you sticking your neck out for me, but we have no idea who's behind this. Up until this minute, I was banking on the full autopsy to reveal a medical issue. But given what happened to you, I tend to agree that those guys might very well have killed Vance in order to steal his car. Maybe they didn't mean to kill him, just drug him, and something went wrong. Guess we won't know that until the toxicology report is in. Meanwhile, I'm still *persona numero uno* as far as the authorities are concerned, and you could be putting yourself in danger poking around here."

"What gets me is why go to all that trouble to steal a Karmann Ghia? True, it's kind of a classic sixties car, but I looked them up and they're not worth much more that fifteen or twenty grand, and that's only if they're in pristine condition."

"People steal stuff for all sorts of reasons. I read somewhere about someone breaking into a house and all they took was the owner's boxer shorts."

"Ew."

"You know, like it or not, what they did falls into the category of assault. You really should call the sheriff's office and report it."

"Um, not a good idea. I was told explicitly by Deputy Hickman to stay out of his investigation and I kind of agreed that I wouldn't contact any of the people Vance had made reference to in his notes."

"His notes? I'm not sure I follow."

"I guess Godfrey didn't tell you, huh?"

"Tell me what? I've been tethered to the lake for close to a week."

"Arrgh. Let me change my clothes and I'll fill you in."

Once inside the tent, Alex handed me the clothes and walked out. "I'll wait for you by that picnic table over there."

"I really appreciate the dry clothes," I said once I had changed. "Nice and comfy. I may even get used to them."

"Consider it a gift from the entomology department. We've got a stockpile. So, what did you mean about Vance's notes?"

I told him everything from Theo and me getting inside the Geneva Historical Society's building to Deputy Hickman catching up with me.

The whole time Alex's eyes got wider and wider, and so did his smile.

"Godfrey told me about you but I thought he was exaggerating. The campsites are at the other end of Kashong Point but I'll see if my students and I can keep an eye out for the two guys fitting that description. Maybe during our breaks or something. Too bad you didn't get a look at their car."

"By the time I got out of the water, they were long gone."

At that moment, the student with the tight blond curls and the wire-rimmed glasses ran over to us. "I'm sorry to interrupt, Dr. Bollinger," she said, "but all of us got to talking and well, if your friend fell headfirst into the water, there's a chance the Naegleria fowleri, or brain-eating amoeba, could have gone up her nostrils to her brain."

Thank you, Little Mary Sunshine, for that.

"Um, I fell in feetfirst," I said. "I'll live. But, um, thanks for the heads-up." *As if I didn't have enough to worry about.*

Alex tried not to laugh. "Tell everyone it's okay, Larissa. I'll be back in a few minutes. And the Naegleria fowleri are found in warm water lakes, not cold ones like Seneca."

The girl nodded a few times and took off.

"Believe it or not," Alex said, "she's the most levelheaded of the group. That's why it's so important for me to demonstrate the correct protocols for a field study."

"How much longer will you be here?"

"If all goes well we should finish up in a few days. Say, I heard the terrific news about Jason's study. Imagine that—he's one step closer to having his name on that new Haemagogus epithet."

"As long as he and my sister are back here before Bastille Day I don't care where they put his name."

"You're a good sport. Even if you deny it. Listen, I would feel horrible if anything happened to you, so let those two sheriff's offices conduct their investigation. I'll be okay. Today was a warning. You're lucky those two men didn't whop you over the head or worse."

"I think they wanted to give me a message, that's all."

"Maybe this time. Be careful who you speak with."

Alex made a good point. There wasn't anyone here at Kashong Point I could really trust as far as finding out what happened to that Karmann Ghia. But maybe I wasn't looking in the right place.

I thanked Alex again for the change of clothes and drove back to the house, where I threw my mud-soaked jeans and top into the wash. Charlie, who was in the side yard, followed me inside in lieu of using his doggie door and plopped himself on the kitchen floor, adjacent to the pantry door.

"I'd better let Cammy know I'm back," I said, "before she sends for the militia."

When I told her what had happened, I thought the line went dead. Finally she spoke. "I hope that teaches you a lesson. You could've been the next victim."

"Nah, I don't think anyone's after my old Toyota, although why they would want an old Karmann Ghia is beyond me. Anyway, I've decided to pick up my search from a different perspective."

"Oh, no."

"Relax. I'm going to drop by the foreign auto dealers in the area to see if they have any classic Karmann Ghias for sale. And while I'm there, I'll sort of snoop around. You know, see if they've got that yellow car stashed somewhere. It's kind of hard to miss."

"I really hate to say this, but I think you're better off having Glenda and that wacky Zenora do one of their séances to contact Vance and get his opinion."

"Very funny. I already did my homework on foreign auto dealers when I first saw that photo in Vance's office. There are only three in the entire Finger Lakes—Watkins Glen, Geneva, and Ithaca. The farthest one is an hour from here. Big deal."

"It *will* be a big deal if it turns out you're right and they're on to you. At least hold off for a while. Until the official cause of death is determined. You could be wasting your time."

"Maybe. But cars don't vanish overnight and people don't get the breath sucked out of them while they sleep. My money's on murder. Plain and simple."

Chapter 19

My money may have been on murder but the headline that appeared in the *Finger Lakes Times* the following morning pointed directly to that stupid curse. It read "Two Witches Curse Looms as Investigation Stalls."

It went on to say that the preliminary toxicology screen did not yield any notable results, thus stymieing the coroner's office while they wait for the in-depth analysis to be completed. I wondered if Deputy Hickman knew about that report yesterday when he showed up at my office with that search warrant. One would think he would have shared it with me as gratitude for giving him the password to Vance's computer. Then again, not placing me under arrest was all the gratitude I was going to get.

The remainder of the article reiterated what everyone knew by now—those two herb-concocting witches from our hill came up with a summer solstice curse because, heaven knows, things must've been awfully boring back in the early 1800s.

I glanced at the article and was about to hand it to Lizzie at the cash register when something a few paragraphs down caught my eye. It was one sentence but it was one sentence too many. "The two witches curse is rumored to have a second part." *Oh, joy of joys. Now everyone knows.*

If that wasn't enough to ruin my morning, it read, "Witch hunters, folklore aficionados, and curiosity seekers, now's your time to find out for yourself."

Were these people insane? They all but invited every lunatic in Western New York to descend on our winery like locusts. Not to mention the Yates County Historical Society. Heck, I don't think their budget can afford all those white gloves. And where'd they get the idea about the second half of the curse? Unless Gladys just *had* to tell someone.

Curse or no curse, I was convinced Vance succumbed to a flesh-and-blood killer and that I needed to follow through with my original plan to find that car of his. Only I couldn't do it alone. I needed someone to distract the salespeople and mechanics at those foreign auto dealers. That way I could sneak around the garage and bays without anyone noticing.

True, I told myself I would never, under any circumstance, involve Stephanie Ipswich in my sleuthing after my last experience with her at the Albright Auditorium at Hobart and William Smith Colleges, but this time it was different. No one else had the looks, sex appeal and come-hither charm that she exuded. The woman was a virtual male magnet. Like Christy Brinkley at the height of her career, Stephanie could turn heads like nobody's business. Maybe it was that back-length blond hair of hers. Or maybe those long shapely legs that made mine look like Mrs. Toad when I was standing next to her. It didn't matter. Whatever she had, I needed.

Wasting no time, I called Gable Hill Winery and asked for her. It was a little before ten and I knew she was bound to be working.

"Hi, Norrie! What's up? Everything okay? I mean, other than today's headline and all that."

"Yeah, the 'all that' is my reason for this call. I need your help. At some point those deputy sheriffs are going to make an arrest in Vance Wexler's death. True, it's inconclusive right now, but trust me, they'll find something and when they do, they'll be after Madeline and a friend of mine from the Experiment Station."

"Not that nice Godfrey Klein?"

"No, one of his coworkers. Another entomologist. Alex Bollinger. Dr. Bollinger. Long story. He's on Kashong Point doing an insect study and he and Vance got into a major brouhaha when Vance showed up with a group of amateur arrowhead hunters and all but wreaked havoc on the insect study. So now, Alex has a motive for murder. And then there's Madeline."

"Madeline has a motive for murder, too?"

"Some snoopy, gossipy board member from the Geneva Historical Society overheard her threatening Vance."

"How do you know this?"

"Because I overheard the snoopy board member. Listen, Stephanie, we don't have much time. I need you to go with me to three foreign automobile dealers in the Finger Lakes. Not far. Geneva, Ithaca, and Watkins Glen."

"I'm totally lost. You'd better slow down."

I took a deep breath and explained about the Karmann Ghia as well as my summer indoctrination into Seneca Lake.

Stephanie all but shrilled her words. "And you want me to go with you into garages to find a killer?"

"Well, not if you put it that way. What I'm trying to do is find that car. Whoever took it did it the night of Vance's death, and that can only mean one thing as far as I'm concerned. Whoever took the car—"

"I know. So what do you want me to do?"

"Nothing that doesn't come natural. I need you to chitchat with the salesmen or mechanics at these places while I sneak around to see if that car is stashed in one of their garages or bays. Use that hair-flipping move of yours."

"My gosh, Norrie, I'm not a femme fatale."

"You're the closest one that I know."

"And what if it's saleswomen and female mechanics? You of all people should be aware of gender equality."

"If that's the case, improvise. Pretend you're interested in buying a foreign car. Ask about the features. And speed. It's always a big deal about speed when it comes to foreign cars."

"When did you say you wanted to do this?"

"Tomorrow if possible. If not, Monday."

"Hmm. I can't do it tomorrow. Even with my mother-in-law watching the boys, I have to work in the tasting room. But I can go with you on Monday as long as it's between nine and two. My mother-in-law can only stay till two."

"Fine. I'll pick you up at nine and we'll start in Ithaca, then work our way back through Watkins Glen and then Geneva. Lunch is on me."

"Good. I'm picking someplace expensive."

Thanks to the *Finger Lakes Times*, the next two days saw more foot traffic in our tasting room than we usually have in late June and early July. That was the good part. The not-so-good part was the foot traffic in our vineyards. John Grishner nearly had a conniption fit.

"I'm making up some signs that read *Verboten*," he told me on Sunday. Vine-tromping tourists had compelled him to stop by on his day off. "If the signs work for Franz in the winery lab, then I can't go wrong. Apparently no one seems to understand *Keep out*."

I stood with him at the midpoint of our hill and glanced at the vineyards. "I hope we didn't have any damage to the vines."

"Not yet."

"What is it these tourists are looking for? Those witches have been dead for two centuries."

John took off his baseball cap and wiped his forehead with a bandana. "You don't know?"

"I'm clueless."

"They're looking for the site of the house where those two women lived. The building was long gone by the time the property changed hands. The farmhouse your family owns isn't it. Your house was built in the late eighteen hundreds and modernized when electricity was introduced to our area."

"Yeah, I knew that. But I have no idea where the original structure is, I mean *was*. Do you?"

"Roughly. When the previous winery owners put in the first rows of vineyards they had to complete all sorts of soil analysis. Those results were included as part of the land sales. It's not a definitive conclusion but, if you take a good look at the property to the far left of your house, you'll notice that no vineyards were established there. The soil analysis had shown nutrient losses. Mainly nitrogen and phosphorous."

"I don't understand."

"Those nutrients are lost during fires. That's why there are so many protocols to follow after a forest fire if the land is going to be reused effectively."

"Forest fire? Our woods are way back."

Suddenly I realized what John was getting at and I nearly jumped out of my skin. "You mean to tell me that Adeliza and Derella's house burned down? I always thought it had, well, you know, crumbled and fell apart over the years."

"It might have," he said, "but the soil points to something else. If, indeed, that was the spot where their house was located."

"I wish I knew more about those two but there wasn't all that much to go on in the Yates County archives at the historical society."

"Did you try looking at old survey maps?"

I shook my head.

"It might be a fun thing to do if you've got the time."

I wanted to tell him that the only *fun thing* I planned to do was track down a car that might have been stolen by a murderer but I decided to keep mum.

"Um, thanks. It's an idea."

As John headed back down the hill toward his truck, I had the strangest thought. *What if someone deliberately set fire to that house?*

That would mean there were two other murders on our property. And while I didn't have the time to find out, I knew someone who'd chomp at the bit to bring justice to a couple of old witches.

Chapter 20

Glenda was arranging wine bottles in our racks when I walked into the tasting room. With her hair tucked behind her ears, I got a good look at her latest earrings—dangling crystal balls that picked up the highlights from her pink and silver hair. She gave each wine bottle a quick wipe down with a cloth before setting it in its place. Behind her, Cammy, Sam, and Roger had customers at their tables while Lizzie was buried under a stack of papers up front.

I walked over to Glenda and whispered, "What do you know about the two witches who used to live on our hill?"

She put a bottle of Cauldron Caper on the rack and tapped her teeth. "Probably the same stuff you do, why? Is there really a second part to that curse? The *Finger Lakes Times* thinks so."

There was no reason to keep the information from Glenda so I told her what Gladys had told me. Then I explained what John had said about soil nutrients and a possible fire. Before I finished, she cut in. "Fire won't destroy a curse. What were they thinking?"

"Huh?" *What did I miss?*

Glenda took a step back from the wine rack and looked directly at me. "People have the misguided notion that setting a witch on fire will end her curses. Is that what happened to the two witches on this hill? They were murdered?"

I shook my head. "I don't know. I need you to find out. I mean, you've got all sorts of connections that, well, most of us don't."

"Zenora told me you'd be seeking my help. Her premonitions are unequaled."

And vague, to say the least. For all she knows, I could be asking Glenda to wipe down the kitchen counter.

"The Yates County Historical Society has anecdotal information in its archives but it's not much. I also checked the Town of Benton records, too. Same deal. I don't think you'll find anything in the conventional places," I said.

"I never do. Hmm, if someone did indeed murder Adeliza and Derella, then their black cloud of death will linger over this hill for an eternity. Unless of course—"

"Unless what? What?"

Glenda took a breath and spoke in a slow, soft voice. "We expose the murderers and make them pay the price."

"Um, you do realize that whoever may or may not have killed the Marsten sisters has been dead himself or herself for over two centuries."

"Physically, yes, but not ephemerally."

Suddenly, all moisture had left my mouth and I wondered if I had made the right decision to ask for Glenda's help. I pictured smudgings, séances, and hypnotic trances resulting in problems the likes of which this winery had never seen.

"Begin with a paper search. Okay? Just the information. Then we can figure out how justice can best be served."

My God, that sounds like a line from a bad Western.

"You can trust me, Norrie. If those witches were murdered, I'll find out."

With Glenda on the hunt to see if there was any validity to what John had told me, I was able to finalize my screenplay proposal and come up with a rough distraction scenario that Stephanie and I could put into play the next day. Needless to say, with the exception of picking Stephanie up at nine, nothing went as planned.

Stephanie breezed out of her house the next morning wearing one of those long flowing summer dresses that clung to all of her best features. "Can we start in Geneva first and then take Routes 96A and 96 into Ithaca?" she asked. "I know you wanted to start in Ithaca but I really need to pick up Derek's dry cleaning on Hamilton Street. The shop will be closed by the time we get back. It'll only take a minute."

Her minute turned out to be fifteen. I waited in the car out front while I watched her through the window. Tilting her head back and laughing, flipping her hair, and waving her hand as if she was casting a spell. The man behind the counter certainly got the full Stephanie Ipswich treatment. I only prayed she'd pull off half as good a job at those car dealers.

When she finally got in the car and we hung Derek's shirts over the backseat, I headed to Geneva Auto Sports on Routes 5 & 20. They specialized in European models including Porsche, Bentley, Audi, and BMW, as well as other unnamed vintage European cars. I figured that had to include Volkswagens.

The dealership resembled an oversized Swiss chalet complete with showroom, a bank of ten bays and a separate body shop and collision center. The new car inventory was housed directly in front of the main building, and unlike the tacky parking lots with balloons and air-filled floaties that waved, this one was tastefully decorated with sculpted trees and bushes.

Thankfully, most of the bays were wide open and the ones that were closed had large glass-paned windows, so looking inside wouldn't pose a problem. I parked directly in front of the main building and waited for Stephanie to go inside before making my move to check out the bays.

"How long do you want me to keep talking?" she asked. "Better yet, text me when you're back in the car."

"Keep an eye out. You'll see me."

No one was in the front parking lot, and once Stephanie had gone inside, I walked toward the bays. Six of them were wide open and I could hear people working. Tools were strewn on the garage floors but I didn't notice the usual oil spills and messes that seemed to come with the territory.

I walked quickly. BMW, Mercedes, Mercedes, Audi, BMW, and a white Alpha Romeo. I'd only seen those in the movies. I looked around and still no one in sight. That's when I peered into the first two closed bays. Empty on both counts. There was a silver Acura in the third bay and I wondered if maybe it belonged to one of the mechanics who was working on his own car. That left one more bay. I leaned forward, almost pressing my nose against the glass when all of a sudden I heard a noise and the garage door started to lift.

Forget that whole flight or fight thing. I opted for the other *F*. I froze with my eyes fixed on a gleaming white BMW X3. "Do you know when we can expect this car to be ready?" I asked the dark-haired man who stood inches away from it. "I'm—"

"I know who you are. You can tell your boss to stop sending over his employees to check on the car. We told him it would be overnight. This isn't Quickie Oil or one of those fast car places. We're specialized technicians who take our time to ensure that quality work is being done."

I nodded. "Got it. Will do. Um, this has nothing to do with my boss," I said, "but do you guys work on old, I mean, vintage Karmann Ghias?"

"We work on all European models. Why? Do you have a Karmann Ghia that needs to be serviced? Depending on the repair, it may take a while for parts. The last one we did took six weeks. And it was body work. Needed a new left fresh air grill. Then the owner decided he wanted the damn thing repainted to Bahia Red from Amber. Go figure."

"Wow. Another Karmann Ghia owner. Do you remember who it was? Are you allowed to tell me?"

"All I know is the guy worked for International Paper and got transferred to someplace in North Carolina."

Terrific. A dead end.

"Thanks. And I'll tell my boss to hold his horses on the Beemer repair."

The man gave me a wave and I walked back to the car. I figured Stephanie was probably anxious to get the heck out of the showroom but I didn't realize how anxious until I saw her getting escorted into a new Mercedes Benz E-Class.

Damn it! She was taking a test drive. A test drive of all things! I'm trying to track down a possible killer and she's what? Christmas shopping in July?

I charged for the Mercedes but it was too late. Stephanie had already executed a left-hand turn out of the place and was now driving on Routes 5 & 20 toward Waterloo. Part of me wanted to get on her tail and honk the horn but I knew better. Instead, I slunk behind the wheel of my car and scrolled through Facebook until I saw her pull back into the dealership.

"I'm so sorry, Norrie," she told me later. "But I ran out of things to ask, so when the salesman insisted I test-drive that new Mercedes, I couldn't very well say no."

"Please don't tell me you couldn't say no when he asked if you intended to purchase it."

"Of course not. I told him I'd be back with my husband. Now all I have to do is pray that salesman doesn't set foot in our winery."

"Oh, brother."

Chapter 21

I took 96A until it veered off to Route 96 and followed it into Ithaca. Like the Geneva foreign car dealership, Ithaca was a total bust, too. No one had seen nor worked on a canary yellow Karmann Ghia, and in fact, no one had serviced any Karmann Ghias in the last six months. On the bright side, Stephanie was offered one hell of a deal on a new BMW 7 series but she'd have to remortgage her house and the winery.

"This is taking longer than expected," Stephanie said when we started for Watkins Glen. *Gee, you think.* "And we haven't even stopped for lunch. Let me see if my mother-in-law can watch the boys until I get home. If not, we'll have to do Watkins Glen another day."

I kept my fingers crossed while Stephanie phoned her mother-in-law because I really wanted to get this trek wrapped up in one day.

"Good news, Norrie. We're all set. Thank goodness Erline agreed to babysit. She adores the boys and has far more patience than I do. Of course, she spoils them like crazy and gives them whatever they want to eat, but still . . . free babysitting is free babysitting."

"Um, yeah."

"What do you say we grab a bite to eat and then check out that last place in Watkins Glen? Maybe I can test-drive a—"

"Don't even go there. Let's just eat. My stomach's been growling since we left Geneva. How about lunch at Wegmans? The one in Ithaca has a huge food court."

"Other than the winery, my whole social life is food courts and pizza parlors with kiddie games. What do you say we try out that new winery on County Route 28? Overlook Glen. Derek ate at their restaurant a few weeks ago and said it was good."

"I'm game."

I took the Finger Lakes version of a roller coaster, aka Route 79, from Ithaca to Watkins Glen, and I thanked the gods my exhaust pipe didn't wind up on the road. Once in town, I took a left-hand turn up a winding street that gradually morphed into a county road. One twist after another and I began to wonder if I'd read the GPS wrong.

"There's the sign," Stephanie said. "On the right. The place looks magical."

Like Two Witches, Overlook Glen stood at the top of a hill with a spectacular view of Seneca Lake. The winery was part of the Seneca Lake Wine Trail but it was fairly new and I wasn't all that familiar with it.

The building was a large converted barn painted in shades of gray and white. A circular sign with a logo of a lake and trees stood above the entrance to the winery. The tasting room was to our right and a rather formal-looking restaurant was situated to our left. Stephanie and I wasted no time heading directly for the food.

The aroma of roasted chicken and garlic filled the room and I all but salivated. It must have shown on my face because the college-aged hostess smiled and said, "The rosemary garlic chicken is our specialty."

"I'm surprised Don and Theo haven't discovered this place," I told Stephanie, "but then again, they've been so busy working at their own winery, they hardly have the time."

Naturally we ordered the house specials coupled with a glass of their Chardonnay. Stephanie wiped the edge of her lip with a cloth napkin and sighed. "We need to do this more often. Heck. What am I saying? We need to do this, period! I never get out anymore."

"Geez, it's almost four. I've got to make a quick pit stop and then we should get to Glen Foreign Motors before they close."

Stephanie gave a nod. "I'm fine. I used the restroom in Ithaca. They actually have scented towels."

With that, I stood and walked to the small corridor where the restrooms were located. No scented towels but sparkling clean facilities. When I exited the room, I stumbled over something and caught myself on the small table outside the restroom. Whatever it was, it felt like a marble.

I bent down to eyeball the culprit and groaned. Some kid had dropped his or her teeny tiny toy car. The words "choking hazard" came to mind and I wondered just how old the kid was. Without scrutinizing the item, I snatched it up and was about to stick it in my pocket when I realized it was a key chain with a small green car attached. And not any old green car. It was a vintage Karmann Ghia and both the car and the chain looked ancient.

The insignia for Karmann Ghia was on the end of the chain, and I noticed that one of the links was broken. I raced back to the restroom and took a closer look under the bright mirror light. Engraved into the surface on the flipside of the insignia were two initials and I knew there was no way in hell this was a coincidence.

It was a good thing no one was in the corridor or near our table or I would have run them down. I held the key chain under Stephanie's nose and couldn't get the words out fast enough. "Stephanie! Take a look! Take a good look!"

"Ugh. Is this some disgusting insect you found? You've been hanging around those entomologists too long."

"No. I think this is Vance's key chain. Or at least part of it. No keys, only the fob and that car charm. But look closely, the initials V.W. are engraved on the backside of the fob."

"Let me see."

Stephanie turned the key chain around in her palm at least a half a dozen times. "It's freaky, isn't it? I mean, it could be *his* or it could belong to someone else with the same initials."

"Oh, come on. How many V.W. Karmann Ghia key chains are out there? It has to be Vance's. Whoever stole his car, not to mention the possible murder bit, was in this winery."

Stephanie sat up straight and turned her head to face the tasting room. "Maybe not *was*, maybe *is*."

I immediately eyeballed their tasting room area but all I saw were a few matronly women and a couple who couldn't keep their hands off of each other. "I don't think the thief is still here."

"It might not be a thief, Norrie. It might be some poor man or woman who happens to have the same initials. You should give that key chain to the hostess."

"Are you nuts? And lose the only clue I have? Besides, it's not as if I've got someone's car keys and they can't drive home."

"Someone may come looking for it. It may have sentimental value."

"Or it may point to a killer. Look, if it will make you feel any better, I'll speak to the hostess."

Stephanie pushed toward the center of the table and reached for a water glass. "It's the right thing to do."

I wanted to heave. Right thing or not, there was no way I was about to part with the only clue I had. "Check out the dessert menu," I said. "If they have anything chocolate, order it for me. I'll go find the hostess."

With that, I retrieved the key chain and walked to the small podium in the front of the building, where the hostess was leafing through some brochures.

"Um, your podium faces the front parking lot; by any chance did you notice a bright yellow Karmann Ghia earlier today?"

"A what?"

"It's a Volkswagen. A vintage Volkswagen."

"I wasn't really looking, but yellow would have stood out and I don't remember any yellow cars, why?"

"It may belong to someone I know. I'm not sure. I found a Karmann Ghia key chain fob on the floor by the restrooms and it may belong to my friend." I held up the key chain and quickly closed my fingers around it. "If it turns out that it's not my friend's, and someone comes looking for it, have them call me at Two Witches Winery in Penn Yan. I'm Norrie Ellington, one of the owners."

"Uh, sure. No problem. Two Witches, huh? Is it really true about that curse? Everyone's been talking about it. It's getting more attention than that Penn Yan kiss-the-gravestone thing. Boy, all we have around here are car races. Although some of the drivers who come in are pretty superstitious. We had one guy who told everyone he wasn't about to change his lucky socks until the racing season was over."

"Yeesh."

At that moment, an older couple walked in and the hostess greeted them.

"Thanks," I said. I turned and walked back to the table with the key chain safely stashed in my pocket and sat back down.

Stephanie slid the dessert menu toward me and shrugged. "Only chocolate mousse, so I ordered it for you. I'm trying their wild berry crumble."

Moments later, I watched as she spooned the first mouthful and closed her lips around it. The groans and moans that followed were almost X-rated.

"Good grief, Stephanie, it's a berry crumble, not—"

"Shh. Don't tell anyone. It might be better."

"I am *so* telling Don and Theo." Then I did the same with the chocolate mousse. It was a blend of bittersweet, milk, and white chocolate in layers that made me forget why we drove to Watkins Glen in the first place.

Stephanie grinned. "See what I mean?"

I was about to reply but in that instant, I caught a movement in the corner of my eye and turned to look. A man and a woman were being escorted to a table at the far end of the room and there was no doubt in my mind that the man was the one who shoved me off the dock at Kashong Point.

"What's wrong?" Stephanie asked.

"I'm not sure, but I'm about to find out."

Chapter 22

Under ordinary circumstances I would have filed a report with the Yates County Sheriff's Office regarding the incident at the dock. And calling out the culprit, even though we were in Schuyler County, would have been a no-brainer. However, that wasn't an option.

Instead, I walked outside and took a good look at the parking lot. Three new cars had arrived since Stephanie and I first showed up. I wasted no time jotting down their makes, colors, and license numbers. Then I walked directly to the table where my assailant was seated.

"Excuse me," I said, "but do you own that white Cadillac parked out front? It looks like one of the tires might be low."

"Oh, my gosh," the woman said. "I need to see for myself."

The man grabbed her by the wrist. "Sit down, Ma. I'll check it out."

Holy cannoli! I took a stab at the car and actually nailed it. Does that qualify as psychic in Zenora's book?

When the man stood and headed for the door, I followed. "Remember me? Or maybe I'd be more recognizable with wet hair."

The man's tan complexion turned ashen and he let out a long sigh. "Hey, I'm sorry about that. It was an accident. My buddy tossed in a line but missed with the hook. Then I lost my balance and toppled into you."

"Then why did the two of you bolt out of there leaving me to drown?"

"Drown? The water by the dock doesn't even come up to your waist. Besides, I did check to see you were all right. And it was my buddy who took off. I was the one who went after him."

"Give me a break. Surely you can come up with a better lie."

"You won't be able to prove anything, you know."

"Are you talking about the misfortune I had in the water or the one Vance Wexler had? Are you two for two?"

"Vance Wexler? The dead guy at Kashong Point? It was all over the news. If you're thinking my buddy and I killed him, you're way off."

"So you knew him?"

"I didn't say that."

"So why the cloak-and-dagger routine when I asked about his car?"

Just then, the man's mother approached us. "Jerome, do I have a flat tire?"

"It was only an optical illusion from the sun," I said. "My apologies for worrying you."

"That's all right. Better safe than sorry." Then she turned to her son. "I'll see you back at the table."

When she was out of earshot, I took a step closer to Jerome. "You can call me or I can call the sheriff's office. I've got your mother's license plate number. Your choice."

Then I handed him one of our Two Witches business cards and winked. "If you must know, I'm one of the witches. I'll expect that call no later than tomorrow."

"I'll expect that call no later than tomorrow"? Who do I think I am? Philip Marlowe?

I seriously couldn't believe what had come out of my mouth. The guy took the card, turned his back to me and walked away. I stood there for a moment, trying to catch my breath. I had no idea who I was dealing with, what possible connection he had with Vance, *if* he did have a connection, or how dangerous he was. If Theo, Don, Godfrey, or Bradley knew about this encounter they'd ring my neck. And Cammy wouldn't be that far behind.

"Everything okay?" Stephanie asked when I got back to our table. "We probably should get going."

I waited until we were in the car and on our way to Glen Foreign Motors before I told her about my second encounter with the dark-haired man.

Her usually soft voice had a tone I wasn't accustomed to hearing. "I'm not telling you what to do, Norrie, but if I were you, I'd take the tongue-lashing from Grizzly Gary and tell him what happened."

"It may come to that, but not right away."

The ride to Glen Foreign Motors was a short one. Back down the winding street and a left on Franklin Street. The dealership was only a few miles from town on Route 14. It was a modest structure that looked like someone had converted an old clapboard house and added a few garage bays. A lineup of sparkling Audis, Beemers, and Mercedes faced the road.

As soon as I shut the ignition off, I turned to Stephanie. "No test drives. Ask a lot of questions, that's all. I won't be long. Only a few bays to check out."

We immediately got to work as soon as I slammed the car door.

Stephanie moseyed into the building while I made a beeline for the garages. Two doors were open but the cars inside were dark-colored. I moved on. The third door was closed but through its glass window I could see it was vacant.

The fourth bay had a red Audi. No prizewinners here. I was about to turn back when I noticed the driveway behind the last bay circled around the building. Maybe there was another, smaller garage. Without hesitating I skirted around the building. The asphalt driveway slowly disintegrated into chucks until it finally became a dirt driveway.

Old automobile parts in various stages of decay were scattered in the weeds, but that's not what caught my attention. There was an old barn with faded red paint that stood on the top of a knoll and well-worn car tracks led directly to it. Not that I was an expert on car tracks, but the indentations on the tracks were still fresh.

I crossed my fingers that Stephanie was able to keep the sales staff occupied and I even began to regret telling her not to take a test drive. I needed the time. With no one around, I crept quietly up the driveway until I reached the barn. The front door was secured with a heavy chain and a huge commercial Master lock. Maybe they were storing valuable auto parts, but I didn't think so. Too cumbersome. Usually those things are stored near the garages.

The weeds were waist-high around the barn, but if I wanted to get a peek at what they had inside, I'd have to peer through the dirt-covered windows. I took the closest side to where I stood and trampled my way through the weeds until I was eye level with the window. Ew! Godfrey would have a field day. It was covered with cluster flies and other assorted insects in various stages of decay.

I tried not to think about it as I placed my hand over my forehead and leaned into the glass pane. Had it not been for the shafts of light that slanted in through the wooden barn slats, I wouldn't have seen the tarp-covered vehicle that took up the entire floor.

There was nothing in the world that indicated the car beneath that old tarp was Vance's Karmann Ghia, but I had a strong feeling it was. Glen Foreign Motors was less than an hour from Kashong Point on a straight-line road, making it the perfect place to stash a stolen vehicle in the wee hours of the morning.

The expression *jumping to conclusions* immediately sprang to mind, but I couldn't shake the nagging feeling I was inches away from the only clue that would lead to Vance's killer. I backed away from the window and started toward the driveway when I heard a soft rustling sound at ground level. My first thought was a snake. But snakes are usually quiet. Maybe it was a rabbit. They were everywhere. But apparently, so were skunks. And the one that was making its way toward me looked like the grand behemoth of his family.

I tried to remember all the things I learned in Girl Scouts about encounters with nature, but the best I could come up with was *stay calm*. Easy for some Girl Scout leader to tell the troop, but considering I could be doused in an ungodly stench at any given second, *stay calm* wasn't exactly something I could control.

When I first arrived to babysit the winery, Charlie had managed to have an encounter with a skunk and it didn't go well. Now, I was about to join him. And while Charlie probably chased his skunk with a gleeful prance, I eyeballed mine as if it was an explosive.

The thing moved slowly and deliberately, inching its way closer and closer to me. One sudden move on my part and it would be all over. I held my breath and started counting. What on earth for, I had no idea, but it was something to keep me from screaming at the top of my lungs.

At twenty-nine, the behemoth was inches from my feet. I looked down and willed my body to stop shaking. Like *that* would work. With no other recourse, I closed my eyes and expected the worst, but it didn't happen.

The skunk continued to meander through the weeds until it veered right and crossed in front of the barn. I could feel cold beads of sweat on my neck, but I was too petrified to make the slightest move to wipe them off.

Finally, when the thing was out of sight, I tiptoed down the driveway with my eyes glued to the ground. That's when I realized I was standing over honest-to-goodness evidence—the tire tracks. I whipped out my cell phone and began clicking photos. If that Karmann Ghia was in the barn, maybe I could prove it by the tire tracks.

Thankfully Stephanie was still keeping the salespeople mesmerized when I returned to the car. I gave a quick honk and hoped she'd come up with an even quicker excuse to get out of there.

Seconds later, I watched her exit the building, but not before turning and waving to whomever she had been with inside.

"I really need a Mercedes," she said when she buckled up her seat belt. "You have no idea how exhilarating it is to be behind the wheel of one of those cars."

"You took it out on a test drive? I didn't hear you."

"Not here. But they have the same make and model like the one I drove in Geneva. Honestly, my pulse was racing and I could feel the hairs on my skin standing at attention. Only a Mercedes can do that to someone."

Or a freaking skunk.

"Stephanie, forget the Mercedes for a minute and focus. I may have located Vance's car. Okay, before you say anything, it's a long shot, but if the tire tracks belong to the same kind of tire that would be on a Karmann Ghia, then I've got to get back here and find a way into their barn."

"Barn? Tire tracks? What are you talking about?"

"A reason for me to go to Cabela's Inc. to see if they sell skunk spray."

Chapter 23

It was past five when I dropped Stephanie off at Gable Hill, and I probably should have gone directly home to conk out. Instead, I decided to see how things were going in our tasting room and got swept into the kitchen by Glenda the minute I set foot in the door.

"Only a few customers left," she said, "and they're busy purchasing wine. No one can hear us in here."

"What is it they can't hear?"

Glenda closed her eyes and rubbed her temples. "I called Zenora the second I got home yesterday and asked her to help me find out who burned down Adeliza and Derella's house. She has a plethora of connections, you know."

"Um, in her spirit circle, or coven?"

"What? No. At the university in their records department. Zenora doesn't just work for the Essential Oils Company, she's been with Cornell for years. First as a file clerk and then a research assistant at Uris Library. Now she even has an office of her own. Granted, it's kind of a cubbyhole in the basement and rumor has it they gave her that office because she kind of scared the students, but it's a lucky break for us."

"That she's in the basement?"

Glenda nodded. "That's where they house all the delicate and ancient tomes. According to Zenora, there's scads of information about the original Benton residents, including the ones on this hill."

"Are you trying to tell me she found something already?"

"Not yet, but she's determined. She's also very concerned about you, Norrie. She has this premonition you're in trouble."

"Tell her it's not a premonition, it's only my relationship with Deputy Hickman."

"I'm serious. *She's* serious. And that's not all. Remember when I told you burning down a witch's house doesn't remove any curses she made?"

"Uh-huh."

"Well, there's more. According to Zenora, it makes the curse or curses even stronger."

Just the thing I need to hear right now.

"Uh, yeah, well, thanks for letting me know. Keep me posted, okay?"

"Sure thing."

I slipped out of the winery before anyone else could give me wonderful tidings. Then I went home to focus on those tire prints. An hour later, after countless Google sites, I was more confused than ever. Width. Ratio. Diameter. I now knew how to read the tire information should I ever need it, but it didn't do me one bit of good as far as those tracks were concerned.

Vance's car was decades old. That meant it would be on its what? Fortieth or fiftieth tire rotation, depending on how often the previous owners replaced the tires? I stared at my iPhone photos and groaned.

The groan was apparently a clue for Charlie to get up from his dog bed and shove his food bowl across the kitchen floor. I immediately replenished it with kibble and stared at the photos again. There was only one person I knew who might have an inkling about car tires, and that was John. I also knew that if I told him my intentions, he'd tell me to stop what I was doing immediately and leave everything to the sheriff's office.

"It's a crapshoot, Charlie," I said when I turned off my phone. "Do I ask Don and Theo or maybe Godfrey or Bradley? Certainly not anyone at the winery. None of our employees are familiar with that sort of thing."

Then, like a flash, it dawned on me—Hank Walden from Walden's Garage. If he didn't have a clue, no one would. I grabbed my phone again and dialed the number. The garage was closed for the day but I left a message about needing an oil change and asked Hank to call me first thing in the morning.

When the landline rang about an hour later, I figured Hank might have been checking his messages and decided to call back, but it was Bradley.

His usual upbeat voice sounded anything but. "You're not going to believe this. Ugh. *I* don't want to believe this. Marvin's sister-in-law fractured her hip and he has to cart his wife back and forth to the hospital in Rochester because she's too frazzled to drive there and visit with the sister."

"Um, yeah. That's too bad but it really shouldn't affect you."

"Oh, hell, it does. Marvin has this major estate settlement in the

Thousand Islands and he was supposed to drive there on Wednesday and stay for the remainder of the week to meet with the family and work out the details. And when I say *family*, I mean wealthy family. Extremely wealthy family. They own their own island up there."

"Oh, no. I think I know where this is going."

"You got it—I'm going. Marvin's secretary rearranged my schedule. I'm taking his reservation at the prestigious Gananoque Inn and Spa in Gananoque, Canada. Listen, Norrie, before you say anything, is there any chance you can join me? I know it's last-minute, but I won't be working twenty-four hours a day. We'd have plenty of time to explore and relax."

The vision of Blind Lady Justice holding the scales immediately popped into my head. On one scale was a fantastic opportunity for a genuine vacation at a ritzy spa during the height of tourist season. On the other was a less-desirable offering—three possible murders to investigate and one winemakers dinner that I absolutely couldn't miss.

"Phooey. Why did that sister-in-law have to break her hip *this* week? I'd love to say yes but I can't. I've got that winemakers dinner and I think I'm getting closer to figuring out who might have killed Vance because I don't, for a minute, believe it was natural causes or that idiotic curse."

"Can't you let the sheriffs' offices deal with it?"

"They'd have Alex under arrest and possibly Madeline. I'm sorry, Bradley. I really am. Maybe some other relative of Marvin's will need assistance in the future."

"We'll figure out something for a getaway weekend. I promise. Look, don't do anything reckless while I'm gone. I'll touch base before I drive up there. I'm missing you already."

"Ditto."

Ditto? Who says ditto when someone throws a romantic line at you?

When I got off the phone, I felt lousy. Not because I couldn't join Bradley, but because I really wasn't sure where we were headed. Francine and Jason would be back by Bastille Day, unless Godfrey was placating me, and if that was the case, I'd fly to that insect-infested rain forest and drag those two home by myself.

Bradley knew when we started to see each other that I would be returning to Manhattan and long-distance relationships weren't in the cards. Then again, it wasn't a hard-and-fast rule.

I had a fitful night's sleep after the phone call and hoped it wasn't the start of a poor sleep pattern. The following morning Hank called. At seventy thirty-three to be exact. He'd just received a cancellation for eight thirty and could do the oil change at that time.

An hour later, I pulled into his garage on Pre-Emption Road.

"This shouldn't take that long," Hank said. "There's coffee on the counter in the front room and some donuts. Help yourself."

Since I was the only one in the garage, I called Gladys at the public safety building to see if she'd learned anything more about the official investigation.

"My goodness, Norrie, if you weren't at the other end of this line, I'd swear you were listening in to Deputy Hickman a few minutes ago. Vance Wexler's death is now officially a homicide. Don't worry. He left the office. I can talk."

"How? What happened? What did they use?"

"I've got the notes in front of me. Horrible scrawls. Someone didn't do a very good job teaching that man penmanship. And now I have to type this up."

"The homicide. Tell me."

"It wasn't detected on the victim's body but traces were found on his bedding. The postmortem toxicology testing took longer than expected due to summer vacation schedules and a decrease in staff."

"What wasn't detected?"

"Chloroform."

"Chloroform? That doesn't kill anyone. It makes them woozy and then—Oh, my gosh. Someone suffocated him with a pillow or something. Am I right?"

"Partially. The chloroform explains the nearly microscopic traces of cotton in the victim's nostrils. Oh, for heaven's sake!"

"What?"

"Deputy Hickman spelled nostrils wrong."

I rolled my eyes and tried to focus. Hank was still under my car but I knew he'd be finishing up quickly.

"Uh, what were you saying about the cotton fibers?"

"According to the deputy's notes, Vance was rendered unconscious by chloroform and then someone shoved cotton balls up his nostrils, spelled with one *l*, not two, and cupped his mouth shut until he suffocated. My, if that isn't gruesome I don't know what is."

"Yeah. Gruesome." *And it was done by a flesh-and-blood human being, and not some witchy spirits back from the dead. Curse or no curse.*

Chapter 24

I thanked Gladys and swore I wouldn't breathe a word of what she said to anyone until it surfaced on the nightly news, which she assured me it would. "Those reporters have been badgering this office for over a week, Norrie. The cause of death is now public information so I'd be channel surfing tonight if I were you."

"Um, one more thing if you don't mind," I said. "Is Deputy Hickman looking into the whereabouts of Vance's car?"

Gladys groaned. "Aargh. *That.* Let me tell you about it. Someone gave the deputy wrong information during the initial questioning at the scene of death. Deputy Hickman was under the impression that Mr. Wexler had been driven to Kashong Point with other members of the historical society's team. He only learned the truth a few days ago and has been scrambling ever since."

I was at a crossroads whether or not to let the sheriff's office know about my encounter with Jerome, who pushed me off a dock when I asked about the car, and the key fob I found at Overlook Glen yesterday, not to mention my suspicion about what was in the barn behind Glen Foreign Motors. I was about to say something when Hank opened the door to the office, where I was seated, and shouted, "Got your car done!"

"I've got to run, Gladys. I'm at Walden's Garage and my car is ready. Good talking with you."

I paid Hank and thanked him for changing the oil on such short notice. Then I pulled up my iPhone and held out the photos of the tire tracks that I took yesterday.

"If you've got a second, can you tell by looking at these photos what kind of car would have the tires that made those tracks?"

"Is this some sort of contest?"

"No. I'm actually trying to locate a missing car that may be involved in a murder."

"Whoa. Shouldn't the sheriff's office be doing that?"

"I think they are, but I may have stumbled upon some information. It's about the person who was found dead at Kashong Point."

"Oh, yeah. That whole curse thing. Gimme another look at that phone."

Hank studied the photos and rubbed his chin. "I'll be darned. Looks like a classic fifteen-inch rim Volkswagen tire. Popular on most models."

"Can you narrow it down to a specific model?"

"I'm afraid not. Tires aren't model-specific. They go by maximum load and car design. Hey, I know this is none of my business, but a word to the wise—don't go looking for trouble where there isn't any."

Oh, trust me. There is.

"Thanks. I appreciate it."

I turned off my phone as soon as Hank was done looking. No sense having it on once I got behind the wheel. The last thing I needed was a hefty fine for getting caught driving while distracted on a county road. I had become worse than a Pavlovian dog lately, snatching up the phone the minute it went off, no matter where I was.

"So, looks like your sister and brother-in-law will be home soon if my memory serves me right," he said.

"I'm counting the days. Not to say this hasn't been an interesting year, but I'm much more of a city girl."

Hank gave me a funny look and smiled. "You could have fooled me."

From the garage, I drove directly to the winery with the hope that maybe Zenora pulled an all-nighter in the Uris Library basement and uncovered some telling information about the fire that destroyed the Marsten residence.

Instead, I was greeted with disturbing information from Cammy. "Godfrey Klein's been trying to reach you for the past half hour. He's on his way to the Yates County Public Safety Building. Something about a search warrant, chloroform, and Alex being arrested for murder."

"Oh, my God! That must have just happened because I was on the phone with Gladys a little while ago and she didn't say anything except that Deputy Hickman wasn't in earshot."

Cammy rolled her eyes. "He wasn't in earshot because he was out making an arrest. According to Godfrey, the Ontario County Sheriff's Office, along with the Geneva Police Department, entered the entomology lab late yesterday evening. They brought a forensic team along and confiscated a vial of chloroform that was found in a foam cooler in Alex's office. They also believe they found the original brown glass bottle in the office as well."

"So what? Those guys use all sorts of chemicals to kill bugs and collect specimens. Godfrey once bored me to death telling me why he preferred ethyl acetate over chloroform when he collected moths because the acetate didn't allow the moth's stomach to separate from the body or something like that."

"That may be the case, but according to Godfrey, chloroform was used to kill Vance. Or to render him unconscious so he could be suffocated. Godfrey tried to reiterate what Alex told him, but he was talking a mile a minute and I didn't get everything except that he wanted you to call his cell right away."

I raced over to the cash register, grabbed a piece of scrap paper and the nearest pen I could find. Lizzie, who was entering something on the computer, jumped back as if I was about to strike her.

"Sorry," I said. "Do whatever it is you're doing."

"Preparing an invoice. Is everything all right?"

"I'm not sure. But I've got it under control."

I charged back to Cammy before Lizzie could launch into one of her Nancy Drew lectures.

"Here," I said. I handed Cammy the paper. "It's Godfrey's number. Phone him for me and tell him I'm on my way." Then I used Cammy's own words when we first met. "Please and thank you."

"Call me when you know something. And don't worry about the winery. We'll be fine."

I was so frazzled I don't even remember driving to the public safety building. I could have run over a cow for all I knew. This entire arrest, as far as I was concerned, was a knee-jerk reaction that made absolutely no sense. Thankfully, I spotted Godfrey's car right away.

It was parked to the left of the lackluster gray building and shaded by the only decent tree in the parking lot. As I pulled up next to it, I had to remind myself to stay calm and not go off the handle as far as Grizzly Gary was concerned.

A glass enclosure separated the visitors from the building's staff and I had to show identification to the woman who was seated behind the panes.

"I need a few minutes with Gladys Pipp," I told her. "I'm Norrie Ellington."

She gave me a nod without saying a word and buzzed Gladys's office. A few seconds later, I was allowed to enter Fort Knox and make my way to the all-familiar cubicle that was Deputy Hickman's office.

Gladys was at her desk in front of his closed doors and ushered me over. "Heavens. I had no idea he was off making an arrest. I thought he was somewhere in the building."

"What about Dr. Klein? Dr. Godfrey Klein. He's one of Dr. Alex Bollinger's coworkers in the entomology department. I got word from him that Alex was arrested."

"Dr. Klein is in with Deputy Hickman at the moment."

"And Alex?"

"On the other side of the building. In lockup."

The last time someone I knew was on the other side of the building in lockup was when Rosalee Marbleton's vineyard manager was held here.

"He's innocent, you know. It's all circumstantial evidence. The guy's an entomologist, for crying out loud. Their labs are loaded with chemicals."

Gladys rubbed her hands together and widened her eyes. "I'm afraid I'm not the one who has to be convinced. And unless other, more compelling evidence surfaces in the very near future, I daresay Dr. Bollinger will stand trial for the murder of Vance Wexler."

"I really need to talk with Deputy Hickman."

Gladys stretched out her neck, looked at the closed office door and returned her gaze my way. "I'm not so sure that's the best idea."

"What if I had evidence to the contrary?"

"And you withheld it?"

"Um, how about if I just found it?"

"Evidence or theory?"

"Burgeoning evidence with strong theory."

"The best thing you can do for Dr. Bollinger, which I presume his colleague is taking care of, is to secure legal counsel. Hold off until you have a burgeoning theory with strong evidence."

"Can Dr. Bollinger receive visitors?"

Gladys shook her head. "Only his legal counsel. And by that, I mean his attorney or someone from his attorney's office."

Last time I needed to speak with a suspect, Bradly snuck me in. Too bad he was on his way to the Thousand Islands thanks to Marvin's sister-in-law.

"I suppose you're right. I'd better duck out of here before your boss opens the door and—"

At that exact moment, Godfrey emerged from the office followed by Deputy Hickman.

"What is it? Some sort of radar with you, Miss Ellington?" the deputy asked.

"Radar? I was only paying Ms. Pipp a social call."

"I'm afraid that's true, Deputy Hickman," Gladys said. "Norrie dropped by to give me her sister's recipe for cold cucumber soup."

Deputy Hickman moaned and turned back to his office, but not before glaring at Gladys and me. "Next time email your recipes. This isn't the nineteenth century."

Chapter 25

"I didn't expect you to race down here," Godfrey said once we were out of the building and in the parking lot. "I wanted to inform you what was going on and tell you that I contacted our department head, who, in turn, secured legal counsel for Alex. His attorney should be arriving this afternoon from Rochester."

"Are they going to post bail?"

"Doubtful. They haven't even had a bail hearing. According to the deputy, that will take place anytime between forty-eight and seventy-two hours, but I'm not hopeful. It's a murder charge, not a burglary."

"What happened exactly? Cammy mentioned a search warrant and chloroform and I found out from Gladys that chloroform may have been used to knock Vance out before killing him, but why suddenly rush in and arrest Alex? It's all circumstantial."

"Except for the eyewitness."

"The what?"

"Come on, let's talk in my car where we won't be overheard."

I was so stunned I didn't say a word until Godfrey held the door open to his sedan and I got in the passenger seat. "What eyewitness?"

"One of the board members for the Geneva Historical Society went to the police station in Geneva with a volunteer from Vance's little arrowhead-hunting group. The volunteer claims he left his tent to make a nature call when he spotted Alex leaving Vance's tent."

"He's lying. He was paid off. Or got bought off. Or blackmailed. Or—"

"Calm down, Norrie. It's not helping."

"Look, if that volunteer saw anything, he would have said something right away. Not waited a week or so. Did Deputy Hickman tell you which board member orchestrated this little charade?"

"According to him, a very reputable woman by the name of Agnes Merryweather."

"Reputable my patootie! Theo and I overheard her when we snuck into the historical society. She was ready to frame Madeline Martinez. I wonder what made her change her mind. He didn't happen to tell you the name of the volunteer who was taking a leak, did he?"

"Uh, no. Look, I really hate to rush off but I've got to cover for Alex at Kashong Point with his field study. His assistant, Cassie, was too flustered to handle things. I knew there was a reason I never saw her outside of the lab. Aargh. Hopefully things will go well and we'll be able to wrap up the study in a few days."

"Is there anything I can do in the meantime?"

"Yes. Keep yourself out of trouble. I don't want to get another call from the Yates County Sheriff's Office."

Then he leaned over and took my wrist. "Seriously, if anything happened to you, I don't know what I'd do. And I'm not just saying that because I swore to Jason I'd keep an eye on you."

My God! Who didn't Francine and Jason commandeer for "Norrie duty"?

I gave his hand a quick pat and got out of the car. "Don't worry. And keep me posted, okay?"

"Okay."

Walking back to my car, I felt like grabbing Agnes by the shoulders and giving her a good shake. It was obvious she and the other Geneva Historical Society board members wanted to cast aspersions on others so they wouldn't be scrutinized as possible suspects, but this went way too far. It seemed as if every time I turned around, someone else had something to hide, including Vance.

That vintage Karmann Ghia of his had to be his prized possession. Why else would he use it as a computer password and keep a framed photo of it on his desk? That, coupled with the fact it disappeared from Kashong Point the night of his death, gave me all the more reason to believe that grand theft auto was the motive for murder. Theo and Don would tell me it was preposterous, but that old adage *People have killed for less* stuck in my mind and wouldn't leave.

Gladys was right about one thing. I didn't have any substantial evidence to prove Glen Foreign Motors stashed Vance's car in their old barn. The tire tracks, although promising, weren't enough. I'd need to get inside that barn myself, but the question was *how?*

I couldn't ask Stephanie to join me again. She might risk chipping one of her fingernails. Besides, it wasn't fair to keep taking advantage of her mother-in-law. Godfrey was a definite no and Bradley was out of town, although something told me he'd be a definite no, too. That meant Theo. And I'd have to be very persuasive. Persuasive with an ironclad plan.

I turned the key in the ignition and drove out of the parking lot. If I *was* going to be persuasive, I'd need to chart the suspects and their actions in such a way that Theo couldn't possibly say no.

Unlike the last time, when I opted to create an oval suspect chart on the mirror in my guest bathroom, I decided to go really old-school and dredge up heavy-duty construction paper for a different approach.

The minute I got in the door, I poured kibble in Charlie's bowl and some horrid organic granola in mine. At least it balanced out the donut I ate at Walden's. Then I scurried around the house gathering paper and markers. With a quick sweep, I moved everything off of the kitchen table and got to work on my chart.

Top of the list was Agnes. And that was because she got some unsuspecting dolt to lie for her. Underneath her name I added Curtis and Mildred. Then it was on to Jerome, along with his "nameless buddy" from the unfortunate dock incident. Farther down on my chart, I wrote, "Glen Foreign Motors" with a question mark. Finally, I added the name of the man whose request for a backyard swimming pool had been denied by Vance's architectural committee. The same man Don thought he recognized that night at Port of Call. Next to the denial Vance had written, "Not enough Prozac for this whack-job."

Satisfied I had accomplished what I set out to do, I opened a bag of potato chips and compensated for the lousy granola lunch I had eaten. I simply couldn't shake the feeling that Vance's car was somehow implicit in his demise and hidden under wraps in that old barn. It was the *why* that didn't make sense. And no suspect chart was going to answer that.

At this juncture I figured I had two options: convince Theo to help me break into a barn or find out more about Agnes Merryweather. Since I didn't want to upset Godfrey any more than he already was today, I chose to focus on Agnes, figuring whatever was beneath that tarp in the barn would still be there for the next few days. Boy, was I wrong.

I started my Agnes search in the usual way, pulling up Geneva Historical Society articles from the internet as well as visiting the society's website. Sure enough, there was a lovely biography about Agnes, who was born in Horseheads, New York, and along with an older sister worked as a secretary for the now defunct Dairylea Company. She moved to Geneva in the 1980s and became active in their historical society. Yawn and double yawn.

Naturally the historical society was going to have a whitewashed version of Agnes Merryweather. I took my chances on social media, only to discover that she was nonexistent on any of the sites, including Pinterest, which is fairly benign. Still, I wasn't about to give up. If Agnes was a Geneva local, then maybe Cammy's family would know more about her.

It was a little past two, and having reached the proverbial dead end, I closed my laptop and walked to the tasting room.

"You just missed Franz," Lizzie said as soon as I stepped inside. "He had us try that new rosé of his."

"The rosé? That can't be. It's not bottled yet. They're waiting for label approval. Are you sure it wasn't something else?"

"It was the rosé, all right, and it was spectacular. Fruity but not overdone. I detected notes of melon and citrus. Lovely. Absolutely lovely."

"He brought over a bottle?"

"No, not a bottle. One of those wine containers. What do you call them? Boxcars?"

"You mean carboys?"

"It was a clear glass gallon jug with a special pourer on top."

"A carboy. Whew. For a minute you had me scared. We're not allowed to bottle and use unlabeled wines. Anyway, have you seen Cammy?"

"In the kitchen. Washing glasses. It's been pretty steady in here today."

"Thanks."

I swung the door open to the kitchen and walked toward her. "Godfrey's a basket case but he's trying not to show it. Alex won't be arraigned for forty-eight to seventy-two hours, but I don't think they let murder suspects out on bail."

Cammy wiped her hands on a terry-cloth dish towel and shook her head. "My God. That's awful."

"You know how Deputy Hickman is once he finds a suspect. That man is so myopic in vision, he refuses to look anywhere else. Meanwhile, I've got two leads to follow and one of them is Agnes Merryweather from Geneva. She's on their historical society board and she was the one responsible for pointing the finger at Alex. Um, is there any chance you can check with your aunts at Rosinetti's and see if they know anything about her?"

"For sure. That family bar's been in business forever and my aunts have had their ears to the local gossip for at least as long. If anyone remotely connected to Agnes set foot in the bar and restaurant, they'd know."

"Good. I can't figure out what she's hiding, but for someone to do something like that, it's got to be pretty important."

"You're not thinking this Agnes person is the killer, are you?"

"Honestly, no. But I think she may know who the real murderer is and that's why she set up Alex."

Chapter 26

I barely finished my thought when Glenda came into the kitchen with another rack of glasses. "Norrie. I didn't see you walk in. Zenora sent me a text a few hours ago. She located letters from some of the original Benton residents. Now she has to decipher them."

"What do you mean, 'decipher them'?"

"Have you ever read something written in the early eighteen hundreds? The handwriting's nearly impossible to figure out. All those wide-swept curves and curls. Zenora said it will take her all night."

"Yeesh. I don't expect her to stay in that basement until the wee hours."

"Oh, she won't. She bought herself a new iPhone X and took photos of those letters."

I gasped. "Won't she get fired for doing something like that?"

Glenda laughed. "Half the staff is petrified she'll put a curse on them and the other staff isn't that far behind. I doubt anyone will question what she does."

"If you say so. But please tell her not to do anything risky."

I, apparently, have dibs on doing that.

"By the way," I asked. "Has a guy named Jerome called?"

Glenda shook her head, while Cammy blurted out, "Not a new love interest? How many guys can you string along?"

"Only Bradley. And I'm not stringing him. I'm dating him. More or less."

"And Godfrey?"

"Friends."

She pulled the deep green ribbon tighter on her bun. "Uh-huh. So who is this Jerome?"

"Not someone any of us wants to deal with, but I think he may know something about Vance's missing car. He's the guy who pushed me off the dock at Kashong Point. Believe it or not, Stephanie and I ran into him when we were in Watkins Glen."

Cammy took a step closer to me. "You drove to those auto dealers after all? And with Stephanie Ipswich?"

"I, uh . . ."

"Much as I'd like to hear this," Glenda said, "I've got to get back to my table. Sam can only cover for me so long before he gets twitchy."

With that, she left the room and Cammy motioned for me to continue. She didn't say a word until I had given her the full rundown.

"You see, until I can learn more about Agnes, I need to focus on the other suspects. I can't afford to waste time."

She put her hands on her hips and did the best imitation of Francine I'd seen in a long time. "Do you have any idea what kind of danger you're putting yourself in? And I don't mean the skunk. The mess you're getting into won't be solved by a can of tomato juice and a hose!"

"First of all, Jerome would be meeting with me, on my terms. Here at the winery. With a zillion people around. That is, if he shows up. And as for the barn, well—How are we going to know if it's Vance's car under that tarp unless we look?—And you know as well as I do that without reasonable cause, no sheriff's office in this state will issue a search warrant."

"So, Theo, huh? Think he'll go with you to that barn?"

"He and Don just bought a new toy. It's a telescoping ladder with comfort treads. Suppose to feel like stairs even though it's a ladder. If I know Theo, he'll want to test it out."

"Yeah, in their winery, not on the backside of a barn. What were you thinking? Climb in from the hayloft?"

"I didn't know you knew anything about barns."

"I don't, but I've seen *Bonanza* and *The Waltons*."

"Then you know most of those lofts have wooden sliders on the outside. All I intend to do is lift the tarp once I'm inside and see what's underneath."

"And if it turns out you're right?"

"Then I'll get photos on my iPhone and confess all to Grizzly Gary. He'll be so happy I found the one clue they're looking for, he'll probably forget about reading me the riot act."

"No, he'll be too busy placing you under arrest. Try to contain yourself. I'll speak with my aunts and see if they know anything about Agnes. That's as good a lead as any. Hey, before I forget, there's a vintage car race at Watkins Glen the same weekend as the winemakers dinner. That's going to bring in some larger crowds. We're definitely going to need you Friday through Sunday."

"No problem." *My barn-busting expedition will need to be put on fast-forward.*

Cammy grabbed a clean rack of glasses and I held the door open for her as she returned to the tasting room. Then I plunked myself at the table and called the Grey Egret. After two rings, Theo picked up.

"Theo, good. I'm glad I got you. I need your help. Alex has been arrested for Vance's murder thanks to Agnes from the historical society. It's too involved. How about if you and Don come over to my house for pizza after work? I'll explain then. Seven o'clock okay? I'll call Cams and pick up two house specials."

"Holy cow. Arrested, huh? Geez, of all things."

"So you and Don will come?"

"Sure. No problem. Remind me not to get on any historical society boards."

• • •

Charlie had been unusually gassy all day and I attributed that to my being slack with the extra treats I doled out. Treats like tidbits of honey ham and Swiss cheese. Not wanting to take a chance he'd ruin our pizza with his gastro overtures, I shut him in my bedroom and prayed for the best. At least it was summer and I could open all the windows and air it out if necessary.

The traditional dough pizzas were weighted down with sausage, pepperoni, meatballs, olives, mushrooms, green peppers and enough mozzarella cheese to sink a ship. I piled napkins on the table and opted for the good Chinet paper plates because I had no intention of doing dishes. I also bought a six-pack of Coors and one of O'Doul's since nothing tasted quite as good as a beer with pizza. Sacrilegious according to the WOW ladies, but they weren't here.

"This is terrible," Don said. "Not the pizza. That's fantastic." He bit off the end of his slice and all but swallowed it whole. "Here we are enjoying Cam's best while Alex is probably eating a white bread sandwich with a slice of cheap bologna."

I watched as Theo wiped the sides of his mouth and took another slice. "What did Agnes do? What happened exactly?" he asked.

I told them about the eyewitness from Vance's amateur archeologist crew and how Agnes brought him to the Geneva police station with some cock-and-bull story—my opinion—about him seeing Alex leave Vance's tent in the middle of the night.

127

Don broke off a slice from the box closest to him and put it on his plate. "That witch! I wonder how much she paid him. Or maybe she held something over his head to get him to lie like that."

I took a giant gulp of O'Doul's and set the bottle down carefully so as not to knock it over on the pizza boxes. "Cammy's going to ask her aunts at Rosinetti's if they've heard any scuttlebutt about Agnes, but until I find out, I need to focus my attention elsewhere. That's why I told Theo I needed your help. It's not exactly kosher."

"Might as well come right out and say it. It's against the law. Whatever little scheme you've got planned."

I winced. "Not quite a scheme. More like a little expedition."

"I don't know what's going to give me more indigestion, the three pieces of pizza I ate or what you're about to propose."

"Like I told Theo, I'm convinced Vance's Karmann Ghia is stashed in that barn behind Glen Foreign Motors. And if that's the case, then it was stolen the night he was killed and most likely the motive for the murder. If I can prove it, maybe it would exonerate Alex."

Don and Theo looked at each other for what seemed to be a painfully long minute. Then Don spoke. "Let me guess. You want us to drive with you to Glen Foreign Motors once they've closed for the day and somehow break into that barn to see what's behind door number three. Am I close?"

"More or less. Not break in. Climb in. From the hayloft window around back. Think of it as a wonderful opportunity to test out your new fold-up-telescoping comfort ladder."

"It's your worst idea yet," Don said, "but I have to admit, it does make sense. But if you think for one second I'm going to be the one on that ladder, you can forget it. Heights and I don't get along."

I smiled. "The loft isn't that high off the ground. I looked. I'll be able to do it unless of course Theo wants to test out that ladder first." I elbowed Theo and waited for his response. It was two words—"Ladies first."

Don moaned. "Guess it's decided, huh? Might as well get this nightmare over with sooner than later. Tomorrow after work? If we leave at six, we can be there by seven. Plenty light outside. If my memory serves me right, Glen Foreign Motors is on that strip of Route 14 with some ice cream stands and a convenience store. If we throw a beach towel over the ladder, I can drop you two off near the car dealership and wait at one of the ice cream stands. I haven't had a banana split in ages."

"See," I said to Theo. "There's a silver lining in all of this, after all. Don gets a banana split and we get—"

"To deal with cobwebs, mice, and whatever else is in that barn."

"Face it. The plan will work. This time of year lots of tourists are coming back from the lake, so having a beach towel hanging over something won't look suspicious. People carry coolers, fold-up chairs, you name it."

Don rubbed the side of his neck and reached for another slice of pizza. "And telescoping ladders for break-ins. Yep, like I said, worst idea ever."

I stood, walked behind him, and gave him a hug. "That's for Alex."

Chapter 27

I could hardly concentrate on anything the next day, knowing that Don, Theo, and I were so close to catching Vance's real killer. No word from Zenora when I got into the tasting room around eleven, but Jerome kept his word.

At a little before noon, when I had left the bistro, having consumed a giant turkey and tomato panini, he was standing by the wine racks looking every bit the tourist. "The lady at the cash register said you'd be right back. I figured I'd check out the wines while I waited."

"Come on, let's talk in my office."

If Glenda, Sam, Roger, or Cammy noticed our interaction, they didn't let on. All of them appeared to be preoccupied with the customers at their tasting tables. I ushered Jerome into the office and motioned for him to grab a chair. Then I pulled mine from behind the desk and sat directly opposite him.

"Let's not waste each other's time. And before this goes any further, I feel I should tell you that the Yates County sheriff's deputy assigned to the Wexler case is a good friend of mine. Then I crossed my middle finger over my index finger and held it up. "In fact, we're like this."

I had to keep myself from bursting out laughing, so I bit my inner cheek and quickly wiped away the tear that had formed in my right eye. "What *do* you know about Vance's car, because it sure hit a nerve back on that dock."

"My buddy and I were paid to keep our mouths shut, that's all. And it won't do you any good to ask who paid us because we don't know. We took the cash and that's all there is to it."

I leaned back in my chair and stretched. "Fine. You can be a bit more up-front with me or I'll have no choice but to call my friend. Did I mention he's the deputy working the case?"

"Yeah. You mentioned it. Look, we got to Kashong Point that Saturday morning while it was still dark out. Best time to get set up for fishing. Once my buddy parked his truck, we grabbed our gear and went straight for the dock. That's when this screaming yellow car comes out from nowhere and nearly runs us over. My buddy thinks fast and whips out his phone. Snaps a photo of the license plate and tucks the phone back in his pocket. Someone must have seen him because shortly afterward, this guy comes up to the dock, shows us four fifty-dollar bills, and tells us he'll give us triple that amount if we keep our mouths shut about the car incident. We figured he was concerned we'd turn the driver in for reckless driving at a community recreation area. Hefty fines for that sort of thing, especially if the driver's been ticketed before."

"Go on," I said.

"Then he tells us he knows about the photo and insists we hand him the phone to delete the pic or the deal's off. Heck, it was a no-brainer. No one got hurt and we'd stand to pick up some fast dough."

"And that's it?" I glared at him and didn't make a move.

"Oh, and there was one more thing. He told us if anyone came snooping around to ask about the car, we were to blow them off."

"Is that new terminology for pushing them off a deck?"

"Hey, I said I was sorry. It was an accident. So, are we good?"

"Not yet. Who was the man who approached you?"

"Damned if I know. He wasn't here for fishing, that much I can tell you."

"What makes you say that?"

"You don't show up to go fishing when you're wearing tailored pants and a collared shirt."

"Can you describe him?"

"Older guy. Heavyset. Early fifties maybe. It was still fairly dark out so I didn't take that good of a look."

"And your friend?"

Jerome laughed. "He was too busy counting money."

I wasn't sure I bought the whole story. Shoving someone off a dock was an awfully strong reaction for blowing them off. I had a nagging feeling Jerome wasn't telling me everything, or maybe he was spinning a fish story of his own. Still, there wasn't much I could do about it.

"If I find out you haven't been honest with me, I'll go ahead with my original plan and have a little conversation with that deputy friend of mine."

"What do you want me to do? Pinky swear on it?"

"Nah. I've got one better. What's your cell phone number?"

"Huh?"

"Your number. In case I need to call you."

As he rattled out the numbers, I added the number to my contacts list. Then I placed the call. Sure enough, his phone rang.

"You don't need to answer," I said. "I guess we're good. For now."

He stood and walked to the door. "You weren't kidding about being one of the witches."

I followed him out the door and watched as he headed toward a black Dodge Ram. Most likely I had hit a dead end, but something told me that might not be the case.

The rest of the day moved at a snail's pace. I fiddled around the winery moving from the tasting room to the storeroom, where I helped Cammy inventory the number of T-shirts and sweatshirts we still had.

"The fall is right around the corner," she said, "and we really should stock up on our holiday-themed shirts. Want to add a new color? The fuchsia's going strong and the green and orange are always good sellers, but I'm thinking black with mixed motifs."

"I'm game. Black's always in style. What were you thinking for motifs?"

"You know, we could capitalize on this whole curse thing and have the words *Beware the Partridge's Eye* written in Old English script on the back of the shirt with a small rendering of two witches holding a bottle of rosé on the front."

"That could kill the sale of our rosé."

Cammy shook her head. "At this point, I think it'll do quite the opposite. We've got the curse. We might as well flaunt it."

"Order two dozen shirts and if they sell, we can triple the order."

"Got it. By the way, you haven't mentioned that barn break-in plan of yours all morning. I take it you came to your senses and decided to forget it."

"Um, actually, I didn't want to mention it because I knew you really objected to it, but I got Theo *and* Don to go along with it."

"Don? You got Don to go along with it? What did you do, spike his drink?"

"I appealed to his sense of chivalry. He doesn't want to see Alex get railroaded for a murder he didn't commit."

"Dare I ask when this clandestine escapade is going to take place?"

"Tonight. After work."

"I figured the encounter with Jerome this morning didn't go all that well or you wouldn't be going full speed ahead tonight. I meant to ask you about it earlier but I was mired under with customers. Thank goodness Sam agreed to work an extra afternoon."

"The encounter, which is a good way to put it, went nowhere. Jerome claims he and his buddy were paid off by someone to keep mum about seeing Vance's Karmann Ghia tear out of Kashong Point at dawn."

"And you don't believe him?"

"Not for a minute. But if Theo, Don, and I uncover Vance's car in that barn, it won't matter. Grand theft auto is all the proof we need for a motive."

"And if the car's not there?"

"I got Jerome to give me his cell phone number. Plus, I've got his mother's license plate number."

"My, my. Guess that Nancy Drew handbook is paying off after all."

"Ugh. Whatever you do, don't tell Lizzie. It's like bat radar with her. One mention of Nancy Drew and I'll never escape. Worse than the time Roger launched into one of his infamous French and Indian War stories and told everyone about the failed attempt of then Lieutenant Colonel George Washington when he tried to get the French out of the Ohio River Valley. Of course, that was at least twenty-five years before the Revolutionary War, when the father of our country was leading the British Colonial forces."

Cammy looked stunned.

"What? You must know this by heart now, too."

"I know the French and Indian War is kind of a passion with Roger, but I let it wash over me when he speaks. The brain can't handle all that information at once. It's like a food tray from a cafeteria. You can only pile on so much before something falls off. Oh, and speaking of information, last night I asked my aunts about Agnes Merryweather. They said they'd see what they could dig up. Especially my aunt Louisa. She's into more gossip than a Twitter feed."

"Oh, my gosh. Feed! I don't remember if I fed Charlie when I left the house. That dog really goes through his kibble. I'd better hightail it out of here and check."

"No problem. At least you're not the one responsible for feeding Alvin. That goat would bust down his fence if his supply got low."

"Or if Glenda decided to hold another séance on the hill."

I handed Cammy the small pad I used to tally the number of T-shirts I counted and headed for the door.

"Be careful tonight, okay? At the first sign of trouble, make a run for it."

"There won't be any trouble."

Hmm, I wonder if Lieutenant Colonel George Washington said that once, too.

Chapter 28

I pulled my Toyota to the front of the Grey Egret at five minutes to six, having loaded the ladder and the beach towel in my trunk a few minutes earlier. Don had left them for me by the side of his porch behind some bushes. I tapped my fingers on the dashboard and took a breath. Seconds later, Don and Theo came out. Then Theo went back inside and returned a minute or so later.

"I wanted to remind our tasting room staff to double-check the locks and the windows when they're done cleaning up," he said, taking the seat directly behind me while Don rode shotgun. "I brought a pocket flashlight with me just in case," he continued. "Much easier than fumbling around with my cell phone light."

Don cleared his throat and glanced back at the Grey Egret as I exited their parking lot. "The two of you better not make this an all-night excursion. In and out. That's it. By the way, I googled the ice cream places and it's the Tasty Tease for me. They've got giant banana splits and something called the Brain Freeze. Norrie can pull in there. It's only a few yards from the car dealership and on the same side of the road."

"I'd ask you to save us some," I said, "but it will be all melty by the time we're done. Theo and I can always get our ice cream fix at another stand closer to Penn Yan. Once we're done snooping we should get out of the vicinity as soon as possible."

Don chuckled. "Amen to that."

Thankfully it was a warm, quiet evening with no looming threats of summer thunderstorms. The road traffic wasn't bad either since it was a weekday and well after five, when most folks headed home from work. Not having school buses all over the place with sports teams was an added boon.

I always liked Route 14 as it hugged Seneca Lake, offering commanding views of vineyards, rolling hills, and the occasional motorboats. But taking in the scenery was the last thing on my mind. I wanted to get this surveillance job over with as fast as possible. To say I was edgy would be an understatement. To make matters worse, Theo kept repeating "the plan" with Don muttering "This better work" every few minutes. When the Tasty Tease finally came into view, I could have kissed the earth.

The building itself was hard to miss. Bright green with a giant cutout of an ice cream cone on the top of the roof. It was one of those seasonal places that appeared to have indoor seating as well as the usual rectangular tables and benches on its front porch. In addition, there were two round tables with green and white umbrellas off to the left.

There was a terrific parking spot shaded by some old maple trees near the round tables and I grabbed it right away.

"Eat slowly," Theo said to Don. He opened the trunk and pulled out the ladder, quickly covering it with the large yellow, orange, and green beach blanket. "And keep your phone on in case we have to call you."

"Oh, brother. Look, if you're having second thoughts, we can all enjoy a giant sundae or banana split and drive home."

"We're not," I said. I yanked Theo's arm and the two of us walked the few yards down the road toward the auto dealership as if we were returning from a swim in the lake. Across the road, a teenage boy with a soaking wet black Lab headed in the opposite direction. A red Frisbee hung from the dog's mouth.

"See," I said. "Lots of lake folk on this road. Take your time. I think we're walking too fast."

"If we walk any slower, we'll be stalled on the road. Come on, Glen Foreign Motors is right over there."

I turned my head just to be sure we weren't being followed or watched. "Okay. Now we can walk fast. The barn's right behind the building. Follow the driveway. Uh-oh."

"Uh-oh what?" Theo rested the ladder on the ground and looked around. "What's the problem?"

"You can see where I was before. In the spots where those high weeds got trampled. I had to look in the windows."

"I doubt anyone will notice. Too bad we can't take the same path. The loft window is around back, right?"

"Uh-huh."

"Then let's not waste time. We've got about an hour and forty minutes of daylight left."

With that, Theo moved through the weeds as if he was stomping grapes. I squelched a giggle and followed him. Next thing I knew, he removed the beach blanket, folded it and tucked it under his arm. Then he unlatched the ladder's locking mechanism and telescoped the thing until the top of it rested against the bottom of the loft window.

"Looks like we're in luck. The window is open a hair. Enough to slide it all the way. You want to go first or do you want me to do the honors?"

"I'll go. This was my idea. Just hold that thing steady."

"It *is* steady. It's designed for outdoor use as well as indoor. Look, it's not even wobbling."

I took hold of the sides and gave it a little shake. "Hmm, you're right. But hold on to it just in case."

Taking a deep breath, I climbed the nine or ten feet until I reached the bottom of the slider. Then I gave it a shove, and sure enough, it started to move. Started, and stopped a few inches later. It was as if it was stuck on something. I gave it another shove and still nothing. *Crap. I don't have time for this.*

I'm sure there was a better way to approach the problem but I wasn't about to figure it out. Instead, I went into panic mode. That meant giving it a yank and waiting to see what would happen. It was a method my father had perfected over the years with his home projects.

Theo's voice sounded muffled from below. "Everything okay?"

"I'm not sure. The slider's stuck. Give me a second."

I grabbed the wooden door with both hands and winced. The aging wood felt like an emery board and I prayed I wouldn't wind up with a zillion splinters. Then I shoved it so hard that for a moment I was scared I was going to fall off the ladder.

This time Theo's voice was louder. "Looks like you got it!"

"I can see the car. Plenty of light coming in from those dirty windows and the gaps in the wall planks. The car's still covered with a tarp. Good news—the loft looks stable. Only a few hay bales stacked up. Probably older than dirt. And the floorboards are all in one piece. No holes or anything. I'm going in."

I stepped gingerly onto the floor of the loft and it felt steady. Peering over the side, I could see a fixed wall-mounted ladder. Old and wooden but not missing any rungs. I went back to the loft window and shouted to Theo, "Come on up. I don't want to be in this barn alone."

I eyeballed the large beams that ran crosswise in the barn and wondered if they were the original ones. No sign of rot or crumbling wood. I knew the beams in our winery barn were chestnut, and according to John would "last for another century."

Theo's voice startled me for a second. "Catch this blanket, will you?

I didn't want to leave it on the ground. You know how Don gets about dirt."

I caught the blanket and shrugged. "It's going to get just as dirty on one of the hay bales."

"Okay, so now what? You want to climb down, pull the tarp and take a look?"

"Yep. And a few pics on my phone if it's a yellow Karmann Ghia under there."

"Fine. Hurry up."

I tossed the blanket onto a hay bale and walked to the edge of the loft. Then I turned around so my back would be to the ladder. Fortunately, the first rung was level with the floor. Whoever built the ladder had the foresight to extend the sides so that someone could easily grasp them when climbing down. I fully expected that splintery feeling when I touched the sides of the ladder but it wasn't as bad as the window slider.

"Piece of cake," I said.

Theo walked closer to the edge and whispered, "Do you hear that? Sounds like a rattle."

"As in snake? Look, I know we get timber rattlers around here, but they don't climb up to haylofts."

"Shh. Okay, I don't hear it anymore."

My right foot landed square on the first rung and I continued down three or four more rungs. By now, my eyes had gotten adjusted to the dim but sufficient light in the barn. So when the entire place lit up like the Star Spangled Banner, I winced. Behind me, I could hear the barn door opening, followed by a man's voice.

Crap. Rattlesnake, hell. How about the chain on the barn door?

"Psst! Norrie! Move it! Move it fast! Get up here!"

My feet had suddenly glued themselves to the rungs and I froze. By now there was another male voice shouting something about rigging. I grabbed the sides of the ladder and prayed that somehow my upper-body strength would compel my frozen feet to move. That's when I heard one of the men ask, "How good is your aim?"

Chapter 29

I don't remember climbing those last few rungs. What I do remember was Theo grabbing my arms and yanking me behind a pile of hay. I expected a gun to go off but nothing happened. All I could hear was the sound of heavy objects being dragged across the barn floor. We were both half crouched down behind the hay so we had no idea what was happening. Finally, I moved my head ever so slightly and looked down. Sure enough, I spied a chain hoist, some large hooks, and a five- or ten-gallon bucket.

This better not be something out of Criminal Minds, *or worse yet, that new FBI show.*

Theo reached in his pocket for his cell phone and motioned for me to do the same. Then he sent a text—*Don will kill me.*

I texted back—*He'll kill the both of us. If those guys below don't do it first. Keep still. Don't breathe.*

With me on one side of the bales and Theo on the other, we allowed ourselves an inch or two at best to peer past the dusty hay to see what was going on. There were three men in all and none of them looked as if they shied away from the dinner table. And while I wouldn't quite use the word *buff*, they were certainly in good physical shape. From a distance it was impossible to gauge their ages but I wagered between late twenties and early forties.

"Someone want to give me a hand with the ladder? Damn thing weighs a ton."

Good. He brought his own ladder. That means he won't be using this one.

I felt my phone vibrate in my back pocket. Another text from Theo—*We can sneak out now. They're too preoccupied.*

And miss what we came to find?—I texted back.

Just then, another voice from below us. "I'll start draining the oil once I find the floor jack to lift the rear end of this baby."

At least that explains the bucket.

"Right behind you."

I had that awful feeling of getting all dressed up only to find the dance, or concert, or whatever it was that I needed to get dressed up for was suddenly canceled. If they were draining the oil, it was probably some old jalopy down there that they were working on. So much for getting one step closer to finding out who killed Vance.

"Okay," the ladder guy shouted, "We haven't got all day. Billy's gonna have his head stuck under the car so it looks like the two of us will have to get this hoisted up to the beam. Like I asked— How good is your aim?"

So that explains it.

"Hell, I think the chain weighs more than the hoist. Think the beam will hold it?" It was the third voice. Raspier than the other two.

"Yeah, it'll hold it. Not like we haven't done this stuff before."

"But only with Bug motors."

"It's the same deal. An air-cooled engine is an air-cooled engine."

I turned to Theo and mouthed, "What are they doing?"

He moved toward the middle of the hay bales, where I could easily read his lips. "They're going to remove the engine. They'll have to disconnect the fuel lines and plug off the tranny lines. That's for starters."

"How do you know about this?"

"From watching my uncles when I was a kid. Look, we need to get out of here while we can."

"Are you sure?" I mouthed back.

"What do you think the hoist is for? It's definitely some type of Volkswagen because that guy is working under the rear of the car, not the hood. And yeah, I'm sure."

This time I exaggerated my facial movements. "That's got to be Vance's Karmann Ghia. We need to stay here for a few more minutes."

Theo resumed his position on the side of the bales. So much for thinking it was some run-down old car under that tarp.

The hoist lifting process seemed to take forever. Even after they got the giant hook over the beam. The chains had to be adjusted along with a lot of other stuff that I didn't recognize.

"This better pay off," the raspy-voiced guy said, "I've got two payments left on this hoist. Can you believe it? A manual ten foot hoist and it cost a fortune. I don't even want to know what one of those electric models go for."

"Yeah, but you bought an Ironton, a top-of-the-line model. And we needed a manual one. It's not like we can count on electricity all the time."

Theo and I looked at each other with dazed expressions. What *were* these guys into? I removed my cell phone from my pocket and pushed the camera app in case I needed to take a picture in a hurry. Then I focused on the car. Billy-whoever-he-was used the floor jack to lift the rear of the car off the ground by a few feet. He stood, brushed himself off, and with both hands slid the tarp across the car. The canary yellow color was unmistakable and my jaw all but dropped.

I motioned to Theo and mouthed, "That's got to be Vance's car. The last time anyone saw that car was when it was being driven out of Kashong Point the night he was murdered."

Before Theo had a chance to respond, Billy spoke from under the car. His voice wasn't quite as audible as the others. Still, what he said was hard to miss. "Good thing you jerks didn't lose the keys attached to that chain or we'd be S-O-L. Last thing I wanted to do was fiddle with the wires in the steering column."

My God! This is Vance's Karmann Ghia.

Then the raspy voice again. "Sorry. Crap happens. The key chain must've fallen out of my pocket when I went to pay for something. It could be anywhere."

My hand began to shake as I inched closer to the edge of the loft to snap a photo. It was evidence if ever there was evidence.

"Watch what you're doing," the ladder guy shouted, and in that instant the phone slipped from my hand. It fell to the front of the loft into a pile of loose hay. It happened so fast I had no idea where it landed. *Terrific. I'll probably step on it and will have to apply for another credit card to buy a new one.*

"You nearly knocked into me," the ladder guy continued. "We don't need to stow the ladder, just get it off to the side."

"Hey," Billy shouted, "someone hand me a large screwdriver. I need to push the torque converter back."

Next thing I heard was the clanging of metal. I figured the men were rummaging through a toolbox. Theo used that opportunity to put his arm on my shoulder and whisper, "Don't make any sudden movements."

Then, the raspy voice. "How long before you can clear the engine bell housing?"

"I'm removing the top nuts from behind the fan shroud. Does that answer your question?"

"It answers mine," Theo mouthed. "It's late. I've got to text Don before he drives over here."

I nodded. I had to figure out a way to sift through the hay to find my cell phone, but the only thing I could think of was to have Theo call me on it, and that would be a death sentence. Instead, I opted for a more conventional approach—getting down on all fours and stretching out my arm to see if it made contact with the phone. It didn't.

After what seemed like an eternity, we heard Billy again. "Engine's dropped onto the dolly but I can't slide it out. Pull the jack stands. The front's got to be lowered back down."

I crinkled my nose and gave Theo one of those "what's going on?" looks to which he mouthed, "They have to lower the front back down so they can slip the engine out from the rear."

And I thought the fermentation process was mind-boggling.

"How long before it gets dark?" I whispered.

Theo glanced at his phone. "Twenty minutes if we're lucky. FYI—Don texted back an angry emoji."

I swallowed and grimaced. Not a single doubt in my mind the car was Vance Wexler's prize Karmann Ghia, and those three men had just removed its engine and were now rolling it toward the front of the barn on a four-wheel dolly. None of this made any sense. Unless they were operating an illegal chop shop. But an old Karmann Ghia? Who's going to want its parts?

With the men otherwise occupied with getting the engine out of the barn, I tried once again to locate my cell phone. This time with both hands. Still no luck. Worse yet, I couldn't get the expression *needle in a haystack* out of my head.

While I was still fumbling to find my phone, I heard ladder guy say, "Yep. *Road and Track* got it right when they called this baby the pinnacle of the classic nine-elevens. And this sweetheart is a Carrera RS two-point-seven. She'll do the trick, all right."

Theo grabbed my arm and mouthed, "Holy cow."

I mouthed back, "What?"

"That was a Porsche engine they removed from the Karmann Ghia. A two-point-seven."

I stared at him but didn't say a word. The numbers didn't mean anything to me. Finally, he mouthed, "Performance racing car," and suddenly everything began to make sense.

By now the men had rolled the engine out of the barn and slid the front door shut behind them. The hook and hoist were still on the beam and the ladder was resting off to the side. It felt like hours since I first climbed through the loft window and my body had stiffened up as if I was ninety years old.

"Call me on my cell," I said to Theo. "It's the only way I'll find my phone. Then we need to follow those guys."

"Follow them? We don't know what they're driving or where they're going."

"It's got to be a truck. One of them said something about getting the dolly up the ramp. Call me, while there's still some light coming in from the loft opening. Then call Don and tell him to get over here ASAP."

Thirty seconds later I located my phone and immediately snapped a few photos of the Karmann Ghia sans its Porsche engine.

"Let's get going." Theo grabbed the beach blanket and was the first one to exit out of the loft. I watched as he got on his knees and swung a leg over the edge of the barn until it made contact with the upper rung. "I'll be right below you to make sure the ladder doesn't wobble."

I hadn't really thought about climbing down, because if I had, I might have opted for another way out, even if it meant breaking an old crusty window.

Chapter 30

I heard that familiar slam of my Toyota's driver's-side door as Don got out and walked around to the passenger side. He had parked in front, a few feet away from the barn door. In front of me, a flustered Theo clutched the telescoping ladder under his arm and tromped across the weeds to the car. I charged ahead, beach blanket in a wad resting on my chest. I tossed it at Don the second I got in the car and quickly buckled up.

As soon as Theo put the ladder in the trunk, he slid behind me and shouted, "What are you waiting for?"

I turned to Don. "Did you see a truck head north right after Theo called?"

"No. What on earth's going on? All I heard was 'Hurry. Make it quick.'"

"We're following the thieves who stole Vance's car. Theo and I saw it in the barn. They took the engine out. It's in their truck. A Porsche engine. Go figure." I turned the key in the ignition and watched the stream of traffic heading south. "If they didn't go north up the lake, they're headed downtown."

Next, I pulled onto Route 14 and stepped on the gas. The sun had already dipped below the horizon but there was still plenty of dim daylight. It was anyone's guess where that truck was headed, but at least I was pretty certain of the general direction.

Without giving any thought to state or local law enforcement, I continued to hammer the gas, passing two sedans and one T-Bird convertible.

"If the truck's on this road, we'll catch up to it," I said. "There were three men, so one of them has to be riding in the bed. Keep your eyes peeled. It's a truck, not a race car. It can't be that far ahead of us. We'll be on its tail in no time."

"If you don't get us all killed first," Don replied. "You all but took the side-view mirror off of that Nissan back there. Will someone please tell me what you saw?"

Theo began to explain while I passed a silver SUV with one of those big family stickers on the rear window. Father, mother, a zillion kids, and two dogs. Yeesh. Seconds later, I spied a faded blue truck.

144

"Up ahead. Two cars in front. Holy cow! I think that's them. Hold on."

The road curved so I had to wait for a clear spot in order to pass the ancient beige Buick that all but slowed me down to a crawl. Once free from the slowest geezer in the Finger Lakes, I sped up to pass a VW Bug, when the road curved again. Coming dead-on in front of me from the opposite lane was a motorcycle. I couldn't slow down, back off, or do anything in between except hold my breath and pray the driver knew how to maneuver his bike.

"Watch what you're doing, Norrie!" Don yelled.

The biker hugged the lakeside of the road and continued north as if nothing had happened.

Then Theo. "There isn't enough insurance in the world to get me in a car with you again."

I was shaken but tried not to show it. "It's okay. We're okay. Look, we're right behind those guys. Don't take your eyes off of them. Besides, the next guy doesn't want to get into an accident any more than we do."

"Where on earth did you hear that?" he asked.

The next few miles went smoothly and I kept a reasonable distance from the faded blue truck.

"What the heck was a Porsche engine doing in Vance's Karmann Ghia?" Don asked. "Could it have been swapped out with a Porsche in some clandestine operation? And maybe that's what got Vance killed?"

Theo leaned over so that his head rested between mine and Don's. "Or maybe he bought it on the up and up and had it dropped into his Karmann Ghia, where no one would suspect what was under the rear." Then, "Slow it down, Norrie. You're right on his tail. Damn, too bad the extra seat belt doesn't reach this far."

"Oh, honestly! If I slow it down, someone will pass me. Those guys don't know who we are. As far as they're concerned, we're just tourists in an innocuous old Toyota."

By now I had passed the Watkins Glen Golf Course on my left and Route 14 became North Madison Avenue. I was now in the village of Watkins Glen, with streets full of tourists enjoying their early evening strolls. The blue truck adhered to the speed limits and I was able to get a better look at the guy who rode in the bed. They'd thrown a tarp over the Porsche engine and he rested one arm on top of it as if it was a settee in someone's formal living room.

"Can either of you make out the license plate? I can barely read it," I said.

Theo nudged Don's head to the right. "That's because it's caked with dirt. Probably on purpose. Its reflective surface won't show up even with your brights on."

Bummer.

North Madison was now North Franklin Street, with Watkins Glen State Park on my left. I was a high school senior the last time I hiked the trails that overlooked its waterfalls and gorges. Funny, I meant to go there with Bradley but we never seemed to find the time.

"Norrie! He's making a sharp left!" Don shouted.

I immediately did the same and held back on the tight curve of Old Corning Road, which branched into Routes 329 and 17. Once the road straightened, I lengthened the distance between my Toyota and their truck, but not to the extent that I'd let them out of my sight.

The truck veered left onto Route 329, and if it wasn't for the lights emanating from the few farms scattered in the area, I would have thought we'd left civilization entirely. I followed the truck's rear lights because it was now impossible to make out the vehicle in the dark.

Theo leaned forward again. "Where the heck do you think they're going?"

"Probably to another old barn. That's my guess. What about you, Don?"

"I stopped guessing five miles ago."

It felt as if we'd never get off Route 329 but the truck turned south on Meads Hill Road and then left on Route 16.

"Shazam!" Theo bumped my shoulder. "They're headed for the raceway. Watkins Glen International Raceway. That's got to be it. A Porsche Carrera RS two-point-seven engine . . . Hmm, now it's beginning to make sense. They've got some vintage car race going on this weekend. Whatever it is they're up to, I doubt it's kosher. By the way, I added a few more part-timers to our tasting room because those things bring in the crowds and Don and I have to leave early Saturday for the winemakers dinner."

Not a single turnoff on Route 16 until we passed Grand Prix Road. "Yep, we're near the race track," I said. I expected the truck to make a right on Bronson Hill, but instead it vanished right in front of me.

"Where'd it go? I don't see it. Did he turn on Bronson Hill or keep going on 16?"

"Whoa. It's like something out of *The Twilight Zone*," Don said. "I swear the truck just vanished in front of us. As if it had a cloaking device like those stealth planes."

Theo leaned over Don's shoulder. "Those things don't have cloaking devices. Only in sci-fi movies. They've got some sort of detection system that delays identification. And, yes, before you or Norrie say anything, I happen to read more than the winery news. And for your information, what those thieves rigged up in their truck is probably nothing more than a toggle switch to their lights. They must have realized at some point Norrie was tailing them."

"Or we lost them on that curve. I'm not so sure I buy that toggle switch idea of yours. So now what?" Don asked. "Pick a road and take a chance?"

I moaned. "We'd be wasting our time. If you ask me, the next time that engine surfaces will be at the raceway. But under whose car is anyone's guess. I can't believe we lost them. I suppose I'd better swing around and head back up the lake. I don't know about either of you, but I'm starving and I saw an Italian restaurant smack dab in the middle of Watkins Glen."

Theo gave my shoulder a poke. "Then what are you waiting for? Turn this sucker around and we can cry in our marinara sauce."

• • •

A few hours later, I pulled up to Don and Theo's house. The meatballs, sausage, and penne pasta settled in the bottom of my stomach and I felt logy. It was an uneventful drive home with the exception of Theo muttering about buying a comprehensive umbrella policy in the event of a catastrophic car accident.

I kept playing the car chase over and over in my mind but the outcome was always the same. I lost them. Somewhere on a stinking road less than a mile from the Watkins Glen International Raceway.

"That engine's going into someone's race car," I announced the second Don unbuckled his seat belt. "When's that race? Saturday?"

"The qualifying race is Saturday. The actual race is Sunday," he said.

Theo reached over the back of my seat and put his arm on my shoulder. "Norrie, there's no way you're going to figure out who's car is the new recipient of a Carrera RS two-point-seven engine. Those guys will have reinstalled it way before the qualifier on Saturday. Heck, the other car is probably sitting in a garage or barn near the raceway. What do you intend to do? Poke around every farm, junkyard, and country house off of Route 329?"

"Not when you put it that way. I just need to come up with another plan, that's all."

The minute I said *plan*, Don and Theo both groaned.

"Word of advice," Don said. "Don't! Don't come up with another plan."

I tried not to sound whiny but I couldn't help it. "We were *so* close. So close. Ugh. I suppose the only recourse I have now is to call Deputy Hickman in the morning and show him the visible proof that it was Vance's car under that tarp in the barn. Don't worry. I'll leave the two of you out of it."

Don chuckled. "Grizzly Gary's not that dense. He'll figure out you couldn't have done that kind of snooping on your own. No sense trying to cover up. What's the worst they can get you and Theo for? Eavesdropping? And what's the worst he can get me for? Cheating on my diet with ice cream?"

Or driving a getaway car to a scene of a crime.

Theo got out of the car and leaned into the driver's side, where I had rolled down the window. "Don's right. Call him and get it over with. Meanwhile, I intend to call my insurance agent about beefing up our policies."

I elbowed him through the door. "Very funny."

Chapter 31

At least Charlie had a good night's sleep. Snoring, grunting, and passing gas as usual. Mine was fitful at best, so it was no surprise that I actually woke up before he did.

"I'm going to the public safety building as soon as I have my morning coffee," I told the dog. "Might as well get this over with. At least it wasn't a total bust. We found Vance's car and a damn good motive for murder."

The dog jumped from the bed, gave me a funny look with those big brown eyes of his, and then charged down the stairs to his doggie door. Forty-five minutes later, once he was fed and I was showered and dressed, I was off to see Deputy Hickman before I lost the nerve.

I literally bumped into Gladys Pipp on my way inside the building.

"Goodness, but you're up early, Norrie. Don't tell me Deputy Hickman made an appointment to see you and forgot to tell me. He does that, you know. Makes all sorts of appointments and then gets grouchy when they coincide with the ones I've made for him."

She held the door for me and we both walked into the lobby.

"Um, no. I've got something really urgent to share with him and it couldn't be done over the phone."

"All right. Follow me. Once I stash my purse, I'll buzz him. Keep your fingers crossed he's had his coffee."

Had his coffee? I'm keeping my fingers crossed he doesn't lock me up.

The moment Grizzly Gary stepped out of his office and eyeballed me, a horrible pit formed in my stomach. I gave him a slight wave and swallowed. "Thanks for seeing me. I came by some information that's pertinent to Vance Wexler's murder."

"Came by or did something illegal?"

I moved my palm up and down. "Maybe a bit of both."

Gladys looked up from her desk and widened her eyes. I was positive Deputy Hickman noticed because he motioned for me to go into his office. "No sense having this conversation out in the open, go inside and have a seat."

The hard metal chair felt as if it came directly from the Spanish Inquisition. Deputy Hickman plunked himself at his desk, propped his elbows on it, and leaned forward. "Out with it. I'm anxious to see how my day is about to unfold."

"Fine. And please keep in mind that old adage about the end justifying the means."

"Oh, for heaven's sake, Miss Ellington, just tell me what you did."

"I found Vance Wexler's car and I can prove it."

There was absolutely no expression on Grizzly Gary's face and I thought perhaps he'd make one hell of a poker player. I took a breath and continued. "I tried to track down that Karmann Ghia by checking out the foreign car dealerships in the area. And, um, one old barn behind the dealership in Watkins Glen. That's where I saw it."

Deputy Hickman's scowl was so intense I thought his eyebrows would touch. "You just happened to walk into someone's barn?"

"Not in so many words."

"Then suppose you give me the words."

For the next two minutes his face fluctuated from scowl to frown as I explained exactly what Don, Theo, and I did. Then he crossed his arms and stood. "Help me understand, Miss Ellington, why you don't simply work on those screenplays of yours or do something at your winery. Surely, you must have enough on your plate without adding amateur detective to the list."

"Oh, trust me. I have lots to do. Lots. But I can't sit by and watch someone I know get railroaded for a murder he didn't commit."

"What you did was breaking and entering. The second time you did that. You were lucky I didn't say a word to anyone at the Geneva Police Department. And now what? The Schuyler County Sheriff's Office? Good grief, Miss Ellington, how many law enforcement agencies do you plan to bring into this tangled mess?"

Yeesh. He's beginning to sound like my parents when I was a kid. "How many times do I have to tell you?" I hope he's not expecting me to give him a number.

"Um, I suppose as many as we need."

Deputy Hickman sank back in his chair and rubbed his temples. "You said you had evidence. Show me the evidence."

Finally!

I whipped out my phone and pulled up the pictures I had snapped. Unfortunately, I wasn't able to adjust the lighting, so what I was stuck with were three grainy photos of a car with a tarp draped over the front.

The scowl never left the deputy's face. "It's a car. I'll give you that much."

"It really is Vance's car. Honestly," I said. "The three men I told you about took out the engine and it was a Porsche engine. A Carrera 911 RS two-point-seven. We overheard them. A two-point-seven engine. That's apparently a big deal. And one of them mentioned losing part of Vance's key chain. Here, I've got it in my pocket."

The tiny Karmann Ghia replica dangled at the end of the key chain as I handed it to Deputy Hickman. "Look at the fob. The initials V.W. are engraved on it."

"V.W., huh? Did you ever stop to think those initials stood for Volkswagen?"

"You've got to believe me. It's his car. Can't you call the Schuyler County Sheriff's Office and get them to get a search warrant or something and check?"

Deputy Hickman shook his head and handed me the fob. "Even if I wanted to, there's not enough evidence to support it. But I will do this much. I know a few deputies in Schuyler County. I'll give one of them a call and see if they can have an unofficial look-see into that barn as a follow up to a tip they got. Of course, it would be up to Glen Foreign Motors to let them inside, but it's the best I can do. Now, before you tempt me to place you under arrest for interfering with an investigation, not to mention breaking and entering, I suggest you let the sheriff's offices handle the investigation."

"But what about Dr. Bollinger?"

"If other, credible evidence surfaces, it would be cause for us to drop the charges."

"Oh, it exists all right or I wouldn't be here. Uh, I suppose it's too late to check for prints on that key chain, huh?"

"Only if you want yours to show up."

I rolled my eyes and put the key chain, fob and all, in my pocket. "Thanks. I appreciate it."

"Consider my decision to not place you under arrest a gift. Have a good day, Miss Ellington."

• • •

At least the morning wasn't a total bust. I stopped at the Penn Yan Diner and ordered a giant stack of blueberry pancakes before returning to Two Witches Hill. The tasting room wouldn't open for another twenty minutes, but I figured I'd bring Cammy up to date on the latest letdown I faced in my attempt to save Alex.

What I didn't figure on was getting greeted by Glenda, who literally shrieked out my name the minute I stepped into the winery. "Noooriece! Noooriee! Did you get my text? Did you get my voicemail? I even left a message on your landline a few seconds ago. Zenora's ensconced with those murders. That's right. Murders. Zenora's positive Adeliza and Derella's deaths weren't accidental. And that's not all, the solstice curse is worse than we originally thought. If I imagined for one single minute—"

"Whoa. Slow down. Calm down. You're going too fast."

She grabbed me by the arm and yanked me to the alcove where the restrooms were. "Shh! Act natural."

"Shh! Act natural"? She's the one bellowing like a banshee.

"Okay. Okay. Suppose you tell me all about this in my office. Lizzie's on the phone and no one else noticed I came in."

Glenda nodded and followed me into the office. I closed the door behind us and pulled my chair closer to the one on the other side of the desk. "Suppose you start with Zenora's findings. Did she locate more letters in Uris Library?"

Glenda took a long, deep breath. "Once she deciphered the letters from the Benton residents, she learned Adeliza and Derella were threatened by Hestherlee Crackstone for allegedly strangling her chickens. Something about the name Crackstone bothered Zenora so she reached out to a friend of hers who works at Widener Library in Boston. The centerpiece of Harvard's libraries or something like that. Zenora was mumbling when she told me."

"Her friend is a research clerk, too?"

"Not exactly. More like part of the housekeeping staff."

Terrific. The cleaning lady.

"I'm not sure I understand."

Glenda clasped her hands together and lowered her head for a moment. "Zenora and her friend are in the same spiritual circle."

And here we go . . .

"Suffice to say, the name Crackstone is quite familiar to them. Painfully long history of witch-hating Crackstones in Salem, Marblehead, and Swampscott, Massachusetts. I'll get to the point—

Hestherlee also moved to the town of Benton to wreak havoc on the Marstens for what she believed was a spell they put on her husband so that he spurned her for another woman."

"So the chicken thing was kind of an afterthought?"

"More like an excuse to burn down their house."

"How does Zenora's friend know this?"

"Because the original Crackstones came over on the *Mayflower* and someone took the time to track their family history. Let's just say the position Zenora's friend holds at Widener Library allows her access to all sorts of documents."

"Holy crud!"

Glenda reached forward and grasped both my wrists. "Norrie, the Two Witches curse needs to be undone before it claims more victims. It's an exponential curse."

Exponential. I knew I hated math for a reason.

"Um, is that the kind of thing that's in Zenora's skill set? Eliminating curses?"

"Oh, heavens, no. Because the unwinding of the curse has to be directed at the last Crackstone descendant in the line."

Let's hope the expression "Live long and multiply" didn't apply to Hestherlee's prodigy.

"Um, not to sound obtuse, but how on earth is Zenora, or her friend, for that matter, going to find the last Crackstone descendant?"

"With your help."

Suddenly, I wished I had another screenplay deadline, because that sounded a whole lot better than what, I'm sure, Glenda was about to propose.

Chapter 32

"Zenora can't do this alone. She's going to be focused on figuring out the best way to unravel a curse. It's not like setting up a DVR or programming a sprinkler system."

"What is it that she needs my help with?" I asked.

"Tracking down Hestherlee's descendants."

"Um, how many of them did she start with before the husband took off?"

"One, by the name of Degory Crackstone. That's as much as I know. Or as far as Zenora got. She emailed me a copy of the family records up until eighteen eighty-nine. Those were the ones she found at Uris Library and I forwarded them to you. She thinks the more recent records must be housed with the Yates County Historical Society."

Uh-oh. I think I know where this is going.

Glenda steepled her hands and smiled. "Once she deciphered the handwriting, she typed everything on her computer. It shouldn't be too difficult to pore through those old ledgers and county records to bring it up to date."

"That's at least a century and a quarter."

"I know. I know. You can thank her. She already did the hard work."

Just then, Cammy knocked on my door. "Is Glenda with you? We need her out here."

"Coming," Glenda shouted. She stood and moved her chair back. "About that curse. I should have mentioned it earlier. According to Zenora's friend, the second part of the curse is really, really powerful. Under no circumstances should anyone be served rosé at the winemakers dinner. Not until after midnight, when the curse vanishes until the next full moon summer solstice."

"No worries. I checked with the WOW ladies and it's summer blends. Plus, our rosé isn't even bottled yet."

"Good. Because last thing we need is another dead body."

Glenda was right about Zenora doing all the legwork. I really did owe her, but how I would repay her was anyone's guess. The woman had bizarre eating habits, so that left out most foods. In addition, she had an equally strange aversion to certain plants and flowers. So much for a nice bouquet.

I stood and rubbed my forehead for a minute before venturing out to the tasting room. No wonder Cammy knocked on the door. All the tables were full and at least six or seven new customers came through the door. For the next two hours, I went from table to table providing relief for our employees so they could grab lunch or take a break.

By a little after one, I moseyed to the bistro and had Fred make me a tuna on rye with extra dill. Our part-time college students arrived shortly after and I took off, once again for the Yates County Historical Society. I hadn't planned on an afternoon poring through their archives, but there was little else I could do to help Alex, or anyone else, for that matter.

It was a tedious and boring process and at one point I almost considered shelling out whatever monies it took to have ancestry.com or one of those places dig into Hestherlee's family tree. It wasn't as if all the Benton records were in one place. Oh, no. That would've been too easy. Instead, I had to sift through the civil records that recorded marriages performed by local clergy.

At a quarter to five, the docent tapped me on my shoulder and informed me that the building would be closed in fifteen minutes. Her voice was low, and for the life of me I couldn't imagine why. It wasn't as if anyone else was in the same basement room with me.

I turned my head and looked up. "What time do you open in the morning?"

"At nine. You're welcome to resume your search at that time. In fact, I can lock those books in our safe and you can ask for them when you get here. That way there won't be any time wasted with reshelving them, only to take them out again."

"Um, that's really nice of you, but can I just finish up? I'm almost done. Looks like these records only go as far as nineteen thirty-five."

The docent leaned over my shoulder and looked. "All right. Another twenty minutes and that's about it. I really do need to lock up. By the way, anything after that date is filed with the town clerk or under vital records with the U.S. government. Up until certain dates, certificates for birth, death and marriage are public information. Usually, but not always, for seventy-five years. It really depends upon the state."

"Thanks. I appreciate it."

"College study?"

"Family history."

"I'm impressed. We don't get many diehards in here. Those genealogy sites make it way too easy to pay the money to let someone else do the work."

Oh, yeah.

I thanked her, finished up, and drove straight home. Charlie immediately pushed his dog dish toward me the second I got in the door.

"Yikes. I'm sorry, buddy. The day kind of crept away from me." I immediately poured him a cup of kibble and then added an extra half cup. He devoured the meal in less time than it took me to pour it.

"You can have some of my eggs, too," I said, reaching for a bowl. "I'm about as hungry as you are so these are getting beaten and microwaved."

I added butter, provolone cheese, and some fake bacon bits to the mix and nuked my dinner, setting aside a heaping spoonful for the dog once it was done. I was so busy writing down names and dates from those old Benton records that I didn't take the time to actually absorb what I had written. In fact, I hadn't even looked at the email Glenda forwarded to me. All I remembered was that Zenora got as far as 1889 before tossing the ball in my court. Thankfully she was right about one thing, the Yates County Historical Society *did* have early marriage records for its Benton residents, but anything after the Great Depression was now part of the Town of Benton records, or worse yet, the federal government.

"I'd better set my alarm clock," I said to Charlie. "If I can't solve Vance's murder, I can at least track down the last Crackstone."

• • •

It was a noble plan for Friday, but not only couldn't I solve Vance's murder, I wasn't able to track down the last Crackstone either. And believe me, I tried. At an ungodly hour of the morning—well, nine-ish, but still early—I drove to the Town of Benton office on the corner of Havens Corners and State Route 14. I was energized and ready to put a stop to the full moon solstice curse. When I left that building, I was worn out, defeated, and cranky. I got as far as 1950, when the records fanned out to a zillion other states because Hestherlee's prodigy wasn't about to live and die in the town of Benton.

Sure, if I was willing to cough up enough money, I probably could have located some of the surviving generations from the *Mayflower,* but who has those kinds of resources? Grumbling and miserable, I returned home to find my landline blinking and the dog shoving his food dish at me. It wasn't even two in the afternoon but Charlie had picked up a habit that I hoped Francine wouldn't notice. He had gotten used to being fed the minute I came through the door. Even if I left for only an hour or two.

"As soon as I listen to this message," I told him, "I'm going over to the winery for a very late lunch."

The dog chomped on his kibble, oblivious to anything I said. I pushed the Play button and groaned the second I heard Deputy Hickman's voice.

"This is a courtesy call, Miss Ellington. The Schuyler County Sheriff's Office sent someone to follow up on your observation. The staff at Glen Foreign Motors insisted there was no car housed in that barn, and in fact, told the deputy that the barn hadn't been used in months. It was for excess storage. Nonetheless, they opened the barn, and indeed, it was empty. I repeat—empty. Devoid of any vehicles. And yes, before you have a tantrum, I do recall seeing that grainy photo you showed me of a car under a tarp. Unfortunately, it's not enough evidence for a search warrant. No judge in his or her right mind would ever issue one. At this juncture, I daresay your so-called lead is a dead end. I suggest you concentrate on your paying job and leave it at that. Have a good day."

Paying job? Leave it at that? He has got *to be kidding.*

I played the message a second time. Heaven knows why. It wasn't as if it was about to change. Maybe I simply needed to have it sink in. And sink in, it did. I was doomed. Worse yet, so was Alex Bollinger.

The combination of having everything crash down on me coupled with intense hunger pangs made for a pounding headache. I took a Tylenol, gave Charlie a pat on the head, and walked directly to the winery.

Lizzie was on the phone with someone but Cammy spied me immediately. She had just stepped out of the kitchen with a tray of wineglasses. "Hey there! I need to catch up with you. Let me put these on Sam's table and we can chat."

"Meet me in the bistro," I said. "I may die of starvation if I wait any longer."

Four bites into a bacon, avocado, and tomato sandwich on sourdough bread, and it was safe for the general public to be near me. Cammy sat across from me and sipped on an iced coffee. "You look like hell. What's going on?"

From the fiasco in Watkins Glen to my futile search for those miserable Crackstones, I relived every lousy moment I faced in the past few days. Not to mention the recent phone message I got from Grizzly Gary.

Cammy pulled her bun tighter and sighed. "Well, maybe this will cheer you up. It's a list of attendees for the winemakers dinner. Madeline dropped it off this morning. I don't know why she doesn't use email."

"I do. It gets her out of her winery so she can pick up the gossip in ours."

"Actually, she was more on the giving end this time than the receiving end."

I put down my sandwich and widened my eyes. "Spill it."

Chapter 33

Cammy crossed her arms and plopped both elbows on the table. "Here goes. In no particular order. Madeline's certain Stephanie is buying a new Mercedes because her tasting room manager, who was off the other day, spotted her taking a test drive in Geneva. He was certain it was Stephanie on the road because, and I quote, 'Not many women can exude that much sex appeal from a distance.' Shall I continue?"

I wanted to heave. "Sure. Might as well. And she's not buying a new high-priced car. We were on a reconnaissance mission. She just took it a bit further than planned."

Cammy's laugh was louder than usual. "I'll bet. Listen, Madeline contracted out to have her porch extended and found out from the contractor that Vance took all sorts of payoffs to look the other way. The contractor told her it was too bad she didn't contact him in the first place. He would have saved her some grief."

"Payoffs? That no good weasel. Oops. Rest his sorry soul. Hmm, no wonder he could afford a Porsche 911 engine. I wonder how many under-the-table deals it took that two-faced liar. Any other tidbits from Madeline?" I asked.

"Only to read the guest list. Something about high-profile attendees."

"You mean fussbudgets, huh?"

"Fussbudgets with money. Other than the winemakers from our six wineries and the owners, I only recognized one of the Finger Lakes bank presidents and the editor from *Wine and Vine* magazine. Maybe you'll have better luck."

She handed me the list and I glanced at the names. "Nope. No one I know. At least the winemakers dinner is Madeline's concern. My mind is boggled as it is. I've got to figure out what those thieves did with Vance's Karmann Ghia because Alex's time is running out. All I know is that sometime between Wednesday night and Friday morning, they took it. But why? Unless someone tipped them off that Stephanie and I were interested in that particular vehicle and they got worried."

"If what you say is true, Norrie, then it had to be someone from that dealership. From Glen Foreign Motors."

"Yeah, but good luck proving it. I'm still trying to wrap my head around the fact that a truck vanished right in front of my eyes."

"Give it a break. You said you were on a curve and they moved fast. Either that or they used a toggle switch. Anyone who knows anything about cars will tell you that."

"That's what Theo said."

Cammy sat straight up and looked directly at me. "They made themselves disappear with some fancy maneuvers because you were getting too close to their location. Think about it. They've stashed a valuable Porsche engine in that truck and now have to deliver it to an undisclosed location. You said it was right by the raceway, didn't you?"

"There's like a zillion barns around there."

"Not a barn. A garage. A garage with all the fixings so that that spicy little engine can be dropped into another car."

"Oh, my gosh. That's exactly what I thought, too. Someone's got a vintage Porsche that needs a new engine. And not just any engine. That super-fast RS two-point-seven. And it's got to be ready for tomorrow's qualifying race. Damn! If I can only track down that garage."

"Forget the garage for a moment. You might have better luck tracking down the drivers who are registered for that race. I know the papers always print the preliminary entry lists for NASCAR and Xfinity, so maybe you can find the one for that vintage race online. And if you're wondering how I know all of this, keep in mind, I've got a zillion male relatives who live for this kind of stuff."

I reached in my pocket for my iPhone before Cammy finished her sentence. "What do I Google? Preliminary entry list along with the name of the race?"

"Yup."

I felt a slight tremor in my hand as I posed the question for Safari. I wasn't sure of the official name for the race, but vintage car race worked just fine. The screen pulled up a six-column list of driver names complete with their entry numbers, the organization sponsoring them, their crew chief, and the car manufacturer and year. It was as if the cloud of doom that had settled over me suddenly dissipated and I was back in business. "Holy cannoli! You were right!"

"You're the Nancy Drew around here, not me. All I did was remind you we're in the twenty-first century and everything's online."

"Not everything. I still have to track down that garage, but at least I've got a fighting chance. Looks like there are at least thirty or forty entries. I need to narrow them down by Porsche. Then figure out which ones are local. This should be a breeze compared to looking for Crackstone descendants. Which reminds me, has Glenda said anything to you today about what Zenora's friend from Boston shared?"

"Good Lord. That widening circle of looney friends just keeps growing. Boston, huh? No, we've been so busy with customers and tastings, we haven't had time to talk. Why? Is it important?"

"More like unnerving. Remember the second part of that curse? The partridge's eye and all that?"

"Uh-huh. Why?"

"Apparently, the damn curse will intensify until midnight. I know it's probably hogwash, but it sure is creepy. I mean, really, really creepy."

"Relax, Norrie. No one's serving rosé."

"No one that we know of."

"I've got to get back to the tasting room. But before I go, please tell me that once you find out if there are any local Porsche drivers on that list, you don't intend to pay them an unannounced visit. These are thieves and one of them could be a killer."

"Don't worry. I'll come up with a plan."

"Make it a written one."

I swished the straw around in my Coke and thought about my next move. There was absolutely no way I was about to beg Don or Theo for another favor, but Godfrey Klein sure owed me big-time for sticking my neck out to save Alex. Without wasting a second, I pulled the iPhone from my pocket and dialed his office.

"Norrie—I planned on giving you a call. Really I did, but things around here have been crazy. I had to cover Alex's field study until they could find a replacement. That meant a zillion schedule changes. Cassie was no help whatsoever, unless you count hand-wringing and sighing 'Poor Dr. Bollinger' every few minutes."

"Yeesh."

"That's not the worst of it. Alex's bail hearing was this morning. I know, I know. I should have called you but it doesn't matter. Bail was set at five hundred thousand dollars. That's half a million! Needless to say, Alex isn't going anywhere."

"That's outrageous."

"Not when you consider the charge—it's first-degree murder. Alex's legal counsel told him they'd be lucky if the charge got dropped to voluntary manslaughter."

"Voluntary manslaughter? That charge should be dropped altogether!"

"Not according to the Yates County Sheriff's Office."

For a brief second I was stunned and momentarily forgot my real reason for calling Godfrey.

"Norrie, are you still on the line?"

"Uh, yeah. I'm here. Tell me, do you have any sort of official identification from the Experiment Station?"

"Of course. All employees do. Uh-oh. I don't think I like where this is going."

"You might change your mind when I point you in the direction of the real killer."

"Don't point me in that direction. Point the sheriff's office. Yates or Ontario County. They're working together on this since Kashong Point is in two counties. Take your pick which office."

"I already did. That's why I need your help."

"Official identification, huh? Please don't tell me I'm going to require legal counsel when this is done."

"I hope not. Bradley's in the Thousand Islands, and besides, he doesn't handle what I'm about to propose."

"Oh, crap!"

Chapter 34

I wasn't exactly up-front with Godfrey when I mentioned pointing him in the direction of the killer. It sort of implied I knew who the killer was, when in fairness all I knew was that it had to be the person responsible for stealing Vance's car and swapping out the engine. But at least it was a start.

"All we need to do," I said, "is drive to the Watkins Glen Raceway tomorrow morning before the qualifying races begin. You explain that we're there on official business from the New York State Agricultural Department and flash them your ID."

Godfrey's voice was explosive. "What possible business is the entomology department going to have at a car race?"

"Not the race. The garage. Tell them the department was contacted by one of the race car drivers regarding airborne insects in the garage."

"You mean flying insects. Although, I have seen that term used when it refers to insects that become airborne as the result of an external stimuli. Now, in the case of the dot echo study that involved nocturnally flying insects—"

"Good. Whatever that is, mention it when you show them your ID. Tell them it's a serious concern for race car drivers should those insects get into the car's interior, or worse yet, its engine."

"No one in their right mind is going to believe that. They don't have glass windows on those cars."

"They'll believe you if you sound authoritarian and assume a hostile resting face."

"A what?"

"Just don't smile."

"I'm not smiling now."

"Trust me. You can pull this off. *We* can pull this off. When they ask who the driver is, tell them it's a Porsche driver. Although, I should have the name before I turn in for the night."

"You mean you don't know?"

"Fine. I don't know but I'm working on it. I have impeccable resources." *Thank you, Safari.*

"Norrie, even if I wanted to join you tomorrow for this wackadoodle plan of yours, I can't. I've got to check on Alex's replacement and

163

finalize a series of reports for the department. And when I say reports, it's not just the Swede midge study. It's also the financial report. Do you have any idea how mentally taxing that is?"

"What about Sunday? Don't tell me you're working on Sunday. It'll be cutting things close but I suppose it's not like we have a choice."

"Sure we do. Let the sheriff's office handle it."

"Come on, you know as well as I do they're not even considering another suspect. So, what do you say? Crack of dawn on Sunday?"

"If it wasn't Alex hanging on the line, I'd never agree to such a preposterous idea. In fact, I'm having second thoughts already."

Second thoughts. That's good. That means he's considering it.

"Look, what's the worst thing that can happen? They won't let us in. Big deal. Lots of ways to get into a Glen race without passing through the official gates," I said.

"I honestly can't believe you're Francine's sister."

"You, and most of the teachers at Penn Yan Academy. So, yes or no, are we in?"

"I suppose. Define 'crack of dawn' for me. Last time it was ten in the morning on your time."

"I was still on New York City time. Get here early. Seven. Seven thirty the latest. Meet me at the winery. I'll get some breakfast rolls and coffee from the bistro. Fred and Emma are there before five."

"I've got a knot in my stomach thinking about this."

"Don't worry. It will go off without a hitch. I'll fill you in on all the details that transpired with Don and Theo when we ride over there on Sunday. I'll also tell you about the winemakers dinner, although there probably won't be much to tell except to describe the food."

"Good. At least we'll have one topic of conversation that doesn't involve a whole lot of drama."

"Admit it. Your life has become a heck of a lot more interesting since I arrived."

"If you're asking, Am I buying more Tums? The answer is yes. In bulk."

At least Godfrey agreed to accompany me to the raceway even though it was a day later than I would have liked. I wanted to nab Vance's killer prior to the actual race in case it turned out to be a messy, time-consuming deal. Now I'd have to settle for pointing the finger at the culprit with a clock ticking and the words *down to the wire* spinning in my head.

With the list of vintage car drivers now on my iPhone screen, I reached for a napkin and begin to write down the names of the ones who were racing Porsches, a popular choice along with Jaguars, MG's, Ferraris, and Corvettes. Too bad I wasn't looking for a Lotus, Shelby or Alfa Romeo because there were only a few of those.

My list consisted of nine names, and that meant nine separate Google searches. The last thing I felt like doing. And the last place I felt like doing it was at the winery, where I'd be interrupted.

I took a long last sip of my Coke before leaving the bistro, waving goodbye to the otherwise occupied tasting room workers, and headed directly home. Once comfortably ensconced on my couch, I began my Google search in earnest, starting with Connor Prendergast. It was a short search. He was from some town near Pittsburgh, Pennsylvania, that I had never heard of and had recently competed in the Pocono Raceway. Cross him off the list.

Next was a woman—Trina Matthews. From North Carolina. I exed her off the list as well but made a mental note that her standing at the Florence Speedway in Timmonsville, South Carolina, was pretty darn good.

Same deal with the next four names on the list—two from California, one from Florida, and one from Michigan. None of them anywhere near this little neck of the woods.

With only three names to go, I wondered if I'd made a mistake thinking whoever stole Vance's engine was a local driver.

"If I pull up a big fat zero," I said to Charlie, "then it's all over for Alex."

The dog ambled over to the couch and gave me the paw treatment. He kept scratching my knee with his paw until I got up, went to the kitchen, and grabbed two doggie treats for him. Once back at the couch, I looked up the seventh name on my list—Augie Lennox. Alabama born and Tennessee raised. I drew a line through his name before bothering to see where he raced before.

With only two names to go, I got really nervous. This wasn't how I expected my Google search to go. Then again, in all the detective movies, the sleuth always found out who the killer was at the last minute. In this case, I didn't.

The last two names were drivers from Wisconsin and Tennessee. I let out a groan that could be heard across the lake. "If this doesn't stink,

Charlie, I don't know what does." I bent my head down and stared at the floor. The dog must have figured it was a golden opportunity for him because, having exhausted the paw treatment on my knee, he tried another tactic—bumping my head with his.

"Aargh. All right. Give me a second."

I went back to the kitchen and brought the bag of all-natural grain-free dog treats with me to the couch. As I reached in to hand him one, I looked at the company information on the back of the bag and paused. It read "Boulder, Colorado," and in big print, "All USA ingredients." Same as always but with one difference. That particular company had been located in Buffalo, New York. I should know. I'd given Charlie lots of those treats in the past few months.

Maybe Colorado offered them a better tax deal. It didn't matter. What mattered was that I was still in the game. Unfortunately, it also meant I had to begin my search all over again, because whoever stole Vance's car might have come from a different state, but they darned well could be living in New York at this time.

It was after four and my brain felt like mush, but I had to expand my search, starting with Connor Prendergast from good old Pennsylvania. Wikipedia highlighted his driving career but not his personal life. I moved through social media as if I was on an archeological dig. First Facebook, then Twitter, and finally LinkedIn.

"Well, isn't that nice," I told Charlie. "Thirty-year-old Connor lives outside of Pittsburgh with his young wife, Elinor. Guess we can toss him in the not-a-killer pile."

From Connor, I tortuously plowed through four more names, including Trina, and got nowhere. Unless developing a stiff neck counted for something. Sure, drivers had relocated, but none of them to New York. Still, I had four more names to go.

Augie Lennox was a bust, but when I pulled up the information for another Pennsylvania driver, Kurt Sherry, I was stunned. His real name was Robert Kurtis Sherry but he had gone with Kurtis as his professional name. I said the name out loud as if to verify what I had discovered—Robert Sherry. R.S. The same initials on that restraining order in Vance's notes. According to what he had written, too much had been invested already. Whatever that meant.

Suddenly, I didn't feel as wiped out as I had an hour ago. I tracked down Kurtis, aka Robert, Sherry like a bloodhound. A social media bloodhound who pored through friends of friends and all sorts of miscellaneous information until I got to that tiny bead I needed— finding out where he lived.

Too bad that morsel of information left me no better off than where I was before. Kurtis Sherry lived in Towanda, Pennsylvania.

Chapter 35

"No sense calling this a day when I can aggravate myself with the last two names," I said to Charlie. "And don't think that means more treats for you."

The dog, who had rolled himself into a ball on the rug by the couch, looked up and then closed his eyes.

The next hour went painstakingly slow. Mainly because I stopped every few minutes to sigh and rub my eyes. The other two drivers were from Wisconsin and Tennessee and nothing on their social media sites indicated they had moved to New York.

It was after five and I felt as if I'd run a marathon but without all the fanfare. Not even someone to hand me a water bottle. I wasn't sure how I was going to broach the subject with Godfrey on Sunday when I all but convinced him I'd have a definitive answer regarding Vance's killer.

Oh, I have a definitive answer all right—I don't know.

Unable to shake the feeling I was defeated, I went upstairs and took a cool shower. If nothing else, I felt somewhat refreshed. As I toweled off, something occurred to me. Sayre, Pennsylvania, was only an hour or two south of the Finger Lakes Region. That's not a very far distance and certainly within reach of engine-swapping on Seneca Lake. With no other recourse, I figured Kurtis Sherry's bay at the raceway would be Godfrey's and my first step when we got in on Sunday. *If* we got in. It all depended on how convincing we were. Or, more specifically, if we didn't muck it up.

I threw on some frayed jeans and a T-shirt before heading downstairs to make myself something to eat. I was tired, cranky, and too darn lazy to defrost anything from the freezer. That left two choices— peanut butter and jelly on bread or peanut butter and jelly on a bagel. The bagel won out and dinner was served.

Sunday seemed eons away and the thought of waiting to continue my so-called investigation made me edgy. I was positive I was missing something, but for the life of me I couldn't figure out what.

For a millennial who prided herself on internet searches, I literally crashed and burned. So much for finding Hestherlee's descendant or a race car driver who lived in close proximity to Seneca Lake, and more specifically, to Glen Foreign Motors.

True, I had plenty of time to work on the never-ending Two Witches curse since next time around would be 2062, but Alex couldn't wait. I brought my knife and plate to the sink and ran water over them. The sticky strawberry jelly was a pain in the neck to remove so I stood there for a while, letting the warm water trickle over my hands. My mind drifted as I absently reached for a sponge to wipe the knife.

At least I'd be dining on gourmet food tomorrow night. Chilean sea bass and Malaysian tamarind prawn. I'd also have to listen to Madeline go on and on about having her porch extended. And then, in the instant I reached for a dish towel, something hit me—the conversation she had with her contractor.

According to Cammy, who spoke with Madeline, the contractor said Vance had accepted all sorts of bribes to look the other way. What if one of them didn't pan out and Vance double-crossed the homeowner? It was certainly a better motive for murder than getting into an argument with someone over interference with an insect study at Kashong Point.

I caught my breath and grabbed the landline. Madeline's number, along with all of the other winery numbers in our WOW group, was on speed dial.

The words raced out of my mouth the second Madeline answered the phone. "Madeline. Hi. It's Norrie. Can you give me the phone number for your contractor? The one who's extending your porch."

"Oh, dear. What happened? A water leak? Dry rot?"

"No, nothing happened, but I think your contractor might have an idea about who killed Vance Wexler."

"What? It's Coby Construction. Out of Bellona. Bill Coby's the owner. I don't understand. How would he know who killed Vance?"

"Um, I don't think he knows in the actual sense of the word. More like having information that would lead to the killer."

"I still don't understand."

"He may know who paid off Vance for approval from the historical society but got burned. It's a hunch."

"Oh, goodness, Norrie. Please don't tell him you heard that from me. I never should have mentioned it to your tasting room manager."

"Don't worry. If what Vance did is common knowledge around here, Bill Coby won't even ask."

"Let's hope you're right. Do you still need his number?"

"Nah. It'll be listed on the internet. Thanks, Madeline."

"Are you all set for tomorrow night? Cammy said someone will be bringing your wine over in the afternoon. Summer Magic, right?"

"Uh-huh. A nice, breezy blend."

"I must say, this is one event I'm really looking forward to hosting. A manageable number of attendees, a renowned chef, and a weather forecast that can't be beat. Not to mention the wines. Glorious summer wines. The perfect way to start the season."

"Um, this is my first winemakers dinner. I should have asked sooner. How dressy is it?"

"Not formal or semi-formal, for that matter, but dressy enough. Like Easter Sunday at church. You *do* have something to wear, don't you?"

"Of course. Naturally." *Francine's closet is a regular treasure trove of gauzy, frilly, flowery summer dresses.* "I'm all set. Just didn't want to overdress." *Like she'll believe that.*

"Wonderful. See you tomorrow night."

I pulled up Coby Construction the second I ended the call with Madeline. It wasn't quite seven so I took a chance and dialed Bill Coby's number. He answered on the second ring.

"Hi! This is Norrie Ellington," I said, "from Two Witches Winery in Penn Yan. I hope I'm not calling you at an inconvenient time, but I really need to speak with you about time-sensitive information."

"Time-sensitive as in something's falling down at your place?"

"Um, no. This isn't business-related. It's personal. Well, not personal-personal, but not business." *Good grief. I'm rattling on like a teenager.*

"I'm not sure I follow."

I took a breath and spoke slowly and succinctly. "Mr. Coby, a good friend of mine has been accused of a murder he didn't commit. The murder of Vance Wexler from the Geneva Historical Society."

Bill Coby's voice was calm and soft. "I'm familiar with Mr. Wexler. Go on."

"My friend is a noted entomologist at Cornell who happened to be at the wrong place at the wrong time. Well, not exactly. He was conducting a field study at Kashong Point when Vance showed up for some historical society arrowhead hunt and got into a verbal altercation with my friend. When Vance's body was found, well, I guess you can figure the rest."

"That's very unfortunate, Miss Ellington, but I don't know how I can help you."

"First of all, I won't tell anyone we had this conversation. Honest." I took a breath and continued before I lost my nerve. "It's no secret Vance took bribes from homeowners who wanted to remodel but needed approval from the historical society. I think one of them may have paid Vance but got stiffed in the end. Is there any way you would know who that could be?"

"Okay. I know this isn't client-patient confidentiality, but we have business ethics that we have to abide by as well."

"I understand. I really do. But we're talking an innocent man who's being framed or I wouldn't ask."

There was a pause on the line and for a minute I was certain Bill Coby would end the call. I bit my lower lip and was about to put the phone down when he spoke.

"I can give you the addresses of pending projects. Pending means prior approval from the historical society before a building permit can be issued. Then on to the village or city planning commission—Geneva, Canandaigua, Penn Yan . . . you get the idea."

"Um, if I understand you, there's a possibility one of those pending projects was waiting for Vance's stamp of approval."

"You understand correctly. Give me a few minutes and I can text you the information."

"Mr. Coby, I don't know how to thank you. And I promise, I won't breathe a word."

"You can relax. The information is not confidential. And please tell Madeline Martinez I said hello when you see her."

"Madeline. So you know?"

"As soon as you said Two Witches Winery I knew Madeline must have spoken with you. Nice lady. And good luck, Miss Ellington. You're doing a decent thing."

"Thanks. And call me Norrie." *It's bad enough Deputy Hickman calls me Miss Ellington.* "And if our winery or our house needs anything done, we'll be sure to call you."

Bill Coby's text message was on my phone a few minutes later. Three addresses with three separate projects. I figured if I couldn't track down the Crackstones or snoop around at Watkins Glen International Raceway tomorrow, I could darn well pay a visit to those residences.

Satisfied the day wasn't a total disaster, I made myself some popcorn and scanned the DVR for a movie. That was the instant the landline rang. It read "private caller," and I was half-tempted to ignore it.

Too bad I didn't. It was Zenora and she sounded as if she was in the midst of an allergy attack.

Chapter 36

"Norrie, is that you?"

Of course it's me. You just called here.

"You sound terrible, Zenora. What's going on?" *And please don't tell me you uncovered another branch on the ever-growing curse tree.*

"I had a spiritual reading this afternoon and my aura is dark. Darker than it's ever been. My spiritualist believes it might have something to do with allowing the Crackstone family to enter my life."

Yikes. It's not as if they're entering her house unannounced with a passel of unruly kids.

"Um, they're dead, aren't they? I mean, with the exception of the last descendant, and no one can figure out who that is, or if they're even alive."

"It doesn't matter. They're linked to that curse and until we put an end to it, I'm afraid it's too late. Once the forces of darkness take hold, it will take an act of epic proportions to set things right again."

My gosh. It's beginning to sound like a Star Wars movie.

"Sure. Fine. Is there anything you want me to do? I kind of reached a dead end tracking down the family."

"You might have reached a dead end but I didn't. That's why my aura is so dark and disturbing."

"You found them? You mean to tell me you found them?"

"That's the beauty and the curse of working in the library system. Someone always finds something. In this case, my friend from Boston got in touch with her, well, let's just say her outreach circle of similar kindred spirits."

Kindred spirits my you-know-what.

"Uh-huh. And then what?"

Zenora wheezed a bit before she answered. And when she finally did answer my question, I almost started to wheeze as well.

"There are Crackstones in our midst. From the original line. Hestherlee's line."

"Who? Where?"

"That part gets blurry. Toss in a few marriages and you've got name changes. I, for one, believe women should keep their maiden names."

Yes, yes. Fine. Keep their maiden names.

"Zenora, was your friend able to get the names? The married names?"

"Yes, but it was a very bad phone connection. Lots of static. I won't be able to get back in touch with her until next week."

"Did she give you a name?"

"Exner. I think she said Exner. Her voice kept cracking up on the line. Something about Abigail Crackstone Exner. Morton was the husband's first name. I heard that loud and clear."

Terrific. The first name. That helps a lot.

"Were you able to hear when?"

"Late nineteen eighties."

"Where?"

"Someplace in Pennsylvania. My friend started to tell me but the line went dead. I tried to call her back but she left for the weekend. A spiritual retreat in Salem."

Salem. Of course.

"Well, can't you call her tonight or tomorrow?"

"It's a spiritual retreat, not a holiday weekend. All worldly devices must be left behind."

Then send a damn smoke signal.

I tried not to display any angst or tension. "I see. When you do hear something, please call me immediately. And, um, I hope your aura improves."

"I'm going to participate in a spiritual cleansing. That should help. And one more thing, Norrie, before I forget. Although I'm sure Glenda warned you. Make sure no one drinks any rosé at your winery. Or at that dinner. It's especially dangerous after dusk."

"Not a problem. None of the wineries will be serving rosé. You can sleep easy on that one."

"I'll try."

When I got off the phone with Zenora, my hands felt clammy and beads of sweat trickled down my cheeks and onto my neck. I was ecstatic she had gotten me closer to finding that Crackstone descendant, but equally eager to visit those residences Bill Coby sent me.

The good news was that the three pending projects Bill sent me were all within close proximity of each other. One a bit north of Kashong Point on Armstrong Road and Route 14, another on the lakeside of Route 14 near Port of Call, and a third located a stone's throw from Geneva on the Lake, where the Chocolate Extravaganza took place a few months ago.

None of the projects listed had names associated with them so I figured it would be a bit tricky when I paid them a visit in the morning. I was up-front and honest with Bill but I wasn't so sure that would be the best tactic with these folks. After all, one of them could be Vance's killer, and the last thing he or she would want to do was help me exonerate someone else.

I decided, instead, on a different approach. I would arrive, clipboard in hand, requesting their signature on a petition to do away with the historical district designation for lakefront and lake view properties along the west side of Seneca Lake. That way, I could easily get them into a conversation about Vance, and if I was lucky, find out which one of them he stiffed.

For the first time since I got that awful call from Godfrey about Vance's death, I slept through the night. Maybe it was because I had an actual plan for the following day, or maybe it was because I was dead tired. It didn't matter. I woke up refreshed and eager to get started on what I hoped would turn out to be a solid lead.

• • •

Once Charlie was fed, I joined him for a brisk walk around the edge of the woods before returning home for a quick breakfast and a second cup of coffee. I left a short message on the winery phone explaining I'd be there to help out in the tasting room after one. I knew they were all set with workers, but still, I wanted to be a part of the everyday business whenever I could.

My first stop was a Georgian-style home that faced Armstrong Road. Only the side of the house could be seen from Route 14, but that was enough to put it on the historical society register. Like all Georgian homes, it was about as symmetrical as any house could get. Two stories, two chimneys, rectangular with paneled front doors, and faded white brick that I imagined was done to give it that early colonial look.

A silver Subaru Forester was parked in the driveway, and for an instant I wondered if there were any restrictions on the color of the owners' cars. I parked behind it and walked directly to the front door before I lost my nerve.

A man who resembled a slightly chunkier version of Zac Efron answered the door. His faded gray SUNY Cortland sweatshirt could have been left over from his college days. Behind him, two toddlers raced around the room.

"Hi! What can I do for you?"

Good. At least he didn't slam the door in my face.

I introduced myself, showed him the petition that I had carefully crafted and printed out last night and asked if he'd be willing to sign it.

"Humph. Funny you should show up with one of these. My wife and I have been thinking about doing the same thing. We bought this house five years ago and have been pouring our blood and sweat, not to mention money, into it ever since. We wanted a great place for our kids to grow up and that included customizing it with a tree house out back. We own all of the wooded property behind us."

"And the tree house got nixed?" I asked.

"Big-time. Hey, I know it's really crass to speak ill of the dead, but that guy Vance from the historical society was a jerk if I ever met one. The way I designed the tree house, no one would even see it."

I reached for a pen and handed him the clipboard. "I don't know why they'd put the kibosh on a kid's playhouse."

"Oh, it's more than that. It's an actual structure that can sleep up to four people. That's why we hired a contractor. But still, it wouldn't take away from the historical charm this house has."

"I guess you must've been pretty upset, huh?"

"Oh, yeah. But we submitted an appeal and maybe Vance's successor will be a bit more lenient. Our contractor suggested greasing the wheels but my wife and I weren't comfortable with that."

Nice guy. Has moral scruples. Got to cross him off the list.

"Well, I hope things work out for you. Maybe this petition will help."

He smiled. "It can't hurt."

The second I left his door I felt a pang of guilt. Talk about moral scruples. Here I was, pretending to take a stance on an unfair ruling, when in reality it was only a ruse. I bit my lip on the way back to the car and decided that, no matter what, I'd follow through with that petition once I found out who really killed Vance.

Next, I drove to a house near Port of Call. It sat directly on Seneca Lake and reminded me of something one of the original homesteaders would build—a simple white clapboard house with a white picket fence.

With pink and red rosebushes under the window, it all but screamed *Snow White Lives Here.*

I felt a bit more confident since this was my second visit with the not-so-bogus-anymore petition. Again, I walked to the front door and rang the bell. This time, a woman answered. She appeared to be in her late fifties or early sixties with highlighted brown hair and hoop earrings. A silky multicolored tunic hung over khaki shorts.

"If you're selling anything," she said, "we're not interested."

"No, I'm here with a petition to have the historical home designation removed for lakefront and lake view properties in Ontario and Yates counties down to Bellona."

The woman all but snatched the clipboard from my hand. "Give me that thing. I can't sign it fast enough."

Before I could say anything, she went on. "That idiotic ruling has made my life a hell during the winters. When we purchased this house we were told we could add a detached garage, but when we finally sought approval, it was after the historical designation and we were turned down. Do you have any idea how impossible it is to scrape your windshield and shovel the damn snow off your car every morning?"

"Um, uh, yeah. I kind of do. I live on Two Witches Hill in Penn Yan and we don't have a garage for our cars."

"Well, unless they change the ruling, you won't be putting one in any time soon. Penn Yan, you said?"

"Uh-huh."

"At least you didn't have to deal with that miserable Vance Wexler at the Geneva Historical Society. You know, other towns and cities use planning boards for that sort of thing. Well, I suppose it doesn't matter. Mr. Wexler was killed not too long ago. That served him right for ticking off the wrong person."

Yeah, but who?

"Um, where does your building request stand now?" I asked.

"Good question. It was denied, which really surprised us since—"

She stopped in her tracks and looked both ways, almost as if she expected someone to overhear our conversation.

"Since what?"

"I shouldn't be telling you this. I don't even know who you are."

"I'm Norrie Ellington. I'm one of the owners of Two Witches Winery."

"Ah. So that explains why you live on that hill."

I nodded. "I can wager a guess. Did you give Vance Wexler some sort of payoff to look the other way? I swear, I won't tell a soul."

"Oh, we gave him a payoff, all right, and he stuck in right back in our noses. I'll say that was a damn good reason to commit murder."

Chapter 37

I couldn't believe what I had just heard. Was this woman admitting to murder? My feet felt glued to the welcome mat on her concrete porch and my mouth had suddenly become as dry as the Sahara, but somehow I was able to respond. "Betrayal is a common motive for murder. And very understandable. Very, very understandable." *Good grief. What else can I possibly say to get her to admit to murder?*

"Tell me about it. For weeks I brooded over that denial notice even though my husband told me to let it go. I even found myself fantasizing about cutting Vance's brake lines or slipping some powerful poison into his coffee. It got to the point where I had to do something."

"Oh, my gosh. You found out he was camping out at Kashong Point and smothered him?"

"Huh? What? Of course not. I convinced my husband we needed to get out of here for a few days, and those few days turned out to be over a week. We went to the Poconos. We left three days before they found Vance's body and didn't get back until a few days later. Stayed at the Cozy Cove Love Nest. Highly recommended. Every casita has its own mini indoor swimming pool and hot tub. Not to mention the Jacuzzi spa adjacent to the gas fireplace. Once we got there, I completely forgot about that denial letter."

"Um, sounds wonderful. The Poconos, I mean. Not the denial."

"Oh, it was. Trust me, honey, it was. In fact, we're booking another getaway for the fall. Please let me know how the petition turns out. Whoever came up with the idea should be congratulated. Along with the person who rid us of Vance Wexler."

"I don't suppose you have any idea who that could have been?"

She shook her head. "If I did, I'd buy them lunch."

I thanked her and trotted back to my car. In less than four minutes, I had gone from euphoria at the thought I'd found the killer to dismay when I learned I hadn't. That left the final house near Geneva on the Lake.

Like the Snow White house, this one was also on the lake side but situated farther back from the road. With its towering pine trees and mulberry bushes surrounding the place, the house's features were definitely concealed from prying neighbors, or worse yet, authoritarian compliance volunteers from the historical society.

Frankly, I failed to understand the big deal if the homeowner wanted to make a change that was not visible from the road. I pulled into the driveway, got out of the car and walked to the front door. The morning newspaper was still on the mat. Not a good sign. I picked it up and rang the bell in lieu of using the polished ring-style door knocker.

No answer. Not a surprise, given the paper on the doorstep. I rang it a second time, and still nothing. Since it was a pleasant summer morning, I thought perhaps someone in the family was around back, maybe even on the lake if they had a dock.

Determined to finish my three-house quest, I ambled around the side of the house and shouted, "Is anyone home?" Again, nothing. By now I was only a few steps from the backyard, so I continued on the concrete pathway that ran from the front door to the rear of the house.

The lawn area had been scraped to bare ground and orange spray paint in the form of a kidney-shaped design encompassed the area. A large excavation truck stood a few feet away. *So that's what this project is—a pool.* Usually, there's a building permit posted somewhere on the site, but I knew better than to look for it. It was a pending project according to Bill Coby, and one that most likely had been nixed.

My view of the lake was unobstructed and there was no sign of anyone on their dock or remotely near it. In fact, the place was about as quiet as could get. Since I'd told Cammy I'd be in the tasting room for the afternoon, I figured I'd swing by here sometime on Monday.

I walked back to the car and was about to get in when I thought of something—the mailbox. With only the number visible on the outside of the box, I assumed the name would be written on the inside lid. Sure enough, I was right. It read "Russell Sweetly and Elysse Knight Sweetly."

Hmm, looks like Robert Kurtis Sherry isn't the only R.S. I've managed to find.

It struck me odd that while I seemed to pull up murder suspects at every turn, Deputy Hickman had latched on to poor Alex and wouldn't let go. Maybe Russell Sweetly didn't take his permit denial as well as the lady from the Snow White cottage or that nice family with the tree house. Then again, maybe the murder had to do with the Porsche engine theft after all. I had two viable theories going and was bound and determined to prove one of them.

If Godfrey and I could pull off our little impersonation tomorrow, at least I'd be one step closer to getting an answer. I still didn't have what I'd like to call a plan of action once we got to the raceway, but there was plenty of time between now and early morning.

• • •

Back at the tasting room, it was customer after customer with little to no time for chatter. The good news was that we made lots of sales on our summer wines. The bad news was that I couldn't commiserate with Cammy until well after five, and by that time, all anyone wanted to do was go home.

Besides, I had a winemakers dinner to get to and I needed to shower, fix my hair, and see which of Francine's summer dresses I wanted to wear. When I got back to the house, the light on the landline was flashing and the caller ID indicated Bradley's number. In my effort to get a Safe Driver Auto Discount from my insurance company, I made it a habit to turn off my cell phone when I drove. I'm sure that made my insurance agent happy, but I wasn't so sure it had the same effect on the guy I was dating.

I tossed a handful of kibble in Charlie's dish, pulled up Bradley's number, and pushed the Talk button. Only voicemail. I'd have to try later. I left a brief message and bounded up the stairs to the shower.

The dinner was to begin at eight thirty but hors d'oeuvres would be served an hour prior. Since most wineries stayed open past five thirty in the summer months, it was customary to begin evening affairs much later.

As I towel-dried my hair and snuggled into an old spa robe, I thought about what it would be like in a few weeks when I'd return to Manhattan and my former way of life. My friends in the city were already badgering me about all sorts of events that were getting underway, wanting to know if they should go ahead and include me in the reservations. It made me realize how much I missed the pulse and excitement of living in a place where someone is always wide awake at any time of the day.

"What do you think, Charlie?" I held up one of Francine's dresses but the dog was too busy cleaning his paws. "I know. I know. The vintage midi isn't really my style, huh? How about this sleeveless sundress?" I waved a lovely print dress in front of him, and for a second he looked up. "Nah. The trouble with these sleeveless things is that it gets cold and then I'd have to cover up with an annoying shawl."

I reached into her closet and moved the hangers around until I spotted something toward the back. The price tag still hung from the ocean blue round-neck maxi dress with a pleated flair bottom. It was elegant yet not over-the-top.

"We've got a winner!" I shouted. Then I studied the dress. "Geez, I hope Francine wasn't planning on taking this back. Oh, what the heck. I'm taking the tag off, and if she puts up a fuss, I'll pay for it. I love this dress. It's the first thing of hers that doesn't have that dowdy factor going for it."

By twenty after seven, I was dressed and out the door. It was one of those perfect summer evenings with a mild breeze and low humidity.

"Be a good boy," I told Charlie. Then, to be sure, I closed his doggie door.

At least a half dozen cars were already parked in Madeline's lot when I arrived, including Don and Theo's. A placard with teal and silver balloons read *Winemakers Dinner* and a large arrow pointed to the path that led to the event.

Finger Lakes Awnings and Pavilions had really outdone themselves. The tent was spectacular—gauzy white with a subtle design element infused in the fabric. A few yards from the entrance, a string quartet played the kind of soft music that usually precedes a wedding.

Thanks for not returning this dress, Francine.

Once inside, a greeter handed me a card with my table number. Thankfully, Madeline had seated me with Don, Theo, Rosalee, and the Ipswiches. The winemakers occupied the place of honor, a dais at the front of the tent. Leandre, Rosalee's winemaker, looked as if he was in a deep conversation with our winemaker, Franz, so I simply waved as I moved past them to the table.

"Whoa," Don said. "That didn't come from your sister's closet, did it?"

I smiled. "Hard to believe, huh?"

Don pulled out the chair and I sat down.

"Madeline's got an army of waitstaff coming around with appetizers, but there's also a buffet off to your left. All sorts of summer salads, breads, and fruits. Theo and I scoped it out a few minutes ago. I wasn't planning on ruining my appetite by filling up on hors d'oeuvres, but what the heck. It's a long night. We probably won't get to the main course until nine."

With that, he stood, gave Theo a poke on the shoulder and walked directly to the buffet. Theo shrugged and motioned for me to join him. "Stephanie, Derek, and Rosalee can catch up when they get here. The Ipswiches are always notoriously late. Must come with the territory of having kids. Oh, look! Rosalee's on her way over. Might as well wait for her."

Thirty seconds later, Rosalee put a white beaded purse on her chair and announced, "What are you two waiting for? If I'm not mistaken, there's a buffet over there. At my age, I choose to eat when I can. For all anyone knows, I could be dead by morning."

Chapter 38

The first time I heard Rosalee say that, I was shocked. Now, not so much. We moseyed to the buffet table, where I helped myself to crab salad and some mini quiches. From what I could tell, the waitstaff was serving hot appetizers like bacon-wrapped shrimp and stuffed pierogis. As I looked around, I noticed the tent had filled up considerably since I arrived.

"I've got another theory," I whispered to Theo.

He and I stepped away from the buffet table to the back corner of the tent. He looked both ways and gave me a nod. "A theory or something more?"

I told him about the payoffs and how I gleaned information from two out of the three names Bill had given me.

"Holy cow. You don't waste any time, do you?"

"I can't afford to. There are two people with the initials R.S. and one of them could very well be Vance's killer. Too bad Russell Sweetly wasn't home. I might have been able to wheedle a confession out of him. I mean, *if* it was him. Now that will have to wait until Monday."

"What's wrong with tomorrow?"

"Uh, yeah. About tomorrow . . . Look, don't get freaked out, but Godfrey and I are going to snoop around one of the Porsche driver's bay at the Watkins Glen Raceway. Sort of a follow-up to where you, Don, and I left off when that truck disappeared."

Theo groaned and rolled his eyes.

"This isn't a stab in the dark," I said. "I did my homework and then some. There's a race car driver named Robert Kurtis Sherry who lives in Tonawanda, Pennsylvania. A close enough distance to have pulled off that engine heist. Think about it—R.S. Like in Vance's note we found."

"Norrie, I don't like where this is going. You really should tell Deputy Hickman."

"I will. Once I'm sure Robert Kurtis Sherry is our guy."

"That may be too late if he's dangerous. Think of all those toxic chemicals in those garages. Not to mention crowbars and—"

"Vance was suffocated, not bludgeoned to death. Whoever the killer is, he or she, although I'm pretty sure it's a *he*, prefers a less violent method to commit murder."

"Very comforting, I must say."

Just then, Stephanie and Derek arrived. One look at her sleeveless form-fitting dress and I knew she wouldn't need a pashmina, shawl, or shrug if it got colder. Her body heat would make up for it. I waved and watched as they seated themselves at our table and studied the wine bottles that had been placed there.

As I started back to our table, Theo took my elbow. "Norrie, if you *do* find incriminating evidence, don't do anything rash. Think it through."

I nodded and returned to our table. Rosalee was right about not taking anything for granted. Her salad/hors d'oeuvre plate resembled a mini Leaning Tower of Pisa anchored by a sea of capers. I guess in her mind, every meal could be a last meal.

"Quite the spread," Derek said. "Madeline certainly raised the bar for this shindig. Good thing we hold them every other year. Hmm, I wonder who's next?"

Don furrowed his brow and then spoke. "Catherine, I think." Then he looked at me. "You can pat yourself on the head, Norrie. You've made it through the year without having Steven Trobert show up."

"Shh! Bite your tongue! Bite it a dozen times! The year's not up yet. Not until Francine and Jason get back. Catherine still has a few weeks to force her son to drop everything in Maine so we can get reacquainted. Yeesh! That's the last thing I need."

Theo choked back a laugh. "It's probably the last thing Steven needs, too. He's probably doing just fine on the dating scene. The guy's a lawyer, right? Trust me, he doesn't need his mother to fix him up."

"Tell her that. And besides, I'm already dating a—Oh, my gosh. Bradley. I never got back in touch with him. Only voicemail. I don't suppose anyone here will miss me for a few minutes. I really should try him again."

A chorus of "no problem," "sure thing," and "go for it" followed. The only exception was Rosalee, who said, "Make him wait. Men enjoy a certain amount of intrigue."

Don uncorked the bottle of Summer Magic that was on our table adjacent to the five other bottles from the different wineries. Then he turned to Rosalee. "Was that intrigue or indigestion? Because Norrie's notorious for the latter."

"Cute. Very cute, guys. Enjoy the wine. I'll be back in a minute."

By now, nearly all of the tables were full and a steady line could be seen by the buffet. The hot hors d'oeuvres continued to be served by the waitstaff as I serpentined around them in an effort to exit the tent gracefully.

Once outside, I walked a few yards past the tent's entrance and started to phone Bradley when a woman rushed past me. I turned for an instant, and when I got a good look at her face I gasped. It was Jerome's mother. A stylish woman in her late sixties or maybe even early seventies. The very same woman I saw at Overlook Glen when Stephanie and I had lunch. This had to be more than coincidence.

Sorry, Bradley. We'll have to chat later.

I followed her inside the tent and frantically began to search the crowd for Jerome. An event like the winemakers dinner usually draws a wealthy crowd. And if Jerome was one of the guests, why then did he need that extra cash to keep his mouth closed about the Karmann Ghia?

Weaving in and out of the tables was easier said than done. I knew at least one attendee from each table, so when I passed by, it was inevitable I'd be dragged into a conversation or at the very least a brief greeting. By the time I got back to my own table, without ever spotting Jerome, Madeline stood from her seat at the dais and tapped on a wineglass with a fork to get everyone's attention.

"Good evening and welcome to our winemakers dinner. My husband, Richard, and I are so pleased you could join us this evening as we celebrate the skill and mastery of our winemakers. As you know, it takes three elements working in unison to produce quality wine—the soil, the weather, and the winemaker. Please welcome the president of the Seneca Lake Wine Association, Henry Speltmore, who will introduce the winemakers."

"God help us," Don whispered in my ear. "Once Henry grabs that microphone, he'll never stop. He once talked so much at a Kiwanis luncheon, it was dinnertime when he finished speaking."

I grabbed a small roll from the bread basket, tore off a piece, and began to chomp on it. Henry stood and puffed out his chest. He was a tall, formidable-looking man with wavy gray hair and deep-set lines on his brow. When he smiled, it was almost as if his mouth could reach the bottom lobes of his ears.

"Thank you, Madeline. It's my pleasure to . . ."

And that's all I heard. Don was right. The words wafted over me.

Not only could Henry speak ad nauseum, but his soft monotone voice could put a room full of insomniacs to sleep in minutes. I caught bits and pieces of the winemakers' backgrounds, coupled with anecdotal references that, for the life of me, I couldn't associate with one winemaker or another.

Finally, when Henry finished with his introduction and Madeline took the microphone from him, I returned to the land of the living and sighed. I wasn't the only one. Rosalee let out a sigh that morphed into a groan. "I could have fallen over dead at the table and Henry would still be speaking."

All of us laughed and nodded in agreement. At that instant, one of the waitstaff placed a bowl of chowder in front of me.

"It's spicy shrimp chowder," Derek said. "With jalapeños and other peppers."

The combination of hot and savory spices hit my palate and I was in heaven. "Wow. The closest I get to this kind of thing is opening a can of Campbell's clam chowder."

It seemed everyone must have felt the same way because no one spoke. They were all too busy tasting the chowder.

"If the soup's this good," Theo said, "I can't wait for the main course."

I watched as two of the waitstaff approached. "You'll have to. They're now serving the salads."

In a split second, my chowder bowl disappeared and was replaced by a stunning roasted pattypan squash salad with pomegranate, baby lettuces, and pecans. I knew I had to pace myself if I was going to enjoy the sea bass and tamarind prawn. I moved the pecans around on my plate when I thought of something.

"Rosalee, you've been around this area for a long time, do you know anything about a woman named Agnes Merryweather? She's on the board at the Geneva Historical Society."

Derek looked up from his plate. "Who's Agnes Merryweather?"

I leaned forward and kept my voice low. "She's the miserable woman who helped frame Alex Bollinger."

Rosalee crinkled her nose. "At least you didn't come right out and say I was long in the tooth. Anyway, I don't know of anyone by that name and don't ask me to call my sister, Marilyn. She's got her nose into everything and I'll be stuck with more scuttlebutt than ears of corn in Kansas. I suggest you get the gossip on Agnes firsthand at the Penn Yan Diner on Monday morning. Those old hens know everything here and in the surrounding counties."

I held back a laugh but made a mental note to add it to my list if things didn't work out as planned tomorrow. I still had the Sweetly house to revisit as well. Too bad they were in opposite directions, and Alex's time was running out.

Chapter 39

Refraining from gobbling up everything on my salad plate and reaching for another dinner roll paid off. The pan-seared Chilean sea bass in garlic and lemon sauce was unbelievable. Sure, everyone uses the expression *melted in my mouth*, but in this case, it really did.

Don kept lifting his eyes to the sky as he ate, as if paying homage to the gods. As for the rest of us, the "oohs" and "ahhs" were enough. I expected to be served the Malaysian tamarind prawn next, but instead the waitstaff brought out champagne-flavored sherbet to cleanse our palates before continuing with the evening meal.

It was almost ten and too late to try Bradley again. Sure, he'd probably be up, but who wants to be bothered late at night? As I let the crisp sherbet liquid roll around on my tongue, I scanned the tent again for Jerome. No dice. Maybe he was on the up-and-up after all, and maybe his mother's presumed wealth had nothing to do with him.

Then, just as I thought the waitstaff would begin serving our next main course, Madeline tapped a wineglass with a fork and introduced the string quartet from Ithaca College, who graciously agreed to delight us with a medley of classical favorites while we let our palates rest.

"Forget my damn palate!" Rosalee announced. "It's my butt that's had too much of a rest. I wish Madeline would serve the rest of the meal already."

"No kidding," Derek said. "Some of us have work tomorrow."

Stephanie nudged his shoulder. "I always have work with the kids. It never stops."

Derek leaned into her shoulder. He kept his voice low but it was pretty audible. "What never stops are the phone calls. Why are all these foreign car dealers asking if we've made up our minds about a Mercedes?"

"Shh. Long story. I was helping Norrie."

Derek turned to me. "You're buying a Mercedes?"

"And now, Beethoven's *Ode to Joy*." Madeline ushered the quartet to the front of the dais and took a step back.

"I'm not buying a Mercedes," I mouthed to Derek. "I'm trying to find a murderer."

"Find your guy without Stephanie. She's got enough problems," he mouthed back.

I did a mental eye roll, leaned back in my chair and listened to the music. Finally, after a few more odes and heaven knows what else, Madeline thanked the quartet and informed us the main course would continue to be served.

"Finally!" Don exclaimed. "I've been dying to try the Malaysian tamarind shrimp."

Less than a minute later, steaming plates of large seared prawns in tamarind sauce appeared in front of us.

Rosalee, who was seated next to Theo, poked him in the elbow. "What's in this stuff?"

He looked at his plate, then at her. "Tamarind pulp, from the tamarind pod, dark soy sauce and sugar for starters. I'm not sure what else. The spices can get really complicated."

Meanwhile, I stabbed one of the prawns with a fork and bit off a piece. It was beyond anything I'd tasted, and that included all sorts of amazing foods back in Manhattan. "Almost makes me want to hang around here for the next winemakers dinner," I said. Then I quickly added, "Only kidding. But seriously, this is wild."

Funny how food can make people forget whatever else is on their minds, because for a brief respite, I found myself immersed in a whole other world that didn't include Jerome, Jerome's mother, the two R.S.'s, and the late Vance Wexler. I had reached that near-Nirvana state of mind when suddenly, without warning, I heard Theo say, "Isn't that Glenda from your tasting room? It *is* Glenda. In that cascading muumuu with the paisley print. And good grief, don't tell me the woman standing behind her in the purple caftan is Zenora?"

I lifted myself from the chair so that I could peer over everyone's head. Then I clasped my hands and prayed a giant sinkhole would take me straight down to the bottom of the earth.

Please do NOT tell me this is happening. Not again. Not in public. This can't be happening again.

Zenora had made a dramatic entrance during the reading of a will a few months ago and I believe most of the attendees haven't, as yet, gotten over it. Now, she appeared again. This time at a fancy winemakers dinner.

I watched, mouth wide open, jaw jutting against my lower neck, as Glenda and Zenora flitted around the room like two possessed fireflies.

"There you are, Norrie!" Glenda rushed to our table with Zenora hovering over her. "We had to see you before it was too late."

I dropped my fork and looked at the two of them. "Too late for what?" They both spoke at once, making it impossible to follow them with my eyes. It was like a Wimbledon tennis match that had gone awry.

"Cowl-neck shawl in the tasting room—"

"Winery lab was open and we saw them—"

"Heard the winemakers first. Alan is really cute."

"Carboys, or was it carboxes?"

"Alan said rosé."

"Stop!" I pleaded. "I have no idea what you're talking about. One person at a time. Glenda, you start."

Glenda shook her entire body and took a few breaths. "I left my beautiful cowl-neck shawl in the tasting room and wanted to wear it later tonight for a little soiree Zenora and I planned to attend. Zenora and I drove back to Two Witches, but of course the tasting room was closed. Then we saw an open door at the winery lab and two cars parked in front. I figured the winemakers were working late and hoped one of them would have the key to the winery building."

By now, everyone at my table focused on Glenda as if she was about to issue a proclamation.

"Go on," I said. *Before you lose your train of thought.*

"I overhead Alan tell Herbert what a wonderful surprise it was going to be when they delivered the first sampling of our new rosé to the winemakers dinner for dessert. That's when I panicked and started shrieking."

"Yes," Zenora said. "That's exactly what she did. Alan thought Glenda saw a rat or a snake and said as much. Meanwhile, before we could do anything, the other winemaker loaded a glass jug-type thing into his car and drove off."

"A carboy," Theo said. "It's called a carboy. A glass bottle with a narrow neck for pouring liquids. We use it for tastings sometimes in lieu of opening bottles. The rosé is in a carboy because it hasn't been bottled yet. Right, Norrie?"

I nodded, too stunned to say anything else.

Glenda grabbed my shoulder and shook my upper torso. "You've got to stop them. They're going to serve that wine and people will be falling over dead on the tables. *Dead*, I tell you. That curse has reached a powerful height. Isn't that so, Zenora?"

Zenora wrung her hands and started humming. "The closer it gets to midnight, the more forceful the curse becomes. What time is it?"

Everyone except Rosalee reached for their cell phones.

"Twenty after eleven," Derek said.

Glenda released the grip she had on my shoulder. "Good, it's not too late."

Then Zenora looked at my plate. "Are those Malaysian tamarind prawns?"

I held out the plate. "Um, did you want to try one?"

Zenora shook her head. "I'm on a liquid cleanse this weekend. It goes hand in hand with the spiritual one. Then she turned to Derek. "What time did you say it was?"

"Now it's twenty-one minutes past eleven," Derek replied.

Zenora all but yanked me from my seat. "Find that wine and pour it on the ground. Hurry. The Two Witches curse isn't going to wait while you dilly-dally around."

"Um, what happens after midnight?" I asked. "Won't the rosé be safe to drink then?"

"Yes, yes." Zenora's voice got shrill and loud. "Hide it until midnight, pour it on the ground, do whatever you have to, but make sure it doesn't touch anyone's lips before that time."

"And what will you and Glenda do?"

"Our soiree can't wait, Norrie," Glenda said. "Zenora and I must leave. You can thank us later."

I turned to Theo and swallowed the salty saliva that had built up in my throat. "We've got to stall the servers and prevent them from pouring that rosé. I'll hunt down the wine while you go up to the dais and talk about something. Anything!"

Theo turned ashen. "What am I supposed to talk about?"

"Oh, for heaven's sake, just bore them. Tell them about the malolactic process in wine. That's always a snoozer."

"I, I, um, er—"

"Just do it!"

As I stood and headed for the rear of the tent, adjacent to the winery kitchen, I could hear Stephanie, Derek, Rosalee, and Don ask each other if they had a clue what was going on. Then I heard the familiar tap of Madeline's fork on a wineglass.

"And now, everyone, a very special treat from Franz Johannes, the esteemed winemaker from Two Witches Winery. He saved this as a special surprise for all of us, including the winery's owner, Norrie Ellington. We are about to taste their newest addition—a robust rosé that's bound to be unforgettable.

Unforgettable, hell. It'll be regrettable if I don't stop Franz in his tracks.

Chapter 40

I ran from the tent like a madwoman. When I glanced back at the dais, Franz was no longer seated there. I figured he had to be in their kitchen making sure the waitstaff was poised and ready to serve his latest blend.

Not if I can help it.

Granted, while I didn't actually believe in curses, or cursed wine, for that matter, I wasn't about to take a chance. The thought of festivity-goers falling down dead after consuming one of our wines was enough to get my adrenaline pumping. Besides, I'd have a heck of a time explaining this to Deputy Hickman.

The tent flap swung open with a swish from my hand and I started for the kitchen. In the background, I heard Theo's voice. "Ladies and gentlemen, before we taste the Two Witches Rosé, I thought it would be interesting to provide you with some background on that particular wine."

Boy, am I going to owe him big-time.

Beads of sweat poured down my cheeks as I thundered toward Billsburrow Winery's kitchen. Inside, the master chef was examining the desserts and snapping his fingers. Franz stood over two large carboys that contained a lovely pinkish liquid.

"You can't serve this!" I shouted. Then I literally threw myself on top of one of the carboys and flung my arm out to block anyone from approaching the other one.

Franz looked stricken. "Did someone tamper with the carboy?" Then he continued to spout in German. *"Mist! Ich glaub mich knutscht ein Elch!"*

"No, the wine is fine. I'm sure the rosé is lovely. We just can't drink it. Not now. Not for at least—" I looked around the kitchen and spied a wall clock. "Ten minutes. At least ten minutes."

"I'm not sure I understand, but Herbert brought the other carboy into the tent a few minutes ago. From the side flap nearest to the caterer's van."

"Oh, no! We have to wait at least ten minutes."

Franz furrowed his brow and shuddered. "It's wine, not beer. We don't have to wait for foam to settle."

By now I was halfway out the door and on my way back to the tent. "Not foam," I shouted. "A witch's curse."

I stormed back inside the tent and watched, horrified, as the servers began to fill wineglasses from one of the carboys and deliver the trays to the tables. Meanwhile, I could hear Theo droning on.

"And so, we can thank the ancient Greeks, who had the foresight to bring wine and vines to southern France when they founded the city of Marseilles . . ."

Without wasting a second, I rushed to the front of the dais and said, "Yes, the ancient Greeks. And together we will toast them and our hosts at Billsburrow Winery." Then I whispered to Theo, "Keep talking for five more minutes."

I worried that Theo might run out of things to say, but I had my own problems. I had to prevent the servers from placing the filled wineglasses on the tables. Like an owl after a field mouse, I moved my head in every which direction to locate the servers.

The first one was a few tables to my left and I all but tackled her. The tray fell, the wineglasses broke, and I sheepishly muttered, "Oops." Then I was off to the only other wine server I saw in the tent—a tall, lanky young man who reminded me of an English butler.

Look out! This ain't Downton Abbey.

Making a mad dive to extricate the tray from his hand, my dress caught on the bottom of one of the chairs, and when the guest pulled the chair closer to the table, I heard the unmistakable sound of fabric being ripped apart.

Oh, no. Francine's dress. Francine's dress with the price tag still on it because I didn't remove it after all. I am so dead.

There was no time to look down and assess the damage. I took hold of the tray and said, "I insist." The server didn't try to stop me, but instead backed off and held his hands as if in surrender once I got hold of the tray.

"And so you see," Theo continued, "the color of the rosé can range from onion-skin orange to deeper pink hues. Transparent to mulled."

Suddenly, I heard Rosalee's voice. "Enough, Theo! Quit describing it and start serving it. We could all be dead by the time you stop talking. This isn't a filibuster."

It had to be past midnight but I wasn't sure. Not without checking my iPhone, but unfortunately *that* was in my bag at the table. Then I realized it would take a few minutes to get the wineglasses on the table and inform Franz we needed those other carboys. The guests were safe.

"Thank you, Mr. Buchman," I shouted as I motioned for the lanky server to take hold of the tray again. He approached me slowly, almost as if he expected me to snap at him or something.

"It's okay," I said, keeping my voice low. "Serve the rosé."

By now, Franz had arrived back at the tent followed by two servers with trays of our wine. Madeline, who looked somewhat shell-shocked, returned to the dais. "And now, the culminating event of the evening, Two Witches Rosé complemented by our heavenly dessert medley—assorted seasonal berries, fruit tarts, mini-strawberry cheesecakes, and of course, our signature chocolate cake. Thank you, everyone, for making this event such a success."

I returned to our table with the hem of Francine's dress in shreds and took my seat.

"Were you trying to impersonate one of the Marx Brothers?" Derek asked. "Because for a while, you gave Harpo and Groucho a run for their money."

"Just a little snafu with the rosé but everything's fine." I lifted my head and glanced around the tent. No one keeled over. "I wanted to be sure it was served at the right temperature."

"Well, it's perfect," Stephanie said. "Absolutely perfect." She took the tiniest piece of cake and a few of the summer berries. "I need to compliment Madeline. Care to join me, Norrie?"

Stephanie stood and I immediately followed. Madeline was seated on the dais but Stephanie walked to a less crowded corner of the tent.

"I wanted to ask you what you found out about that car engine but Derek overhears everything and overreacts."

I gave her the abridged version and added, "If we don't mess things up, Godfrey and I will finagle our way into one of the bays at the raceway tomorrow. I think I know where Vance's engine wound up."

"You mean who killed him and stole it?"

"Not sure about the murder part, but the theft, maybe."

"You'd better be really careful, Norrie. You don't know who you're dealing with."

"I'll have Godfrey with me. Maybe he can bring along a tarantula or something."

Stephanie blanched.

"Relax, I'm only kidding. Look, we should go over to Madeline so we don't raise any suspicions as far as your husband is concerned. He's probably furious you went with me to those car dealers."

"Actually, he was relieved I didn't purchase anything. By the way, what *was* that hubbub with the wine? Room temperature my butt."

"Long story. The curse was a two-parter but we circumvented it."

"You really believe that stuff? You're as bad as my twins."

"Oh, I don't believe it, but why take the chance?"

When we got back to our table, everyone was finishing up. Rosalee announced that if she stayed seated any longer, she'd need to soak her hemorrhoids in a sitz bath. Her comment resulted in the fastest exit any table made from a wine trail gala.

As Don, Theo, and I strolled to the parking lot we kept our voices low. There were wine patrons all over the place, and the last thing we needed was for some stray comment to wind up on a Twitter feed. It wasn't until we neared our cars that Don said, "Remember that guy I said looked familiar at Port of Call? The one who told Vance to watch his back?"

I moved closer to Don. "Ruddy complexion? Outdoorsy?"

"Uh-huh. Don't make a scene, but that's him to your right. Thanks to Madeline's outdoor lighting, I can see every detail of his face. I finally remembered why he looked familiar. He was in front of me at the DMV last month. Had a conniption fit about having to pay the extra twenty-five bucks for the enhanced travel license. I thought he was going to lean over and punch the man behind the desk."

"Yeesh. I only saw him that once, when we were all at Port of Call and he got into it with Vance. Over his request to build a swimming pool. Oh, my gosh! That guy could be Russell Sweetly. You know, one of the three people I had to track down. He wasn't home but there was a backhoe in his backyard and the layout for the pool was spray-painted on the ground."

"Looks like whoever he is, he's a loose cannon. Best to keep away."

"You don't suppose he's our killer, do you?"

Don shook his head. "Nah. These explosive types don't wait until the middle of the night. And they don't come prepared with chloroform."

Chapter 41

"I wish we could find out if Vance stiffed him over the swimming pool permit, but if he's that unhinged, I'm not so sure I want to get into a conversation with him on Monday."

"Then don't," Don said. "I'm sure we can think of another way to find out if Vance pulled a quick one over him."

"I suppose. Anyway, we might as well call it a night. Godfrey's picking me up really early tomorrow. Maybe we'll have better luck if Robert Kurtis Sherry turns out to be our guy."

"You mean *your murderer*?"

"Engine thief, murderer . . ."

Theo looked at Don. Then back to me. "You know we're both really uncomfortable with this. At the very least, you're dealing with a sophisticated car thief who had the wherewithal to swap out a rare and expensive Porsche engine. Wait. Not car thief. Thieves. As I recall, there were three of them. And if those guys were responsible for killing Vance, who knows what they'll do if someone rats them out tomorrow."

"That's right," Don said. "Do you and Godfrey have a calculated plan of action in the event you discover the truth?"

In the past, whenever Godfrey came to my rescue, it was by the seat of his pants. Like pretending he had a container of dangerous bees when he was merely transporting ladybird beetles for relocation.

I gulped. "More like an ever-developing, malleable plan."

"That's reassuring. Look, just make sure your cell phones are charged, okay?"

"Don't worry. No one's going to do anything to us in front of a zillion people. It's not like we're going to snoop around in some dark alley." *It'll be in some garage bay where no one can hear me scream with all that engine noise.*

Theo put his arm on my shoulder. "Sure you want to do this?"

"Uh-huh. I think Godfrey and I are Alex's only hope."

When I turned in for the night, my mind was on overdrive. Little snippets of information bounced back and forth as I tried to pull them all together. Too bad I wasn't writing a mystery, or worse yet, a horror screenplay. Russell Sweetly's temper, Jerome's flimsy explanation about the dock incident, and Agnes's false accusation. Throw in that engine swap and I'd have fodder for a few screenplays.

At least I managed to stave off that curse thanks to Glenda, Zenora, and Theo. Frankly, I was fine letting it ride until 2062. I didn't want to end the curse by killing off the last Crackstone descendant. The mere thought of it gave me the willies. Still, I was curious to learn who was at the end of the family line.

No wonder I couldn't fall asleep. I was too tired to read and too exhausted to do anything physical like clean the house or bake cookies. Instead, I tossed from side to side to the extent that Charlie got annoyed and slept on the floor. Sometime after three, I fell asleep. I know it was after three because the last time I looked at the alarm clock it read 2:41.

At precisely 4:48, the alarm went off. Dazed, I dragged myself into the shower and brushed my teeth. It was such an obscene hour that even the dog refused to get up. By five thirty I was dressed and fumbling to make my first cup of coffee. Charlie finally made his way out the doggie door, returned a few minutes later, and devoured the kibble I poured for him.

• • •

Godfrey and I agreed that if we were going to pull off this impersonation stunt, we'd have to look the part—professional and all business. That meant no jeans or T-shirts. I'd chosen a white button-down top that went nicely with my dark gray linen slacks, but I still opted to wear ankle boots since Watkins Glen Raceway was notorious for muddy surfaces. As I glanced down at my top, I wondered if I would have been better off with a darker color. Too late—Godfrey was at the door.

I ushered him in and motioned to the table. "Want a cup of coffee? It's early. We've got plenty of time. I've got a box of Entenmann's donuts, too."

"Can't refuse that. Tell me, how did the dinner go? Spectacular, I bet."

"We circumvented the latter part of that curse and the food was amazing, so yeah, overall it was a good evening."

Godfrey bit into a chocolate donut and washed it down with a gulp of coffee. "You don't sound convincing."

"Oh, no. That part *was* fine. It's just all the other stuff."

Then I told him about Russell and what Don had said about the guy's short fuse.

"Yeah, best to keep a distance. This whole thing's a tangled mess, that's for sure. Maybe we can unravel some of it today. Might as well get going, huh?"

I rinsed out our coffee cups, put them in the drainer and stashed the donut box back in the pantry. Last thing I needed was Charlie getting into them.

"If you don't mind," Godfrey said, "I'd rather drive. I've seen you behind the wheel before."

You don't know the half of it.

"Fine. Let's go."

The sun was at the horizon, providing enough light for me to get a good look at the car—a dark four-door sedan with a metallic banner on the side that read *New York State Agricultural Department.*

"An official state vehicle? You're driving an official state vehicle?"

"I always take the state vehicle when I'm on business."

"You're really getting into this, aren't you?"

"I have to. We're running out of options."

"Geez, I just hope they'll believe you when we get to the gate."

Godfrey smiled. "They won't have to. I've got us another way into the raceway. Come on, get in the car and I'll tell you about it."

No sooner had I buckled my seat belt than Godfrey explained he was in possession of campground passes and three-day tickets to the event.

"Huh?" I was flabbergasted. "How'd you manage that?"

"Remember Arvin Pincus? He was supposed to oversee the Kashong Point project along with Alex but got poison oak from that spider mite study."

"Um, yeah. What about Arvin?"

"Turns out he bought three-day passes to the raceway as well as a campground permit. I had no idea. I called him yesterday to ask about his schedule for the week and he moaned and groaned about his poison oak and how he had to lose out on his weekend at the raceway. Long story short, he gave me the passes."

"Passes? As in plural?"

"Yeah. His fiancée wasn't about to go without him. I offered to compensate him but he refused when I explained what we were up to. Said he'd do anything to get Alex off the hook."

"That's fantastic. We can get in without a hitch."

"Into the raceway and the campground, yeah. But the bays where the drivers work on their cars are a different story. To be honest, I'd rather take my chances climbing fences and skirting under those track tunnels than giving false information at the gate."

Climbing fences and skirting under tunnels? Now he tells me. There's no way around it, I'm going to ruin another one of Francine's outfits.

Chapter 42

Godfrey handed me the lanyard with my three-day pass on it. I put it around my neck and watched him do the same as we approached the attendant at the gate. I looked down at the ticket and saw the notation that read "Reserved Camping Area G."

"Need another map or are you okay?" the attendant asked Godfrey.

"Might as well grab another map. These things have a way of disappearing."

"Sure thing."

As soon as we pulled away from the gate, Godfrey reached over and I took the map. "Guess I'd better figure out where the bays are located, huh?"

"Good idea, Norrie. I'll park in the general admission area and we can go from there."

"Hold on. Don't park in general admission. We've got tickets to a reserve area that's near the paddocks where the bays are located. I can see it clearly on the map. All we need to do is take the pedestrian tunnel and we'll be within a stone's throw of those bays."

"Got it."

The tunnel was located between raceway turns three and four, also known as the *esses*, and although it looked like a short distance on the map, it wasn't. At least Godfrey had the foresight to carry bottled water in an over-the-shoulder specimen bag. It was one of those summer days that started out with mild humidity but I knew what was coming. I'd be sticky, sweaty, and smelly in no time. Thankfully it wasn't raining. From what I've been told, it wasn't a race at Watkins Glen without at least one downpour.

"Hey, there's a restroom off to the left. I'm going to use it because who knows when the next opportunity will come along."

Godfrey nodded. "Okay. Meet you back here in a minute or two."

I absolutely abhor public restrooms. Especially restrooms at venues like concerts, races, and amusement parks. The fact it was fairly early in the day gave me hope that the place wouldn't be too gross.

A few cars were running practice laps as Godfrey and I rejoined each other and trudged past the displays and vendor section on our way to the paddocks. I elbowed Godfrey. "Remind me never to use a public restroom again."

"Really bad?"

"Worse than that."

"Ugh."

The whishing noise as the cars passed us was deafening and I couldn't imagine what it would sound like when all of them were on the track. According to the schedule, the race was to begin at three p.m., and while that seemed like ample time to snoop around, I worried something would go wrong.

"I can see the pit terrace from here," Godfrey said. "Looks like the garages are to its right, behind the south paddock."

I squinted. "All I can see is the grandstand."

"Look just past it. On the right."

"Wow. That fence looks more intimidating than the proposed border wall with Mexico."

Godfrey studied the scene in front of us. "Let me take a look at the map for a second. Hmm, I may have found a chink in the armor. There's a media center to our left and just beyond it is the back of a garage. If we can get into that area without getting caught, we may have a good chance of tracking down the Porsche that's registered to Kurtis Sherry."

There was a moderate crowd in the vendor area and we moved along at a decent clip. When we reached the media area, the sign in front indicated access only with appropriate credentials. A handful of men stood off to the side looking at what appeared to be a printout of something.

Small beads of sweat trickled down my neck. "Those must be reporters. Or sports editors. I don't suppose Cornell's entomology journal qualifies, huh?"

"No," Godfrey said, "but this might."

Before I got the chance to ask him what he had in mind, he motioned for one of the men to approach.

"Excuse me, I'm with the state agricultural department. Entomology to be more specific." Immediately, he whipped out his official identification and held it up. "I was supposed to confer with a Mr. Bardslow regarding some brown recluse spiders that were found in the building but we must have crossed paths. Any idea where my colleague and I can find him?"

"Did you say *brown recluse*?" one of the reporters asked. "Those suckers are dangerous. Flesh-eating if I recall correctly."

Godfrey nodded. "Uh-huh. That's why my department was contacted. I drew the short straw and had to give up my weekend."

"I work for the Associated Press so I'm not familiar with the management here," the man said, "but go inside and ask around. Show the raceway official your state ID and he'll take it from there."

The man unlatched the gate and ushered us into the compound. Another car whished by but I was pretty sure I heard Godfrey thank him.

"I thought you weren't going to pull the entomologist card," I whispered when we were out of earshot.

"What can I say? Sometimes we have to work with the gifts we have."

"Oh, brother."

"Hurry up, while no one's looking. There's a direct access to the bays from the side of the media center. Next time get your producer in Toronto to issue you a press pass."

"Right. What am I going to tell Renee? That I'm researching the love interests of race car drivers?"

"You've done worse."

"Don't remind me."

Godfrey took the lead across the walkway that connected the media center to the large paddock area with garages and bays. The sound of drills, air compressors, and hammers combined with the raceway noise to create an irritating cacophony.

"There are nine Porsche drivers," I said as we approached the first bay. "I wish I could remember what Kurtis Sherry looked like. I was so overtired when I pulled up that information online, I didn't pay too much attention to any of the photos. Besides, the drivers all looked the same—fit thirty-something men with close-cropped mustaches and beards."

"It doesn't matter. We'll find him. Someone's bound to know which bay he's using. We'll ask the first person we—"

"What? What's wrong?" I asked.

"If I'm not mistaken, isn't that Deputy Hickman over there conferring with a Schuyler County deputy? He's not in uniform like the other guy, but that's him, all right. Grizzly as ever."

"Oh, hell, no. It *is* him. What's he doing here? The man doesn't strike me as someone interested in car races. Or any other form of entertainment, for that matter."

Godfrey grabbed me by the wrist and we ducked behind three large trash barrels filled with icky automotive stuff and lots of empty coffee cups. "Maybe he's following up on that lead you gave him. You know, the key chain."

I shook my head. "He wouldn't even take it to check for prints. So now what?"

"We wait until he leaves. He can't stand around and gab forever."

Famous last words. For a man who was all business, Deputy Hickman certainly took his time yakking with that other deputy. Then again, it could have been business. But what? My back began to ache from being hunched over behind those trash barrels and my knees stiffened from the awkward position I was in.

"They're heading past the front lineup of bays," Godfrey said. "You can stand up, but don't move. Wait until they're out of sight."

"This is like my worst nightmare. If I didn't know any better, I'd swear the guy was tracking me."

"Okay, we're good. But walk slowly."

We took a few tentative steps until we were certain Deputy Hickman was a good ways ahead of us. Still, I kept an eye out for Dumpsters and large trash receptacles that we could use in the event Grizzly Gary doubled back.

Again, Godfrey grabbed me by the wrist. "What do you plan on asking Kurtis once we find him? Or do you plan on winging it?"

"I was hoping something brilliant would occur to me once I was face-to-face with him."

He rubbed one of his temples and moaned as we kept walking. Two men with oil-stained coveralls passed us and nodded. We nodded back. Then Godfrey pointed to a bay on his left. "Something brilliant, huh? Good luck."

I stepped in front of him and walked into the garage. Sure enough, a guy who looked like the proverbial poster child for a race car driver was standing behind the rear of the car peering into the engine. On the front left-hand side, another man was inflating one of the tires.

"Um, excuse me," I said. "I'm looking for Kurtis Sherry."

The man flashed a million-dollar smile and I wondered if he had veneers. "At your service, but fans aren't allowed back here. How'd you get past security?"

"Oh, we're not fans. I mean, we *are* fans, but we're not here as fans." *Can I possibly babble any worse than a high school sophomore?* "We're here on official county business. Investigating the murder of Vance Wexler." *Oh, no. Impersonating an officer of the law. I think that's a felony.*

Kurtis shrugged and had a perplexed look on his face. "I'm sorry. I don't know anyone by that name."

"Then maybe you'd know him by the Porsche 911 Carrera RS two-point-seven engine you've got under your hood."

"Not me," Kurtis said. "I'm running with an RSR Turbo. Made it through the qualifying round without a hitch. Now all I need to do is beat the 1974 record at Le Mans."

"An RSR Turbo, you said?"

Kurtis gave a nod, looked down, and actually smiled at the engine.

So much for brilliance. I'm back at square one.

I backed out of the garage, all but bumping into Godfrey. "Sorry for your trouble. Good luck this afternoon."

We were on the macadam in front of the garage when the man who was inflating the tire called out to us, "Hey, if you're looking for a Carrera RS two-point-seven, you might try Augie Lennox, three or four bays down. I heard he was racing with a two-point-seven."

"Is he the only one?" Godfrey asked.

"Only one I know of."

"Thanks!" I shouted. "Good luck!"

Chapter 43

"Augie Lennox didn't even appear on my radar," I said to Godfrey when we were six or seven yards past Kurtis's garage. "I can't even remember where he was from. Tennessee? Alabama? Someplace in the south. And how would he have a connection with Vance?"

"Only one way to find out. Come on. We can't afford to dawdle around."

"I think I'm going to try a different approach when we find him."

Godfrey laughed. "Can't be any worse than what you've done already."

We were now a few feet away from the fourth bay down. The two garages we passed belonged to Trina Matthews and Connor Prendergast. Had I been observant in the first place, I would have noticed the *Official Use* sign tacked to the side of the building with the race car driver's name on it. At least Godfrey paid attention.

I peered into the garage and turned to Godfrey. "This doesn't make sense, you know. Augie Lennox."

Just then, I heard a raspy voice, and in that split second I knew where I'd heard it before. This time, I was the one who grabbed Godfrey by the wrist.

"Shh. That grating voice. Inside the garage. It's one of the car thieves."

"Are you sure?"

"Uh-huh. It's the kind of irritating voice you can't forget. Theo and I heard him when we staked out that barn behind Glen Foreign Motors. The guy was talking with someone named Billy and another guy we called 'ladder guy' because they never called him by name."

"Maybe now would be the time to let the sheriff's office do their job. I say we either find Deputy Hickman and his counterpart from Schuyler County or call one of their offices."

"Are you nuts? We'll be the ones who are arrested. Trespass for one thing. Besides, we need definitive proof. And this time, I may have a plan that really works."

I never gave Godfrey a chance to respond. I walked directly into the garage and stood there, mouth open wide, as the raspy-voiced man and the one I'd nicknamed "ladder guy" were at opposite ends of the gleaming vintage Porsche 911 Carrera, checking tire pressure.

"I'm looking for Augie Lennox," I said. "It's important I speak with him."

"He left a few minutes ago to grab something to eat," the ladder guy said. "Should be back in a bit. You guys with the press?"

Before I could answer, a third man walked in and this time I didn't have to rely on a voice to recognize him. It was Billy. Billy from under the engine in that barn. "Damn latrines," he said. "They're overflowing like usual. Should have used one of the Port-O-Potties. Oops. Didn't expect company." He looked directly at Godfrey and me. Then squinted and scratched the back of his head. "Do I know you folks?"

"They came to see Augie," the ladder guy said. Then he wiped his hands on his jeans and sighed. "Augie's under a hell of a lot of pressure. Not a good time to interview him. Tell you what, give us your names and we'll pass it along."

I glanced at the workbench to the right of the car and bit my lower lip. Behind a wad of greasy rags, a small brown glass bottle was wedged between some tin cans. At first I thought it might have been cough medicine, but then I remembered Godfrey's description of the chloroform bottle from Alex's lab. I tried to sound nonchalant but my heart was pumping like crazy. "Um, sure thing. But maybe one of you can answer something for us. Is that a Carrera RS two-point-seven?"

"Damn straight it is," he said. His response, coupled with the bottle of chloroform, left no doubt in my mind—Godfrey and I were standing in front of three murderers.

That instant I felt my phone vibrate in my pocket. I pulled it out and saw the incoming call was from Theo. I was tempted to let it go to voicemail, but since Augie wasn't in the garage and he was the player I needed to make my plan work, I decided to get the heck out of there. Godfrey and I were no match for three well-built men who were used to wielding heavy tools, and if I was right, smothering someone in their sleep.

I stepped back and held the phone in front of me. "Got to take this call. We'll check in later."

Without wasting a second, I turned and exited the garage with Godfrey a few feet behind. "It's Theo," I said. Then I answered his call.

"What's up? Whatever it is, we've got you beat. We found the three guys from the barn. They're on the pit crew for a race car driver named Augie Lennox. Godfrey and I have to find a way to stop the race."

"What?" Godfrey shouted in my free ear. "Stop the race?"

"Shh," I whispered to him. "I need to find out why Theo called."

Theo's voice was louder than usual. "I heard you. And I called because we made a mistake."

"About the three men?"

"No, about Vance's notes. Don and I went over them again. Remember that night when we looked through them at the house? Don mentioned Vance's copier being low on toner. Well, lack of toner means some letters and words are really light or missing. We didn't catch it at the time but we did just now. That R.S., as in the R.S. with the restraining order, isn't R.S. at all. It's B.S. Don was able to get a better look."

"B.S.? Are you serious? You mean I wasted all my time looking for an R.S. connected to today's race? And worse yet, pinpointing poor Kurtis Sherry? And, oh, no. I also had Russell Sweetly fingered. But now you're telling me they don't belong on my suspect list?"

"All I'm telling you is that the person Vance thought would get even isn't an R.S. It's a—"

"I know. Someone whose first name starts with B. Aargh."

"Hey, don't get in a total tizzy. Don and I went through the names associated with building requests that Vance turned down and there was no one with that first initial in those notes of his. But get this—not all of the notes dealt with historical society stuff. Vance used that personal sounding-off file of his to blow steam about all sorts of folks who ticked him off."

As Theo and I continued to banter over the phone, Godfrey nudged me. "Norrie! Think! You told me one of those men in that garage is named Billy. Duh! You've got your answer. Now, can we please call the sheriff's office?"

I've heard of cars not firing on all cylinders, but this time it wasn't a car. It was my brain. I was so obsessed with the thought of starting over on my search that I completely ignored the one important clue that stared me in the face—Billy. Billy whoever-he-was had to be the person Vance was concerned would get even.

"Good grief, Theo," I said. "Did you hear Godfrey? That's definitive proof, isn't it? All the more reason for me to stop this race. Gotta run."

I ended the call, stashed the phone back in my pocket and looked directly at Godfrey. "It's a stolen engine, for crying out loud. Stolen by Vance's killers. Even if we do find Deputy Hickman, he's only going to pooh-pooh it."

"As opposed to what? Making an accusation that could result in absolute chaos at this raceway? What do you propose to do? Stand in front of the starting gate or whatever they call it?"

"Don't be ridiculous. We just have to find Augie Lennox and let him take it from there."

"Take it from where?" came a booming voice behind me. "I'm Augie Lennox."

I swear I never spun my head around so fast in my life. Augie Lennox looked nothing like the other thirty-something race car drivers. With golden red hair framing his face and freckles on his nose and cheeks, he appeared to be more of a Disney character than a seasoned race car driver.

Without wasting a second, I reached into the side pocket opposite from where I had put my iPhone, pulled out the key chain, and dangled it in front of him. "This look familiar?"

"Where did you find that?"

"Never mind where I found it, if you don't tell me the truth about that engine in the Porsche you're about to race, the next time you get behind the wheel of a car will be twenty or thirty years from now when they release you from prison."

"Prison? Who are you people? And for your information, the Carrera two-point-seven *is* my engine."

"Then why did those three men in your garage steal it from a Karmann Ghia and kill the owner?"

"Oh, crap. I knew I should have flown up here sooner."

"So you know about the car theft and the murder."

Augie winced and rubbed the back of his neck. "Humrph. I knew it was too good to be true when he offered to do me a favor."

"Who? Vance or the guy who killed him?"

"Hey, it's a long story and I've got a race to run, so—"

"Hey! Augie! Thought I heard your voice. We've got to get moving if you expect to be in the starting lineup. You can gab with the reporters later."

Augie turned to Billy, who was standing a few feet away, before returning his gaze to us. "Reporters? Just what this country needs—more fake news."

"Come on," Billy said, "we don't have all day."

I poked Godfrey in the arm. "Neither do we. Let's get moving."

Chapter 44

"Godfrey, listen up. We've got to find the track officials and put the kibosh on Augie Lennox and his crew. That was a chloroform bottle I spied on their workbench. And before you tell me it's a solvent for removing grease, I'll tell you what I know. That stuff isn't supposed to be used. Oh, sure, it can be used in your lab for insect stomach removal or whatever the heck that was, but it's supposedly off the market for consumer use."

"It's certainly evidence. I'll give you that much."

"Holy crap. What's the quickest route to the grandstand? That's where the lineup begins, right?"

Godfrey shrugged. "I'm not all that familiar with motor sports if you must know the truth, but yeah, the main grandstand makes sense. We're in the paddock area behind the media building. According to the map, the pit area and front stretch grandstand are to our left."

"We'd better hurry. I don't even know what time it is but Billy was in a rush."

"It's only one forty-five."

"One forty-five?" I practically shrieked. "The race starts at three. They'll be lining up any minute now. Yeesh. I can't believe it's one forty-five already. It took us forever to trek around this place."

"Yeah, well, it's a mega raceway, not the local amusement park."

"Just point me in the right direction, and so help me, if I hear the words *Ladies and gentlemen, start your engines*, I'll heave."

"Uh, I believe the command is now 'Drivers, start your engines.'"

"Whatever. I'm not going to let them get away with this. And I'm not referring to Vance's unfortunate demise, I'm talking about Alex's."

"Gotcha. But one more thing. Promise me you won't do anything to disrupt the race or make a blazing spectacle out of us. I'm a tenured research entomologist and I intend to keep it that way."

"No problem."

Godfrey motioned me to follow him as he hugged the fence that separated the bays and media building from the track. Unfortunately, he wasn't alone. Throngs of raceway aficionados flooded the area. It was as if they came out of nowhere along with their kids. And not just kids. They came with kid paraphernalia—strollers, baskets that turned into strollers, and small rolling carts filled with God knows what.

I'm going to put off parenthood indefinitely.

Then there were the handholding couples who wouldn't dare let go of each other to let us pass by, not to mention the packs of teens and the guys who just turned twenty-one. Easy to differentiate. The legal drinkers held up their beer cans like trophies.

A few cars were on the track but a quick look told me they weren't the race cars. Godfrey mentioned official track cars checking the road surface and things like that, but I didn't pay attention. I was focused on getting to the pit area, where I could convince whoever was in charge to prevent Augie Lennox from racing. In retrospect, I would have had better luck launching the space shuttle.

"There's a break in the crowd," Godfrey announced. "But don't get your hopes up. We'd have to get over the two fences that separate us from the track. And before you say *climb them*, take another look. They've got hardware cloth wrapped around them. Impossible to get a foothold."

"You can hoist me over. I don't weigh that much. All I want to do is inform one of those men what's going on. It'll be simple. He'll radio to whoever's in charge and they'll be forced to talk with us and confront Augie and his crew. It's not as if we can go straight to the top, so to speak, because we don't know where or who the top is."

Godfrey groaned and looked in both directions. "Okay. Fine. Might as well get it over with. But I can only get you past one fence. The rest is up to you."

"Wait! I don't think you'll need to boost me over the fence. There's a gate a few yards away."

There was a gate, all right. And it was guarded by Hagrid's dog. Okay, fine. Maybe the guy wasn't quite as intimidating but he was formidable enough. At least six foot tall and no stranger to bench pressing weights.

I gave Godfrey a quick tap on the arm and raced to the gate. Still panting, I looked directly at the guy. "I need to get inside the fence and speak with one of the officials. It's urgent."

The man gave me a cursory look and turned to face the track. "You have to wait with the rest of the press in the media area," he said with his back facing away from me. That was the instant I realized the gate wasn't locked and he wasn't looking. I shoved it open with a kick and an elbow before running between the two fence lines. The hum of engine motors from the track vehicles drowned out his words but I could pretty much ascertain what he was yelling about.

Without bothering to answer, I charged ahead. Two men were leaning over the fence a few feet away from the track. Both of them had radios pressed to their ears, and in my mind it couldn't get any more official than that. I immediately shook the nearest shoulder and the guy spun around in a nanosecond.

"You're off-limits," he said. "Don't know who let you in but you need to return to the grandstand."

Just then, the announcer's voice blared, "Drivers, begin lining up in position. Drivers, begin lining up in position."

I had every intention of providing a clear, succinct explanation of events leading up to my discovery regarding Augie Lennox's crew. Unfortunately, the minute I heard "begin lining up," words spewed out of my mouth like a geyser. And they didn't just spew.

I screamed, "Stolen engine . . . murderers . . . Vance Wexler . . . chloroform . . . Augie Lennox, but not him, I don't think, his crew . . ."

"Whoa, whoa," one of the men said. "Slow down. How much have you been drinking?"

"I'm not drunk, you moron! I'm telling you that one of the pit crews murdered someone and I can prove it. They stole the guy's engine, too. Listen, you have to contact the officials and stop this race."

"No one's stopping the race," the other guy said. "You can wait in Hospitality and have a nice chat with one of our deputies once we call security."

"I don't want a nice chat with one of your deputies. I want the men responsible for committing a crime to be arrested."

My words fell on deaf ears, and it didn't look as if I had any other options. That was the moment Godfrey shouted from his side of the fence. He was out of breath from running but that didn't stop him from bellowing, "Who knows what they could have done with their engine!"

In that second, one of the men got on his radio and the next announcement I heard was, "The lineup is delayed by thirty minutes. Repeat—the lineup is delayed by thirty minutes."

"Find me the nearest track official," I said. But before either of the men could answer, a sheriff's cruiser with his red and blue lights flashing made its way to the grandstand.

"There's your nearest official," the first guy said. "Stay put until your escort arrives."

Godfrey held up his hands and shrugged from the other side of the fence while I stood motionless waiting to be taken into custody. Minutes later, we were seated in a restricted security area not far from the pit terrace and media area.

A lone deputy sheriff paced back and forth shaking his head. "Once again, if you don't mind. From the top."

I pinched back my shoulder blades and groaned. "We already explained. And we wrote down statements for you. We have undeniable evidence that one of the race car drivers and his crew was involved in grand theft auto and murder."

The deputy shook his head. "A bottle of chloroform on a workbench in a garage is not evidence of theft. Unless it was *your* chloroform bottle. And as for murder, what evidence should I be looking at?"

In my wildest imagination I never thought I'd mutter the following words, "Call Deputy Gary Hickman from Yates County. He's at this race. Someone in your office is bound to have his number. He knows what's going on."

The call to Deputy Hickman took less than five minutes, but I figured I must have hit a nerve with the Schuyler County deputy because the next announcement coming from the raceway was loud and clear: "There is another thirty-minute delay until lineup. Repeat— another thirty-minute delay until lineup."

I turned to Godfrey, who was seated next to me on a wooden bench, and whispered, "Finally. They're taking us seriously."

Godfrey whispered back, "Don't get your hopes up. My money is on county lockup. That's where they'll take us."

Chapter 45

"Miss Ellington!" The deputy's voice cut through the room like a razor. "God forbid I get to enjoy a day off."

"You'll thank me. Honestly, you will."

Deputy Hickman rubbed his chin with such force I thought he'd scrape the skin off. Then he pulled a wooden chair close to the bench where Godfrey and I were seated. "I'm reading the notes the Schuyler County deputy handed me but I'll need more. Start at the beginning."

I always thought the expression *start at the beginning* was reserved for old 1940s crime movies, but apparently not. For the next seven or eight minutes, Godfrey and I told him about Augie recognizing the key chain and the absolute positive ID I had on those three guys in his pit crew.

"Augie knew Vance," I said. "He pretty much admitted as much. Don't you see? They were all in cahoots."

Deputy Hickman looked at his watch. "That may or may not be the case, but no one is in imminent danger and there's no reason the race can't go on as usual." With that, he stood and walked over to the Schuyler County deputy. While they talked, the announcer came on again. This time to get the race underway.

When Deputy Hickman returned, he held out his hand. "Guess I'll need that little key chain you've been carrying after all."

I turned it over without saying a word.

"Thank you, Miss Ellington. And now, if you don't mind, the Schuyler County deputies and I will take it from here."

"Does that mean you're going to arrest Augie and that pit crew? Does it mean you're going to release Alex?"

He shook his head. "It means . . . you need to go back home and let us proceed without any further interference."

"But, but—"

"Miss Ellington, these county deputies can have you arrested for disturbing the peace. And trespass as well, unless those tickets the both of you are wearing are legitimate."

"They are. Arvin Pincus gave them to us. He's an entomologist in Dr. Klein's office. Got poison oak."

Deputy Hickman closed his eyes and took a deep breath. "I see.

Now, before either of you say or do anything that would give anyone reason to detain you further, I suggest you return home. Am I clear?"

Godfrey and I nodded simultaneously. When we exited the building, the familiar "Drivers, start your engines" came on the loudspeaker.

"I don't suppose you want to stay and watch the race?" I asked Godfrey.

"I'd rather deal with an infestation of bedbugs."

It was easier trekking our way back to the parking lot because everyone was gathered around the track. We walked in silence except for the occasional groan. Once on Route 14, we stopped for burgers and ice cream at a roadside stand but neither of us felt like talking.

"I'll call Gladys Pipp in the morning," I said. "She'll know what's going on. I can't believe we were so close and then, *poof!* Nothing."

Godfrey reached over and put his hand on my knee. "Quit beating yourself up. You were amazing. A tad reckless, mind you, but still, amazing."

His words, coupled with that reassuring feeling of his hand on my knee, made me wonder if maybe I should reconsider my relationship with him. Then thoughts of Bradley came to mind and I knew I'd be better off leaving things as is.

When we reached Two Witches, I invited Godfrey in for some iced tea or even one of our wines, but he said he was exhausted and needed to head back to Geneva. With the winery closed for the night, I figured I'd let Cammy and the gang know what happened when Monday morning came around, but I couldn't wait as far as Don and Theo were concerned. I was about to pick up the phone when Theo beat me to the call.

"Good. You're home. Don turned on the news and they had a special announcement regarding today's race at Watkins Glen. The starting time kept getting pushed back. Don was adamant you had something to do with it but I told him you weren't *that* nutsy-koo-koo. Were you?"

"Arrgh. It's a long, painful story. Good news is, Godfrey and I weren't taken into custody."

Theo must have moaned at least half a dozen times when I explained what happened.

"Poor Alex is going to rot in a cell thanks to me," I said. Then Don got on the line and reassured me it wouldn't be all that bad and that we'd revisit things in the morning.

Once I said good night to them, I opened a bag of Wise potato chips, inhaled the aroma and dug in. Later, I sank down on the couch and channel surfed while Charlie snored at my feet. At some point I must have dozed off, because when I woke, it was pitch-black outside and I'd neglected to turn on any lights. At least the TV screen gave off enough light for me to pull the chain on the table lamp.

No sooner had the light flooded the room than I saw another light—this time headlights coming up our driveway. I moved closer to the window and gulped. It was an official county car and I recognized it as the off-duty car Deputy Hickman drove.

Oh, no. Now what?

Without wasting a second, I flipped on the kitchen lights and opened the door to let him in.

"I knew you'd badger my secretary first thing in the morning," he said, "so I figured I might as well spare her the agony and let you know what ensued."

"Uh, great. Sure. Do you want something to drink? Iced tea? Water?"

"I'm fine, thanks. I need to be getting home but felt I owed you this much."

Owed me this much? Oh, my gosh. Maybe it's good news.

We sat at the kitchen table and I forced myself to let him speak without interrupting him.

"As it turns out, Miss Ellington, and believe me, I hate to say it, but you were right."

"Oh, my gosh! They killed Vance. And stole his car. And removed the engine. And—"

"Hold your horses. The pit crew in question admitted to knocking out Mr. Wexler with chloroform while he was sleeping in his tent, and they confessed to stealing his car, which by the way has been located in a barn near the raceway. They also confessed to removing the engine and reinstalling it in Augie Lennox's Porsche. But they emphatically denied smothering him to death. Had no reason to do so. They got what they wanted. Or in this case, what rightfully belonged to them."

"Huh?"

"You heard me. The engine belonged to Billy Sullivan and Augie Lennox. Quite a pricey piece of machinery if you ask me," he said.

"So what was it doing in Vance's Karmann Ghia?"

"Aha. The million-dollar question. It appeared Mr. Sullivan and Mr.

Lennox had a number of gambling debts and the holder of their markers wasn't about to take it lightly. The men were afraid their bookie would get ahold of that high-priced engine, car and all, so they approached Vance about doing them a favor."

"I don't get it. Vance is in Geneva. Augie's in Tennessee."

"Apparently, Vance is from the same hometown as Augie. They grew up together and were friends. Somehow Augie was able to convince Vance to let him replace his Karmann Ghia engine with the souped-up Porsche one. On a temporary basis only. Vance drove down there for an extended weekend and returned with a different engine under the rear."

"Holy cow!"

"Vance was to remain mum about the swap and wait until the pit crew arrived in the Finger Lakes, where they would swap back the original engines."

"What about the other guys?"

"Mr. Sullivan knew them from prior races. They worked for Glen Foreign Motors. Convenient, I'd say."

"So why steal the engine when it was going to be swapped back?"

"Humph. Greed. It seemed the late Vance Wexler refused to give it up. Threatened them, in fact, if they tried to make a move near his car. Went so far as to suggest slapping them with a restraining order."

"Yeesh."

"According to Mr. Lennox and Mr. Sullivan, they felt they had no recourse but to steal it back. When they learned Vance was going to be camping out at Kashong Point, they devised a plan to steal the car. Even went so far as to pay off a couple of local fishermen to keep an eye out for anyone coming around asking questions."

Jerome and his buddy. So Jerome isn't a liar after all.

"Um, isn't that enough of an admission to arrest them for murder and drop the charges on Alex?"

"Like I said, they had no reason to kill Mr. Wexler. Unlike Dr. Bollinger, who had an ironclad motive—preserving his insect study. Most likely, Dr. Bollinger went to use the restroom, saw what was going on in Vance's tent and took advantage of the opportunity to murder him. And yes, although we had initially booked him for premeditated murder, the charges will be changed to murder in the second degree."

"That's ridiculous. Absolutely ridiculous."

"I'm afraid, Miss Ellington, the arrest stands; but if it will make you feel any better, the gentlemen we have in custody have agreed to polygraph tests tomorrow. All the more reason I do not suspect them of murder."

"That's splendid news," I mumbled under my breath before thanking Grizzly Gary for paying me a visit.

Chapter 46

"Of all the insane theories," I said to Charlie once the deputy got into his car and drove off. "First they think it was premeditated murder since Alex's lab uses chloroform, and now they think he piggybacked on someone else's actions. Oh, brother."

My mind was now on overdrive with an appetite to match. I nuked a frozen macaroni and cheese dinner, grabbed a Coke, and consumed everything in record time. "Imagine," I told the dog again, "discovering someone being knocked unconscious with chloroform and then deciding to take advantage of that by smothering him with a pillow. As if Alex would ever— Oh. my gosh, not Alex, but someone else!"

Suddenly Deputy Hickman's theory was in full play. The only trouble was, I didn't know who the someone else was. Certainly lots of people had motives, especially the ones Vance nixed regarding their building permits. I had to talk it out, and the only way I could was with someone who could distance himself from the situation yet provide me with the insight and direction I needed.

Thirty seconds later I was on the phone with Bradley.

"Norrie! Don't you check your voicemail? I must have left at least three messages. Miss you like crazy and going crazy here at the same time."

"I miss you, too. And I'm going crazy. In fact, I nearly got arrested today."

"What?"

"It's all right, but it'll take time to explain."

The alarm in Bradley's voice turned to concern. "I've got all night. Start talking."

Start talking I did. And I didn't stop for a solid twenty minutes.

"Okay. The sheriff's office is trying to make a theory stick even if they have to reinvent one. Won't be the first time. Look, you can figure this out. I know you, Norrie. Think of the smallest details. The ones you might have thought didn't matter at the time. Mull it over in your mind and don't force it. The connections will come."

"Yeah, when they put Alex on death row."

"Not in New York for second-degree murder."

"That's not encouraging."

"You can do this. I have faith in you."

"Wish you were here."

"Yeah, me too."

Bradley wouldn't be back for a few days so I was on my own. Unless of course I wanted to drag Don, Theo, Godfrey, and my tasting room crew into the mire with me.

Exhausted from fatigue, it took me over an hour to finally conk out. Unfortunately, sleep was short-lived. At exactly five thirty the next morning the landline rang and it was Zenora.

My voice was hoarse and low. "Do you have any idea what time it is? This better be important because I lost some decent REM sleep."

"I have news for you that can't wait! Norrie, my friend in Boston tracked down the last surviving member of Hestherlee's family tree and you'll never believe it! And here's the best news of all—we don't have to kill him to end the curse. He's already dead."

"He's already dead? Who's already dead? You mean to tell me all that hullabaloo I went through at the winemakers dinner was for nothing? Nothing! We could have drunk that rosé without dropping dead? That's what you called to tell me?"

"I thought you'd be ecstatic. I know Glenda and I are. And my spiritualist said the dark aura I experienced was from stress, not the uninvited curse. You should be jumping for joy."

"I'm sorry, Zenora, really I am. I just get grumpy when I'm woken out of a deep sleep. Um, I don't suppose you know who this surviving Crackstone is? Did your friend tell you?"

"Oh, she told me, all right. And here's the astonishing thing— remember when she said Abigail Crackstone Exner?"

"Uh-huh."

"Well, there was so much static on the line I didn't hear her right. She confirmed the name later. It wasn't Exner. It was Wexler. The last survivor was Vance Wexler from Tennessee."

For the first, and hopefully last time in my life, words couldn't form in my mouth.

"Norrie? Are you okay? Norrie?"

I don't think I'll be okay for a long, long time.

"Um, yeah. But I'm confused. If the curse ended when he was smothered to death that night, wouldn't we have known? Like a giant thunderstorm? Or hail falling from the skies? Or maybe a wild comet?

Or better yet, plumes of smoke emanating from his tent?"

"Darn those Disney movies. It doesn't work like that. It's much more subtle. In this case, the way you'll know is to check the land where the house once stood. By now, it should start to fill in with fresh green grass."

"That's it? Green grass?"

"Uh-huh. Hope you don't mind but I asked Glenda to scope it out for me once she gets out of work today."

"Okay."

"There's more."

I knew it wouldn't be this easy.

"What? What more?"

"Since the ground is no longer cursed, Glenda and I thought perhaps we could hold a purifying celebration on it. I have a friend who plays lovely lyrical music on the lute and that, in combination with the burning of lavender and sage, would be the perfect ending to that centuries-old damnation."

The last time Glenda and her crew performed a ritualistic chant, Alvin went berserk and broke out of his pen. I didn't need to repeat that nightmare. Still, I couldn't very well refuse Zenora's request. Not after all the trouble she and her friend in Boston went to. I figured I'd ask John to have one or two of the vineyard workers keep an eye on the goat while the wackadoodle crew sanctified the plot of land.

"Sure. Fine. Just let me know when. I'll need at least a two- or three-day notice. And again, thanks, Zenora. I mean it."

I was wide awake when we ended the call and anxious to let Don and Theo know what Zenora found out. Boy, talk about poetic justice. Vance rubbed me the wrong way when I met him, but I had no idea that little weasel was generations down the line that murdered the two witches from our hill. Well, at least Adeliza and Derella Marsten can rest in peace.

It was still too early to bother the guys so I made myself some coffee, fed the dog, and took a quick shower. Then I broke the news to Theo, who answered the phone.

"Are you kidding me? I can't believe it. You mean to tell me I made an absolute fool of myself at the winemakers dinner for no reason?"

"Uh, um, er, well, not really. People were really impressed about how much you knew about the history of rosé."

"Give me a break. All they wanted was to eat the dessert and get out of there."

"Forget about the winemakers dinner for a minute, and the curse. Which, thankfully, is now gone. It was too late to call you last night but Deputy Hickman paid me a visit and you're never going to believe what he told me. He said—"

Theo didn't wait. "Hang on. I'm putting you on speakerphone."

I recounted every word Deputy Hickman said, including some that I added for emphasis. By the time I finished, both of the guys were astonished. I could hear Theo spouting off in the background as Don spoke. "They still want to keep Alex locked up, but for second-degree murder this time? They're crazy."

Then Theo spoke. "Hey, it's bad, but it's not all that bad. It's like that Meat Loaf song. You know, 'Two Out of Three Ain't Bad.' You got to the bottom of the car theft and ended the curse."

"Tell that to Alex."

"Look, we'll figure something out. We've got to get ready for work but we'll talk to you later, okay?"

"Uh-huh. Later."

I knew the tasting room crew would be anxious to hear about the arrest at the raceway, not to mention the end of the curse, so I made sure to get into the tasting room a good forty minutes before we opened.

"Glenda told us about Vance," Lizzie said the minute I got in the door. "Imagine that. Now all your worries are over."

I sighed. "Not all of them. We still don't know who murdered him."

She gave me a funny look. "I thought some arrests were made. It was on the early-morning news."

"Yeah. Car theft and whatever charge they give you for knocking someone out with chloroform. But not murder."

"Tsk-tsk. It had to be someone who was threatened by him. Or someone who owed him money and couldn't pay up. Hmm, maybe he was about to put something on social media. They do that nowadays. Put horrid things on the computer. Too bad he didn't run a business or it could have been someone who was dipping into the till and afraid they'd be found out."

Dipping into the till. The oldest motive in the book.

"Oh, my gosh, Lizzie. You may be on to something."

Chapter 47

I held my breath and prayed Deputy Hickman had left his office. Then I dialed Gladys Pipp from my office. After the usual banter about calling 911 if it was an emergency, she finally said hello.

"Gladys, it's me. Norrie Ellington. Please tell me Deputy Hickman is nowhere in sight."

"The coast is clear. He's out on a call. What's going on?"

"Listen, I know there are all sorts of confidentiality laws involved when someone shares information with the sheriff's office, but I really need a name. Only a name. And I swear I won't ever divulge where I got it."

"A name? What name?"

"Remember when Agnes Merryweather went to the police station in Geneva with a volunteer from the Geneva Historical Society? And that volunteer told the police he saw Alex leaving Vance's tent? I know the police shared that information with your office and Ontario's because they're working the case together. Can you tell me who that volunteer was?"

"You know I can't do that, Norrie. Hmm, hold on a moment, will you? I have to rearrange some notes in alphabetical order and it can't wait. Excuse me for a moment while I do that. Just stay on the line."

The next thing I heard was Gladys humming to herself. Then I heard her mumble, "Hmm, Appleton . . . Appleworth . . . Toby Belcher, yes, that belongs with the B's," before she got back on the line with me.

"So sorry, I can't help you, dear, but I do hope you understand."

"Perfectly. And thanks, Gladys. Have a great day!"

Belcher! I knew where I'd heard that name. It was the night Theo and I broke into the Geneva Historical Society. Curtis Bloor, one of the board members, complained about their office secretary, Doris Belcher. Could it be that simple?

By now I could feel my pulse quicken. The list of Geneva Historical Society members that Theo and I found was tucked in the top drawer of my desk. Thank goodness he thought to make a copy. My fingers fumbled as I scanned it. Sure enough, Toby Belcher's name all but exploded from the page. Complete with an email address, a college dorm address, and cell phone number.

I took a deep breath, let it out slowly, and phoned. Miraculously, he answered on the second ring.

"Toby Belcher?"

"Uh-huh. Who's this?"

"I'm Norrie Ellington and I'm calling to inform you that providing a false statement to the police is punishable under the law. It's a felony."

Or maybe a misdemeanor. Or maybe even nothing, but what the heck.

"Who are you?"

"I'm the person who's going to see that you're locked up for the next decade unless you tell me the truth about what and who you saw or didn't see at Kashong Point the night Vance Wexler was killed. Meet me at the Dunkin' on Hamilton Street in half an hour. And don't be late. Oh, and you'll recognize me. I'll be wearing a Two Witches T-shirt and a scowl on my face. If you don't show up, I will see to it a warrant is issued for your arrest."

"I, um, I'm, uh . . ."

"Just be there. Your dorm is walking distance."

I ended the call before I lost the nerve. Then I took off for Geneva like the proverbial bat out of hell.

Toby Belcher was all of five feet tall with curly brown hair and a mild case of acne. His Hobart College T-shirt looked as if it hadn't seen a washing machine in weeks and his khaki shorts were rumpled. He jumped up from his seat at a rear table the second he spied me walk in the door.

"Sit down," I said. "And tell me the truth."

"Are you with the police department?"

"No."

"Then I don't have to tell you anything."

"True, but you'll wish you did. Listen, there's an innocent man sitting in jail because of a lie you helped fabricate. I need the truth. Why did you tell the police you saw that entomologist leaving Vance's tent?"

Toby made two fists and pounded them together. "Because if I didn't, Agnes Merryweather would've made sure my mom lost her job at the historical society. It's only my mom and me. My dad died last year. Heart attack. If she can't keep her job, I'll have to drop out of college."

I looked at the kid and tried not to show any emotion. "Tell me, what did you see the night Vance was killed? *If* you saw anything at all."

"Oh, I did. But like I said, my mom will lose her job."

"I'll do everything I can to make sure that doesn't happen, but you need to tell the truth. Again, what did you see?"

Toby reached for an old napkin that someone had left on the table and tore the corners off. "I camped out with the rest of the crew on that archeological expedition. And I told the truth about getting up to take a leak."

"But it wasn't Alex Bollinger you saw, was it?"

"No. It was Mrs. Merryweather. She came out of the tent, saw me a few feet away and grabbed me by my nightshirt. Said to keep my mouth shut about what I saw inside the tent or she'd see to it my mother was fired. I think she thought I was in the tent and she didn't give me a chance to tell her I wasn't. Honestly, I had no idea Vance was killed. Not until the next day when we all found out. Later on, Mrs. Merryweather contacted me and insisted I tell the police it was Alex I saw leaving the tent. I'm sorry. Really sorry, but my mom needs that job."

"Did she say anything else? Did you see anything else?"

"Um, yeah. Sort of. I watched her get into her car, and even though it was dark, it wasn't pitch-black. There was plenty of moonlight. Enough for me to see her take off the scarf she had around her neck and stuff it under the driver's seat. Weird, huh? I don't suppose that means anything."

It sure does to me. That scarf is the murder weapon. Why else does someone stuff a scarf under the driver's seat?

"It means everything! Come on. We're heading right to the police station, where you're going to make a full confession if you know what's good for you. And you're coming with me. In my car. I'll drop you off when we're done." *Because the last thing I need is for you to slip away.*

The second we were both buckled up in my car, I phoned the Yates County Sheriff's Office and all but shrieked in Gladys's ear.

"Gladys! It's me again. Norrie. This time I need Deputy Hickman. Please tell me he's back in the office."

"I'm afraid not, but I can call him if it's an emergency."

"Tell him to meet me at the Geneva police station. Tell him I can prove Alex didn't kill Vance. And I know who the real killer is."

An hour and twenty-six minutes later, the Geneva Police Department brought Agnes in for questioning. Too bad when someone is brought in for questioning they're not handcuffed. As the officer walked alongside Agnes, she immediately saw Toby and me seated against a wall where we were asked to wait, and dove at him like a ravenous seagull at a picnic.

"What did you tell them, you rotten miscreant?" she yelled.

Toby turned ashen. "I, I, um, uh . . ."

She grabbed the collar of his T-shirt before the officer could stop her. "So help me I'll deny everything." Then she shook poor Toby by his shoulders until the officer pulled her away. As he led her to another room, I heard her say, "That jackass had it coming," but I wasn't sure if she meant Toby or Vance.

"Are you okay?" I asked Toby.

"Yeah, I'm fine. Geez, she's really unhinged, isn't she?"

I nodded. "Unhinged and hopefully under arrest."

We sat for another twenty minutes before Deputy Hickman arrived. Apparently, he was on the other side of Yates County dealing with a hit-and-run on a back road. When he walked inside the police station, his only words were, "Stay right where you are until I get back."

From that point on, Grizzly Gary was behind closed doors with some officers but did come out once to let me know that a search warrant had been issued to check Agnes's car. He was accompanied by a police officer who informed Toby and me that we were free to go, having given our statements.

I dropped a stunned Toby off at his dorm and told him he'd done the right thing. I even offered to give him a Two Witches T-shirt to replace the one that Agnes apparently ripped when she accosted him.

It wasn't until much later in the day when I learned the scarf was under the driver's seat and on its way to the forensic lab. And I learned *that* from Gladys. In the interim, I left messages for Don, Theo, Bradley, and Godfrey.

I had to wait until the next day for confirmation, but sure enough, it came. Her scarf was permeated with the chloroform Augie Lennox's crew used on Vance. Agnes merely took advantage of the situation once she overheard the plans to steal Vance's car while she traipsed about Kashong Point earlier in the day. Working at the historical society, she knew about the 1948 smothering death of Eldridge McComb and used it to her advantage by suffocating an unconscious Vance with her scarf.

According to Gladys, Agnes made a full confession in exchange for leniency when it came to sentencing.

"So what did she do?" I asked. "Embezzle money? Steal some valuable artifact from the historical society? What? What?"

"She stole donation monies. And we're not talking petty cash. She feared Mr. Wexler would discover the truth and either blackmail her or turn her over to the authorities. He kept impeccable financial records so it was only a matter of time."

That explains the paper I saw her stuff into her blouse the night Theo and I broke into the historical society.

The good news was that Alex was released the same day the forensic report came back, even though Agnes pretty much admitted to killing Vance. A few days later, the entomology department held a celebration at Uncle Joe's restaurant and all of us went—Don, Theo, Cammy, Godfrey, and even Stephanie. The only one missing was Bradley, and that was because he got tied up with paperwork for Marvin.

Before I left Uncle Joe's that night, I made it a point to reiterate what I had told Godfrey earlier. "Francine and Jason had better darn well get back here before Bastille Day and that's coming up pretty soon."

Epilogue

"It's the darnedest thing," John said to me as we stared at the plot of land where the two witches' house had once stood. "The grass looks like green fuzz. Bright green fuzz and it's growing like mad. We didn't seed it or anything."

It was a full week after our night at Uncle Joe's and the news of Agnes's confession had already peaked in the media.

I scratched my arm where a mosquito had just bitten me. "Think there's any validity to that curse?"

John crossed his arms and shook his head. "I don't believe in that mumbo-jumbo, but still . . . makes you wonder, huh?"

I let Zenora and Glenda hold their purifying celebration even though the music from the lute annoyed Alvin to the point where he rammed part of his fence and it had to be repaired. I also kept the promise I made to myself about the petition. By week's end, I had over ninety-six signatures.

In the days that followed, I went about the task of saying my goodbyes to everyone since my sister would be back to take the helm at Two Witches Winery and I'd be free to return to my quirky sanctuary in Manhattan.

"I feel like this is the finale of *The Wizard of Oz*," I told Theo.

He laughed. "You're going back to Manhattan. A day's drive from here. Not Kansas."

The toughest part was saying goodbye to Charlie. I threw my arms around that smelly old Plott hound and hugged him close to me. "I'm going to miss you, buddy. Even if you get my bed muddy and bring in all sorts of yucky stuff." The dog slobbered my cheeks and I tried not to cry.

A few seconds later, I felt the vibration of my cell phone in my pocket and read the text message. It was from Godfrey.

Satellite call from Costa Rica. They want Jason to take a three-week hiatus in Madagascar. Hissing cockroaches. Call me.

Call him? I'll murder him! And the entire entomology department!

Endnotes

The haunted gravestone legend mentioned in this novel is based on a real one—the "Lady in Granite" gravestone found at the Lakeview Cemetery on Elm Street in Penn Yan, New York. The gravestone belongs to the Gillette family, and more information can be found at: hauntedhistorytrail.com/explore/bishop-gillette-headstone

About the Author

J. C. Eaton is the pen name of husband-and-wife writing team Ann I. Goldfarb and James E. Clapp.

A New York native, Ann spent most of her life in education, first as a classroom teacher and later as a middle school principal and professional staff developer. Writing as J. C. Eaton, she and James have authored the Sophie Kimball Mysteries, the first book of which, *Booked 4 Murder*, took first place in the 2018 New Mexico-Arizona Book Awards in the Cozy Mystery category. They are also the authors of the Wine Trail Mysteries and the Marcie Rayner Mysteries. In addition, Ann has published nine YA time travel mysteries under her own name.

When James E. Clapp retired as the tasting room manager for a large upstate New York winery, he never imagined he'd be co-authoring cozy mysteries with his wife. Nonfiction in the form of informational brochures and workshop materials treating the winery industry were his forte, along with an extensive background and experience in construction that started with his service in the U.S. Navy and included vocational school classroom teaching.

You can visit Ann and James at www.jceatonmysteries.com, www.jceatonauthor.com, www.facebook.com/JCEatonauthor/, and www.timetravelmysteries.com.

www.ingramcontent.com/pod-product-compliance
Lightning Source LLC
Chambersburg PA
CBHW022134240626
47153CB00007B/2365